LOVE LUST & BEAUTIFUL LIARS

SHAKIR RASHAAN

nebu publishing

COVER DESIGN by J.L. Woodson/Woodson Creative Studio

PUBLISHED BY NEBU PUBLISHING, LLC

PRINTED IN THE UNITED STATES OF AMERICA

ISBN 978-0-578-67452-0

ALSO BY SHAKIR RASHAAN

CHRONICLES OF THE NUBIAN UNDERWORLD

The Awakening
Legacy
Tempest
Samois

THE KINK, P.I. SERIES

Obsession
Deception
Reckoning

NOVELS

In Service to the Senator
The Devil's All-American
Unthinkable

NOVELLAS

The SHEOL Corporation
The Perfect Set-Up & The Perfect Lesson
Carnal Confections
GFE Interrupted

Anthologies

Z-Rated: Chocolate Flava 3
Cougar Cocktales
Lies Told in the Bedroom

For my Beloved...

"Never go to war ... especially with yourself."

Yuri Orlov – Lord of War

ACKNOWLEDGEMENTS

23 March 2020
0235hrs (2:35AM)

Happy 2020! Man, it has been a while since I've had a chance to holla at you!

I've been a bit, well, distracted, I guess, over the past year. A lot has happened in such a short time. I helped Beloved through breast cancer treatment, watched my father transition due to complications from lung cancer, dealt with a variety of other challenges over the course of 2019, and a host of other things that I won't bore you with right now.

I know we're in the midst of this pandemic right now, and I don't know when the curve will flatten, but I hope that this story will be something that will help you pass the time, and possibly provide a little excitement and escapism. After all, that's what books are all about!

I am trying to find my rhythm again. Sometimes, even in tragedy and strife, the most beautiful things can come to light. That's how this particular project came to fruition. I needed to step outside of myself a little bit, and Dorian became the newest in a line of complicated men who I think you will fall in love with. We will see, but I enjoyed this journey with him.

So, you know what comes next, so let's get to it, shall we?

To my mother, thank you for everything. You've been there since the beginning of the journey, and I hope I have made you proud. I love you.

To my father … this is the first novel I've written since you've been gone. It wasn't easy, but I got it done. I'll come through to have a long talk with you soon.

To my sister, Rae Lamar, I love you. Thank you for being as much my hero as I hope I have been for you.

To my Beloved, there's not much more to say that hasn't already been said in the past, but it bears repeating: I love you more than life itself.

And finally, I'm going to end this in the usual fashion because we'd be here forever while you had me gushing over folks, so do me the usual solid and insert your name in the following statement;

I'd like to thank ________________________________ for the support and love. I hope to continue to put books out that you will always want to tell your fellow bookworms about.

Thank you and God bless,

LOVE

LUST

&

BEAUTIFUL

LIARS

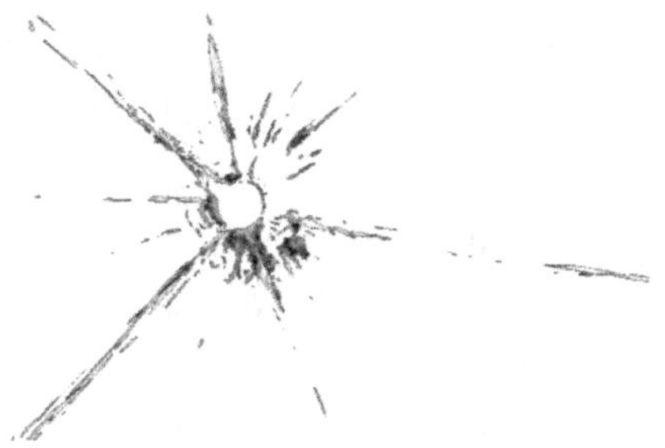

Prologue

The ones who knew didn't care, and the ones who cared didn't know.

It was because of that statement Dorian Bentley was as good at what he did. In fact, it was one of the reasons he was one of the most notorious illegal weapons dealers and gun runners in the world.

The reason he was that damn good was simple: no one believed in ghosts.

And he was a ghost—so much so that he took on the moniker of "The Wraith."

The mantra, "real G's move in silence" influenced his choice of name, while watching old gangster movies as a youth. With Capone, Gotti, and a few other fictional and real crime bosses as indirect mentors, he quickly understood the concept of never drawing too much attention to himself.

For the most part, the philosophy stuck: he drove rentals that were paid for with ghost accounts, with one of his lieutenants, Ishmael or Kale, usually making the rental transaction, using their own carefully crafted aliases. Even in the unlikely event that someone wanted to find the paper trail, all they would find was a "young, gifted, and black" man enjoying the sites of the city he happened to be in at that time.

Many claimed to know who the Wraith was and had never laid eyes on him before, and of those who knew who the Wraith truly was, they would commit perjury under oath before they would admit they have any connection to him whatsoever.

It's not because they feared him, although that's one of the reasons they would risk incarceration. The one reason above all else was also simplistic: it's bad for business, and when in the business of financing and supplying wars and conflicts, the last thing one wanted to do was "bite the hand that feeds you" or even worse, try to kill your merchant of death. There's enough going on as it was with all of the leaders of the free world trying to spread peace all over the planet.

Yeah, right, like that's going to happen. With the current US administration in place, along with the other regimes around the world still dealing with different tensions and aggressions, there was no way in hell that would even be a possibility. With all the moves being made throughout the usual hotbeds of violent outbreaks, it would only be a matter of time before business would be booming all over again.

He wasn't the typical criminal mastermind, considering his upbringing. He was born in London, England, the product of an African-American father and Brazilian mother before moving to his father's hometown of San Diego, California at age seven. He graduated from high school at sixteen, getting accepted into Princeton on a full academic scholarship, graduating with honors with a dual major B.A. degree in economics and public affairs at nineteen. He finished graduate school with an M.P.A. – Master's in Public Affairs – at twenty-one before being accepted into Oxford University, studying in the prestigious Ruskin Fine Arts program, graduating with a BFA at twenty-four.

In order for him to move the way he did, he realized he needed some other skills and assets at his disposal: he spoke seven different languages, had a trust of untold millions set aside for him by his grandfather, one of the wealthiest businessmen—and crime bosses—in Rio, and learned the business of illegal weapons transactions from none other than his father, Donovan Bentley, who originally learned the art of illegal weapons dealing after leaving a civilian defense contractor who worked for the US Department of Defense.

His only weakness—well, what most men's weaknesses were—was his taste for women. His tastes were not of the common variety—he enjoyed the convenience and beauty of high-priced escorts. In his line of work, attachments could get a man in his line of work killed. His father was able to survive because he managed to get his weapons deals done without stepping on toes and keep anyone from having a reason to seek out his wife and only son.

Dorian, however, was never one to agree with "going along to get along."

By the time he'd taken over for his father and really gotten entrenched in the illegal weapons trade, he'd turned the game on its ear, using his Oxford and Princeton connections—who by now had become high ranking officials in different countries throughout the world—to all but obliterate the arms embargos that members of Parliament, Congress, and any other legislative bodies had bothered to write, thanks to loopholes that were always meant for the governments to exploit.

As long as he kept to his principles and kept his connections uncomplicated, he would continue to stay at the top of his game. The thing about rules, though, is eventually there's an exception.

In his mind, it had better be one hell of an exception.

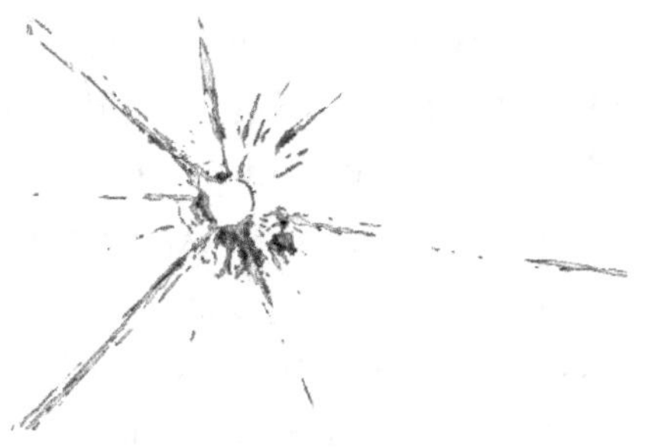

Chapter One

Dorian Bentley knew they were in trouble before the first grenade fell. It was all instinct and adrenaline from there, and they had to use every drop of it to get out of that clusterfuck alive.

The transaction was supposed to go off without a hitch, just another routine day in the stifling heat of Cameroon—only, it wasn't another routine day. The terms of the agreement weren't even routine. In hindsight, that should have been the harbinger of things to come.

The terms were explicit: ten million in uncut blood diamonds, another five million in US dollars, in exchange for a half-dozen cases of RPGs, or rocket-propelled grenade launchers, and a couple of SAMS—surface-to-air missiles. The only thing left to do was drop off the merchandise and get out of the country before the client's enemies tried to close in on the location.

What deepened the tensions in the negotiations for the exchange was what might have caused things to go left. In hindsight, he probably would have admitted that he could have handled things a bit better. The fact, for him, was that the Central African Franc wasn't worth the conversion; Dorian insisted on US currency, or Euro, whichever they could get their hands on first. Considering the poor conversion rate of the CAF by comparison, coming up with the requisite asking price would cause a problem for a regime whose dictator was under fire for not delivering on the promise of revolution.

That might have been his major mistake—allowing his privilege to show and forgetting the hostilities within the current global climate. Under normal circumstances, he would have taken the payment and converted it on the open market. He had several brokers already lined up to handle the diamonds and turn a handsome profit. He realized he was taking a risk by asking for the payment in the manner he did; the international hatred for the US was at an all-time high, despite the current Yeager Administration's best efforts to stem the tide from the previous presidency.

The weather held no high hopes for the possibility for a positive outcome, either. The scorching sun and 110-degree heat lent no relief to the intensity of the meeting. If anything, it served to shorten the tempers of all parties involved.

The deal went south when the Selakah rebels—more specifically, their leader, Akbar Adam—tried to engineer a double-cross with the attendance of one of the lieutenants to broker the deal instead of Adam himself. Adam's lieutenant tried to play a shell game with Juan Carlos, Dorian's right hand, giving him what he thought was the full payment on the weapons being delivered. Harry, Dorian's bodyguard, was slow to react to the situation as it played out in front of him, which only enraged his employer further. From the moment the bag of diamonds was placed in his hand, the incredulous look on Juan Carlos's face was enough for the man known as "The Wraith" to realize alternative methods for collection were in order.

There was no doubt in Dorian's mind the transaction was a bust, and he had no choice but to risk a firefight to get full payment. He yelled out in French that the lieutenant had thirty seconds to produce the payment. When the lieutenant responded that the payment was there in full, Dorian's anger rose to critical levels. He shot the lieutenant at point blank range, startling the other Selakah soldiers and causing confusion in the mind of his protection. There was no confusion in Dorian's mind, however, and he had to send a message that he was not to be trifled with.

Things escalated faster than it took a Ferrari F8 Spider to accelerate from zero to sixty.

Harry pushed Dorian out of the path of the grenade

thrown by one of the Selekah soldiers, taking cover behind a stone wall only seconds before it exploded. The force of the explosion weakened the foundation, with only a few more grenades threatening to reduce the wall to rubble. The three of them did their best to take shelter as the grenades exploded, with Harry and Juan Carlos glaring at Dorian the entire time, wondering how they got into another fine mess.

"What the hell were you thinking?!" Juan Carlos yelled at his employer. "You had to say something about the diamonds, didn't you?!"

"They shafted us on the diamonds, JC!" Dorian yelled in response, shielding his eyes from the small pebbles falling from the grenade blast. "They thought they were getting over on us, I did what needed to be done!"

"Well, we're fucked if we don't get back to our ride, DK!" Juan Carlos looked up and quickly pulled Dorian away from the wall, running as fast as they could taking cover by jumping into a nearby doorway. Seconds later, half the wall tipped over from the second grenade blast.

The gunshots ringing in the distance pierced through the walls of the room, causing the men to drop to the floor to avoid getting struck. Harry barely got inside the door before a hail of bullets sliced through the adjoining wall, coming within inches of grazing his neck and shoulder. Juan Carlos quickly peeked around the door, blindly firing in the direction of the gunfire, trying to buy them a temporary window to move from their cornered position.

He scowled at Dorian, his anger mounting with each bullet penetrating the walls. "You're gonna get us killed one day!"

Harry joined in on the dogpile while wasting blind rounds in the direction of the soldiers shooting into the room. "You should have taken the damn diamonds, Dorian! Now we have to shoot our way out of a fucking war zone!"

"Quit your bitching and run, dammit! We have a bird to catch!"

Getting to their feet, the men ran down the corridor, the hail of gunfire nipping at their footsteps. They weaved to keep from providing static targets for their pursuers, picking up the pace to get to the awaiting helicopter several yards away.

"DK, look out!" Juan Carlos yelled as one of the pursuers had somehow gotten ahead of them and stood in the path of their escape.

"Fuck!" Dorian yelled as the gunman adjusted the rifle in his hand, aiming to fire.

He pulled the Glock G30S out of his shoulder harness in mid-stride, firing toward the gunman, hoping to hit with as many bullets as was left in the magazine. The slumping body dropping like a sack of potatoes was the result of several bullets hitting center mass, providing an instant kill as the three of them jumped over the corpse.

Dorian cursed at having to empty his magazine to hit one target. *They're never gonna let me live that one down.* He glanced behind him, realizing Juan Carlos was firing back at their attackers while in a reverse sprint. He grabbed another magazine from his pocket, ejecting the empty one, unconcerned with keeping the discarded equipment as he would under normal circumstances. It was messy, but he didn't have a choice in the matter. He reasoned that no one would bother to come for any of the equipment anyway, not in this region.

"The whole damn mag, DK?!" Harry yelled ahead of him. "What's the point of going to the range if you have to unload the whole bloody thing?!"

"Shut up and run!" Dorian shouted behind him, never breaking his stride. "I killed him, didn't I?!"

The helicopter was in sight. The pilot saw the pending drama unfolding and started the rotors, with hopes they would be able to take flight in time to escape with the precious cargo on board. Dorian was relieved to see Kale, his contingency plan in case anything went awry, sitting with his sniper rifle at the ready.

Before Dorian could give the signal to fire, Kale's eye had already focused on the closest target, squeezing the trigger and watching the advancing target fall from the kill shot. He took notice of the throng of pursuers closing the gap on his employer and signaled the pilot to take off.

"Get this bird in the air. Prepare for a close proximity hot pickup, Ishmael." Kale instructed. The helicopter lifted off, hovering about ten feet in the air, maintaining the altitude while he surveyed the landscape and the players on it. Once they were close enough, the expertise of both pilot and gunner took center stage of this unfolding drama.

Kale always took pride in his sniper skill, and rarely rushed when focusing on his targets. However, he had to make an exception based on the circumstances. His employer was in immediate danger, and he needed to ensure Dorian's safety. He put down the sniper rifle, shifting his body behind the machine gun on the side of the helicopter and sprayed bullets in the direction of the pursuing masses.

The rebel gunmen fell like weeds being sliced down with a sickle as Kale spared no one in the path of the firestorm he rained down. The shells falling from the chamber of the gun sounded off against the landing slide, the metal clanking like pennies on a tile floor.

The men made it to the helicopter, jumping up on the landing slide and quickly slipping inside the cabin as Ishmael picked up altitude to get them to safety.

"What the hell was all that about, sir?" Kale asked as he shut the door and put the headphones on so they could hear each other. "Did the rebels try to pull a fast one?"

"Yeah, Kale, but they didn't get away with it," Dorian replied as he pulled another bag of diamonds from the inside of his jacket pocket. Harry's eyes widened as he pulled a similar bag of diamonds from his pocket, wondering whether the bag he had possessed the real package.

Juan Carlos shook his head as he took a look at the bag. "Goddamn Adam. Where did he leave the actual payment, and how did you find it before we got out of the drop site?"

"Adam is a lot of things, including very gullible and very predictable," Dorian replied as he continued to examine the payment. Satisfied that the weight was as originally agreed upon, he turned his attention to Juan Carlos. "He trusts the women in his organization more than the men; the woman who was being ignored was the one who was holding the authentic payload."

"How did you know they were willing to pull a double cross?" Harry asked as he produced the other bag of diamonds. "And if you have the actual payment, what the hell have I been trying to hold on to this whole time? You got us in the middle of a firefight over a fucked-up shell game?"

"The lieutenant's body language gave him away," Dorian explained. "If that bastard Adam had done the deal himself, they would have been one day gone before we'd realized we'd been had. I would have never known the female soldier was the one holding the payment because my focus would have been on Adam. For all we know, both bags might be full of fake stones. He sent a boy to do a man's job."

"He's never done that before, Dorian," Juan Carlos objected. "Every time we've completed the transaction in the past, everything was on the level."

"If everything was on the level, JC, why the shell game, right?" Dorian was always one to make sure every detail was covered, and the last-minute switch was a dead giveaway. "The least his lieutenant could have done was acted like he had the actual diamonds in hand. He was supposed to have five million in cash, but you know how hard it is to convert US money, but the weight of this bag will more than suffice, but we weren't supposed to know that she had them in the first place. The point is, Adam is getting desperate. He's robbing Peter to pay Paul, as my abuela used to say. The CAR security teams must be catching on to his teams' robberies of their treasuries."

"So, what happens now, sir?" Kale inquired, smiling as he looked down over the carnage he'd created, admiring his handy work. "Adam is gonna be pissed when he finds out what happened today."

"He won't do anything, Kale," Dorian retorted, inspecting the diamonds more closely with the jeweler's loupe in his briefcase. Upon rough observation, a smile spread across his lips. "He's getting quality product, courtesy of the US Armed Forces, to continue his cause. Losing a lieutenant means nothing in the grand scheme of doing business. Make no mistake, playa: it's always business, never personal."

CHAPTER TWO

"So, now that we're safe and sound, what the fuck was that back there, DK?"

The standard debriefing between Dorian, Kale, Harry and Juan Carlos was always one that provided as much entertainment as it provided its usual tension. As the stakes have risen, thanks to Dorian's shrewd business connections over the past few years, the areas where they have been doing business had become more contentious and dangerous with each passing transaction. It was bad enough they had to do what was necessary to stay off Interpol's radar, but there was the competition that made things difficult.

The location always rotated, as each man had his designated rendezvous point where everyone was to meet, even if things went left and the need to abort was necessary. The idea was to ensure that no one could, or would, be able to track them. This meant that the locales could lead to some nondescript areas, which suited everyone fine. This time, it was Kale's location; he made the choice to debrief at his secured cottage in Costa Rica.

As each man made their way through the series of stepping stones, following Kale's specific instructions to the letter, there was a sense of mild irritation that threatened to consume the group. They weren't entirely certain of where Dorian's current line of thought was taking them, and they needed answers.

"Did you have to set up the bloody trail to your cottage like this, kid?" Harry's tone was a mix of trepidation and aggravation. "From where I'm standing, no one would want to come this deep inside the country anyway, too much fucking rainforest to brush through. I'm wondering if you all are taking this old cloak-and-dagger shit too far."

Kale gave a wry smile as he welcomed each of them inside. "You can never be too careful, old man. If anything, things have gotten more difficult than when you had to go through the paces. GPS screws up a whole lot of things; which reminds me, gentlemen, my apologies for requesting the cell phones be left in Panama. It is a necessary evil, especially considering we seem to have a target on our backs as of lately."

Dorian nodded as he made his way into the cottage. "It isn't a problem, Kale. The connections we've made in the past few months have yielded some desirable results—and some undesirable ones, too. But it isn't anything we can't handle or stay ahead of, so, we'll do what we've always done."

"Absolutely, nephew." Juan Carlos wasn't too far behind the group, taking his time to keep from stepping on the wrong stone. He shook his head as he saw the remnants of an animal that came too close to the cottage. "Kale, remind me to get you to safeguard my house in Joburg. It's obvious your measures do not discriminate."

The men finally settled into the living area as Kale grabbed beers from the large cooler in the kitchen, handing the preferred brand to each man before taking his seat. Dorian took out the notes he wrote down while in route to Kale's location, reviewing them one more time before he addressed his lieutenants.

"Gentlemen, yesterday was quite the time, wasn't it?"

The group erupted in laughter for a few moments before things quieted a bit. Juan Carlos took a swig of his beer and continued to relax, while Harry sat stone-faced, his body language in direct contrast to the rest of his comrades.

Dorian gave Harry a look before he referred to his notes. "Okay, so, Cameroon didn't go exactly as planned, but there was no other choice but to improvise in the manner that I did. We still got out of there with the payment, although it wasn't what was discussed, but I'll take that up with Adam when he reaches out again for the next shipment."

"Next shipment? If you think for a minute that I'm going back in there to deal with Adam and his undisciplined lot, you've got another thing coming, bruv." Harry's voice conveyed his annoyance with the whole situation. "The tensions are rising to a fevered pitch, and there's no telling what those diamonds will fetch on the dark web, if they come close to what was negotiated. He should have come up with the fucking payment as agreed, in the currency that was agreed upon."

"Harry, DK had it under control, all right?" Juan Carlos' aggressive tone matched Harry's in intensity, causing Kale and Dorian to pause a moment and wonder if there was something else going on that they weren't aware of. "The last two jobs, you've been acting like you're a rookie or something, bruv. Why are you acting all skittish like we didn't know what could have gone wrong and made the adjustments? We got out of there in one piece."

"That's a crock and you know it," Harry replied. "Adam's soldiers were more than a few sandwiches short of a bloody picnic, and you want to question my ability to handle a fucked-up situation? If you and I hadn't thought fast while Dorian was playing fast and loose, we would have dropped a major clanger down there."

"Gentlemen, gentlemen, take it easy, it's not as bad

as you thought it was." Dorian felt it best to keep an even tone to bring the heightened emotions in the room down a couple notches. He didn't appreciate Harry's assessment of the situation, but this wasn't the time nor place to address it. "I made sure to check with my normal connections once we got out of Cameroon. We only lost five percent of what we would have normally taken in euros, so I'll know what to tax when it's time to renegotiate."

Harry wasn't convinced, no matter how smoothly Dorian tried to make it sound. "Fair enough, but we shouldn't have to go gallivanting around the globe trying to fence illegal contraband. You've never adjusted like this before, what's the change of heart about?"

Dorian stayed silent for a few moments, closing his eyes and nodding as though he'd made his mind up that he would finally divulge what he knew. "Rainier tried to backdoor me by going to Adam himself and accepting the blood diamonds as payment. Adam called me as a courtesy of the party he was hosting as a test of his loyalty to our business dealings."

"Rainier is as much a myth as anyone," Harry scoffed. "He doesn't exist. Hell, no one knows who the blighter is, much less what he looks like."

"The same can be said of me, Harry, or have you forgotten my reputation?" Dorian was reaching the point to where he would have to cut Harry down so they could stay on task. "According to the outside world, I don't exist, either. It's obvious Rainier has learned that stealth and anonymity are rather powerful tools to use."

"All I'm saying is that Adam might be drawing up an imaginary friend to drive up the price. This is shite, I can't abide by it."

"Then it is a good thing you aren't the one who has to make that decision, innit?" Dorian's Cockney accent pronounced itself, throwing Harry off balance. "Now, stop waffling on before I lose the fucking plot. This isn't doing any of us any fucking good."

Juan Carlos couldn't stop laughing as he listened to Harry and Dorian argue like he and Kale weren't in the room. "Okay, can you two travel back to where we are right now, please? You're not in the UK."

Dorian extended his hand toward Harry in a goodwill gesture. "Sorry, Harry, didn't mean to toss about like that. We have a lot to cover in a short time, and I still have an appointment I have to make before I meet with the German Ministry of Defence in the next few days."

That information caught Kale's attention. "When did you make inroads with Germany? If you solidify that relationship, it could open up business in Eastern Europe. If you need an interpreter, I can recommend family I have in the area."

"I'll be using that connection, or shall I say, you will be using that connection, Kale," Dorian remarked, watching Kale's face light up over the correction in speech. "You know better than anyone how the Germans are about anyone non-German handling back-channel deals, much less a Black man."

Kale nodded. "Unfortunate truth, but a reality to deal with nonetheless. So, I'll be playing you to get this deal handled, I can do that."

"And what will the rest of us be doing while Kale is handling the German negotiations?" Juan Carlos considered the new information being disseminated. "I don't know about you, but I would love to take some time off until the next transaction is set up. There are some things I need to see about."

Harry nodded at that suggestion. "It might take the edge off, DK. We've been going pretty hard the past couple of months. Would love to spend some money on some creature comforts and such, and enjoy them for a few weeks."

"I'm already ahead of you, gentlemen." Dorian took a look at his timepiece, smiling as he considered his next words. "We still have to wait for DoD to re-up, and that's going to take a couple of weeks, so, let's use that downtime to indulge and decompress. See you then, and be careful out there."

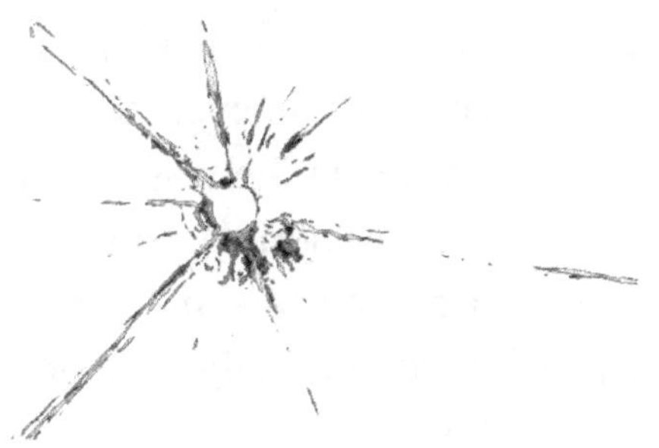

Chapter Three

Dorian was a creature of habit when it came to his confections and proclivities. Once something—or someone—caught his discerning eye, he made sure it stayed in his permanent mental rolodex, to be used over and over again. That included his tastes in jewelry, where Cartier, Rolex, Bulgari and Arum Brothers dominated his repertoire, the art pieces he kept in his home or the ones he purchased for his mother when she wasn't creating pieces for different art galleries across the world, and his tastes in high-priced escorts. One high-priced escort in particular— his favorite paramour, Samara D'Acosta.

The outside world knew her by her industry name, Arianna Lamonte, but she still offered her carte du jour of carnal delights to discerning gentlemen on very rare occasions. That list was small and mysterious, much like the men—and women—who would clear out their schedules to indulge for lavish and luxurious rendezvous.

She was the one who gave him the GFE—the Girlfriend Experience—whenever he needed to feel "normal". That's not to say he wasn't normal, but he wasn't in a business any normal person would select for themselves. After five years of "dating" him, she'd become adept at knowing exactly what he needed after an intense transaction.

They first met when they were teenagers, their paths crossing when Dorian was in her native Brazil. She helped him escape the favelas, barely getting out of the infamous "Cidade de Deus" (City of God) alive. Dorian was in a desperate search for his father, who'd been kidnapped and held for ransom over a weapons deal that had gone south. They'd fallen in love almost immediately, but lost touch after he'd gotten his father Stateside, despite his pleas for her to come home with him to San Diego.

They'd crossed paths again by pure happenstance, as Samara had been making her name in the world of high-class escorting, and Dorian, under one of his assumed aliases, contracted her services. Their unexpected reunion was emotionally and sexually charged, as their unresolved feelings made a furious rise to the surface. What was supposed to be a one-night affair turned into a weeks-long escape from the worries of their worlds, with Dorian making explicitly clear that he wanted her to himself—and if he couldn't have that, he wanted her as his personal paramour.

Samara resisted his advances for as long as she could, realizing that it would be bad for business. She tried coming up with smokescreens over the real reason she couldn't completely extract herself from her occupation. Despite her rebuffs, Dorian had worn her down to where she decided to parlay her exotic beauty and adept ability to role-play into an acting and modeling career, using her escorting income to build her more "legitimate" career to the point to where she didn't need to go on calls as much as she needed to. She still needed to ensure her employer wouldn't find her expendable. The end result would be unimaginable.

He was happy about their compromise, cutting off the majority of his other feminine indulgences so he could focus on making a future with her. In his mind, there was no one else who would fit in his world—even if he was dragging his feet about it. That was the way he preferred it, and as much as she didn't want to admit it, she loved fulfilling his wishes. It was a precarious balance struck between them, but it was only a matter of time before that balance would shift one way or the other.

Walking into the atrium of the Armani Hotel in downtown Dubai, he smiled as he approached the front desk to go through the usual protocol so he could take some well-earned days off before the next transaction he'd set up. He enjoyed taking these excursions; they'd become much-needed escapes from the realities he faced daily.

His smile was returned along with the most mesmerizing eyes he'd encountered in a while. "Good evening, and welcome back. Would you like your usual suite, Mr. Nagi?"

He looked at the stunning Somali desk agent and replied, "Yes, the usual suite will do fine, thank you, Alma? Did I remember your name this time?"

She blushed at his recollection since his last stay at the hotel. He should remember her well, considering she spent a rather pleasurable night with him on her day off. The sensuality dripped from her lips as the tone in her heavily accented voice conveyed the *extra* services that she was more than willing to take another chance to deliver. "Would there be anything else that I can provide for you to make your stay more enjoyable, sir?"

He took in her features, noticing the skirt she wore was much shorter than he remembered, but then again, that skirt wasn't worth remembering except when it was in a heap with the rest of her uniform. He also remembered how aggressive she was, which was the way he liked his women, and how insatiable her appetite was, too.

He would have to disappoint her this time around. He had something a bit more familiar on his mind, but he didn't put the idea out of his mind in case that initial plan fell through.

"Alma, if I need anything—and I mean *anything*—you will be the only one I call," Dorian answered as he took the key and headed up to his suite on the 40th floor. He blew a kiss in her direction as he made his way to the elevator, making eye contact with her before ascending to his destination.

As he sat in the penthouse suite to enjoy a few days to unwind and relax before the next deal, he'd contemplated either flying Samara in or indulging in the pleasures of the local delicacies on the menu.

African-Brazilian or East African? Familiar or the semi-familiar? In his mind it was a no-brainer, but the decision would come with a bit of patience on his part, and he was not a patient man. However, Samara was the exception to any rule he may have created for himself, and he was willing to make it more than worth her while for interrupting her schedule.

He knew where she was at all times; it was a part of their arrangement, as it were. She was in in Naples, Italy on a photo shoot at current, and he'd sent his private jet to bring her to him. In a little over five hours, she would be naked in his room doing unspeakably nasty things. Until then, he decided to work through his idle time setting up for the next transaction.

He looked at the laptop screen, trying to ignore the beauty of his surroundings, but it would be impossible to do. The ultra-modern suite—from its unique circular entrance hall, to its unobstructed, spectacular view of the Arabian Gulf, to its private gym area with the latest cardio equipment—it was opulent, yet it was too genteel, too impeccable.

Maybe that was his problem with the room. There were no flaws anywhere in the room. Everything was in its proper place. Even if someone may have had a wild night and used every room in the suite, once housekeeping had run through it to clean and restore the suite, there was nothing out of place. Ever.

While Dorian enjoyed the rare sights of perfection as much as the next man, without some havoc to wreak, even something as small as putting a cushion on the sofa out of place, life would be boring, and he was anything but boring.

To keep from feeling like he was comfortable being an obsessive compulsive, he got up from the desk in the office area, stalking each room in the suite, doing as much minor damage as he felt comfortable with, especially considering the company that would be escorted to his door in a few hours.

Satisfied with his efforts, he finally reentered the office area, studying the notes he'd composed on the next locale and buyer, which would take him back to the States. He'd been pleased with the inroads he'd been able to make with different companies on the West Coast, mostly federal contractors who needed to run tests under the radar. The truth be told, he was getting a bit weary of the constant intensity that came with dealing only with warring nations.

Initially, he had managed to not develop a conscience when it came to selling to both sides of a conflict on the African continent, but even that was slowly eating away at his moral compass. He needed a way to diversify his business interests, and do so without having to circumvent the different international laws from countries who actually did mind it when people dealt in premium weapons and munitions.

Still, providing weapons to both the new regime and the rebel cause would net him untold millions for years to come, as long as he played his cards right and kept those that needed to know in the loop to ensure a seamless transaction. There was very little room for error, and he detested mistakes. In fact, even though his memory was razor-sharp and he could rely on it to recount details at a moment's notice, he made sure it wasn't his only means of recalling information, which minimized his mistakes in the field.

In the illegal side of this business, mistakes cost lives, or worse, mistakes cost you your freedom. Since neither death nor incarceration was an option, the alternative was to be as meticulous as possible in every aspect of his operations, and he made sure his employees were as meticulous as he was. This new undertaking would be his endgame, a way for him to turn his more nefarious arm of the empire over to those who'd had a stronger constitution. He'd then go and take the money he'd housed in different overseas banking institutions and make the rest of his life, the best of his life.

With a few more hours to kill, he decided to freshen up before his companion arrived. No matter the heat of the water in the shower, it wasn't enough to temper the anticipation of the debauchery he had in store for her. It took everything within him to resist the urge to elicit an eruption out of his system. He couldn't wait to feel her again; it had been weeks since the last time they were together.

Toweling himself dry, he slipped on one of the plush hotel robes and stood in the window, admiring the view of downtown, watching the ships in the Gulf sailing in the distance, allowing his mind to rest, if only for a moment or two.

We can't afford a fuck up like that again, Bentley. His mind took him to the deal in Cameroon and what could have gone wrong instead of what went right. *Harry's slipping, kid, and you know it. He's getting slow in his old age, regardless of your loyalty to him, you have to see that he's not the one to replace you at the top.*

He shook his thoughts, closing his eyes tightly in an attempt to erase it from his memory.

That deal was done. The only thing that mattered was moving forward to the next deal. His patience was running out, and he knew it was due to having too much time on his hands waiting on Samara's arrival. Instinctively, he looked at his wrist and, forgetting he didn't put his watch back on, he walked over to the desk to retrieve it.

He heard a noise that was foreign to him as he picked up his watch. According to the time, the object of his desire's arrival would be imminent. The continuous ringing from the desk phone proved the source of his confusion. "This is Nagi."

"Sir, your guest has arrived and is being escorted to your suite, per your instructions. Please let us know if there is anything else we can do to accommodate you," Alma stated. "Enjoy the rest of your evening."

"Thank you, Alma, I will be sure to remember that." He disconnected the call, doing his best to suppress his excitement. He hadn't seen her in a couple of months due to their hectic schedules. It took everything within him to keep from meeting her out in the hallway, digging deep to extend his patience for a few more minutes. After that, he would not be held responsible for anything that would or would not happen.

Chapter Four

There was a sudden soft tapping of knuckles against the thick oak door, a distinctive cadence that made him stop in mid-stride. He smiled at its familiarity, realizing his prize awaited him on the other side of the door.

He didn't bother trying to be cool about it. They were beyond the point of putting on pretenses or hiding nervousness or anything of the sort. He gripped the metallic door handle, swinging the heavy door open, preparing his eyes to behold the beauty that lay on the other side of the threshold. No matter how much he prepared, no matter how many times they'd seen each other over the years, she still took his breath away.

She stood in the doorway with a smile that illuminated the Arabian night sky. Her hair was tousled, giving her a wild and untamed look as it flowed past her shoulders, draping pert breasts that were barely covered by the string bikini top she wore. Her narrowed, slanted eyes tried to hide the smoldering desire beneath, but he knew her better than to think she wasn't happy to see him.

While the wrap skirt hid the bikini bottom he assumed was as flimsy as the top, it couldn't hide the roundness of her ample hips. It was easy to deduce that she was pulled from a swimsuit photo shoot and she didn't bother to change while on the flight. Her bronzed skin took on a radiant sheen against the ambient lighting in the hallway, giving her a mysteriously stunning look. He wanted to take her before the door shut, her thighs pleading to be wrapped around his waist. Nothing would please him more than to answer their pleas and then some.

"Hi, baby." Samara sounded rested, leading Dorian to believe she slept most of the flight. "Did you miss me?"

Dorian loosened the tie on his robe, letting it fall to the floor at his feet. The grin on his face widened as Samara bit her lip to stifle the lustful expression on her face at his response to her question.

She jumped into his arms, kissing him deeply, her legs tightly wrapped around his waist as he released the door to shut itself. He slammed her against the wall, returning the intensity in her kisses, desperately trying to slide the fabric of the bikini bottom to the side to slip his length as far inside her as he could. He knew he found his mark when she moaned loudly through the kiss.

"Damn, baby." She tried to breathe as much as she could as he continued to drive inside of her. "You have missed me!"

"Yes, I missed you, sexy." Dorian continued to kiss her deeply as he slammed her against the wall to slip deeper inside her.

"Show me how much! I'm yours, baby, take it!"

Samara cried out from the impact but never stopped kissing him, squeezing her legs tighter around him. She didn't want him to slip out of her, not until she'd drained him of every ounce of energy he had to give her.

"You like that?" Dorian whispered in her ear.

"Fuck yes, baby, give it to me!"

He broke from their kiss, looking into her eyes. The words nearly splashed from his lips, and it took everything within him to keep from saying them. She felt exquisite as he pushed deeper inside her, using the wall to keep her in place. He needed her to feel everything he wanted to say to her, but too afraid to give voice to them.

"You like fucking your nasty slut, don't you, baby?" She said. "I love being your personal slut, baby. Don't stop fucking me!"

He lifted her from the wall, walking her to the nearby bedroom, kissing and holding her as he strode.

She trembled under his touch, surprised at his ability to keep her floating on air – literally and figuratively – as they tumbled onto the bed.

Getting their bearings, he slipped back inside, finding his rhythm again.

"I love … fucking … you!" He growled as each stroke was punctuated by the sound of skin slapping skin. He'd found his zone again, getting lost inside of her in every way possible. He pounded inside her walls as though he were trying to find a permanent escape from the madness of his world. "Fuck, you're so wet, baby!"

"Always wet for you, baby!" Samara screamed out. "Oh my God oh shit oh fuck oh goddammit you're making me come!"

She couldn't do anything more than hold on for dear life as Dorian had her legs pinned against his shoulders and her arms pinned down with his own. There was no escape, no reprieve, until he felt like he was ready to erupt. It only turned her on more, cheering him on with every feverish stroke inside her.

"Fuck me harder!" She urged. "Come on, baby, get it!"

"Oh, God, Mara, I'm gonna come!"

"Oh, yeah, baby, come on me," she said, hoping to time her climax with his. Her thick island accent pronounced itself as she felt his pending explosion. "Shoot it all over me, baby! Fuck me good!"

Dorian went in as hard as he could. Finding her legs

no longer pinned, Samara wrapped her legs around his waist again as the sweat from their bodies caused them to slip effortlessly against each other. As he grunted and growled from the intensity of the wave threatening to crash inside of him, she needed him to hold on a little bit longer. She wasn't ready for him to stop, and she was willing to do whatever it took to keep him revved up.

An orgasm of her own ripped through Samara, causing her to shout to the heavens of how good he made her feel. She squeezed tightly against his shaft, triggering the eruption from within. He pulled out to expel his juices, but she took hold of his shaft and jacked him off until she directed his stream all over her ample chest.

"Damn, baby, it's so thick and creamy!" Her accent was even more pronounced, making it difficult for the untrained ear to understand the words she screamed. "You held all this for me? Give it to me, baby!"

Exhausted, he collapsed, falling to her side as she used the sheets to wipe the remnants of his juices off her chest before snuggling up to his side. Before long, their quiet snores filled the room, signaling a serene ending to a carnally-driven night.

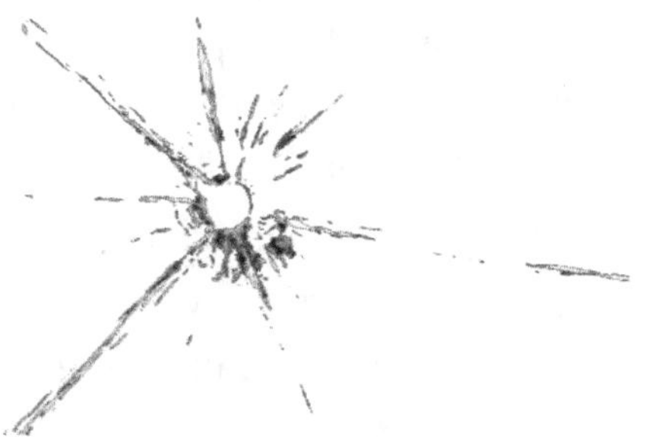

CHAPTER FIVE

The stifling heat that came with a normal Dubai morning was nothing compared to the sweltering haze inside the bedroom of the suite. The radiance of the midmorning sun poured in, its brilliance spreading throughout the massive space, a reminder that the day had already started whether the slumbering couple wanted it to, or not. Samara stirred, but Dorian held her close, not wanting her to move from where she nestled next to his hip.

It was times like this that made him wish for simpler days. She felt so perfect in his arms, like her body was tailor-made to fit against his. He couldn't think of a better place to indulge his fantasies, and no one else could star in those dreams but the woman lying in his bed.

Samara would make a man very happy, and not only

on a physical level. She was business savvy, learning the other side of the film industry almost from the moment she entered it. She didn't want to be known as another pretty face in a sea of pretty faces. Thanks to some investment tips Dorian slipped her from his colleagues on Wall Street, she'd become comfortably wealthy. She was of child-bearing age, which appealed to him immensely. He honestly wanted to settle down and have a family, but the truth of the matter was startling: the lure of business was too seductive to resist.

Hopefully, he'd be able to enjoy those simpler days soon. As lucrative as this life was, it began to wear on him. Selling legal and illegal weapons inside hostile nations—and to both sides of the conflict—was not an industry from which many got the chance to retire. It was only a matter of time before he got distracted and made a mistake that could cost him everything. He'd come too far to have it all come crashing down now.

He nudged the gorgeous creature lying next to him to awaken her. Her honey-bronzed skin melted wonderfully against his chiseled muscles and milk-chocolate hue. "Good morning, sexy."

"Mmm, good morning to you, too." Samara stretched as she struggled to cover her nude form. "What time is it?"

Peeking under the covers to enjoy her nakedness, a slick grin spread across his face. "I'd say it's time for round three, but I don't want to wear you out before you have to go back to your shoot."

"I don't want to go back to work, and I don't want you to, either. I was hoping that we could … well, you know."

Dorian stroked his chin, wondering how far he wanted to take the teasing between them. "Persuade me."

"And how can I do that?"

"Use your imagination."

She leaned in, daring him to press his lips against hers. "Will you to stop me once I try to convince you?"

"Maybe I will, maybe I won't, but there's only one way to find out."

"Allow me to, in my own way, but you can't stop me once I start."

"I have a feeling I won't like where this is going."

"Yes, you will. I promise you will."

Samara straddled his lap before he could protest further, staring into his eyes with an intensity he didn't anticipate. She traced a finger across his chin, lightly kissing his lips a few times, moving to his neck, then closing his eyes, fluttering her eyelids against his like a butterfly breezing in the wind. He tried to resist her advances, but she playfully forced him to clasp both sides of her waist. She cupped his face in her hands as she pressed her lips against his once more, parting them with her tongue, to get inside and kiss him with everything she had to offer.

"Mara—"

"No, baby, you can't stop me, remember?"

She continued tempting him, and as much as he wanted to reciprocate, he couldn't. No matter how badly he wanted to let himself go, he couldn't. He struggled to regain some semblance of control over the situation by slipping her off his lap at the very least, but Samara was unwilling to yield it to him.

"Kiss me, DK. Kiss me the way you kissed me when we were kids back in Rio," she implored. "Kiss me like you want to make me yours. I'm all yours. I've always been yours."

He hesitated as the memories of the first night they made love—the night he fell in love with her—flooded his psyche. He was weak for her, desperate to allow his emotions to rise to the surface, but he wasn't ready to let that happen. He needed to turn over the operations to one of his lieutenants before he could step away permanently and give himself completely to her.

His other dilemma: could he kill "The Wraith"—a persona he'd embodied for nearly his entire adult life? It was the one thing Samara didn't know about him, the one secret he'd kept from everyone he held dear, except his father. His mother was convinced he worked for the State Department all these years, and he refused to allow her to believe anything different.

"Dorian … kiss me. It's only a kiss, baby. I know you want to; I can see it in your eyes. Don't hold back, darling. Kiss me."

Dorian sank his fingers in her hair and pulled her

down to him. He held her in place as he licked her lips, then slid his tongue deep in her mouth. He kept his kisses soft, slow, not wanting the moment to end for either of them. One hand kept a firm grip on her silky mane while the other wrapped securely around her waist. The longer they kissed, the tighter he held on to her.

"Mmm, Daddy, damn. Stay here with me, please? Just for a few days? I've missed you terribly."

"You know you make me weak when you call me that."

She brushed her lips against his as she murmured, "Please stay with me a few more days. I really need you."

He snapped his fingers as he remembered the other reason he'd chosen their current locale. "Only if you accompany me to an art gala later tonight. After that, you'll have my undivided attention."

"But what if I just want to stay in this beautiful suite and make love to you instead? Would you tell me no?"

"You know I can't say no to you now, sexy, so that's not fair."

Samara giggled at the thought. "D'you have something for me to wear?"

"Always, but what about your shoot?"

"The shoot is over, baby," Samara answered. "Yesterday was the last day. Your timing couldn't have been more impeccable."

Dorian's phone rang, interrupting their conversation. "Yes? Ah, yes, Yves, how are you doing, darling? Yes, she'll be returned to you in the next few days, and yes, I do appreciate you extending your schedule for me, love. I promise to make it worth your while very soon."

Samara looked bemused. "How do you know Yves Paladin? For that matter, how in the world did you get her to extend her shoot to include me?"

Dorian pecked her lips as he placed his smartphone on the night stand. "Yves and I met at an art benefit some years ago to launch my mother's collection. We've been friends for a while now, baby."

"Have you been doing this the whole time? I don't need you doing that for me. I didn't ask you to do that for me." Samara's indifference to Dorian's gesture wasn't what he had in mind when he had her brought to him. "You've been watching over me this entire time?"

He tried to keep the mood light, incredulous over her intimations. "Have I done this to you before? Flown you where I was, to an exotic location, at a moment's notice?"

"Don't do that, DK. You know bloody well what I'm talking about," Samara's anger rushed to the surface. "I've done everything I can to get to where I am without any undue influence. If I'd known you'd convinced Yves to postpone things so I could be here, I would have stayed there and convinced you to let me be here after I was done."

Dorian did his best to keep his calm, but deep down, he was disturbed—more than he wanted to admit. He glared at Samara, irritated by her outburst. From her reaction—pulling away and turning wary eyes on him—it was a pretty good guess she couldn't decipher his mood. "We've known each other since we were kids, Mara, and I've never done anything to compromise you or your professional growth. What you're accusing me of doing is not what I was doing."

"Then, what the hell were you doing? Tell me what was going through your mind when you put all of this in motion."

The one thing Dorian kept under control, regardless of the circumstances, was his temper. To lose control was to tip his hand, giving his client the advantage and leading them to believe he had something to hide. It was one of the things that kept him alive, especially in regions where hesitation in front of the wrong despot meant an immediate death sentence.

This wasn't a business deal, however. This was an affair of the heart, and as much as he wanted to keep it locked away for safe keeping, eventually emotions would spill over when he least expected it. He almost regretted his outburst, but he made the promise to himself that he would never hide his true feelings from her. He couldn't hide from her, no matter how hard he tried.

"Fine, your mind is made up that I've been somehow calling the shots on your professional career, there's obviously nothing I can do to change it." He reached for his clothes to ger dressed, avoiding eye contact with her the entire time. "I can do a lot of things, but there are some things that I would never be so callous to consider. I'm not as narcissistic as you're making me out to be. But this *one* time, I wanted to see you because I needed to see you. If that makes me a bad man, I'll take that."

The pregnant pause between them was palpable, to the point to where Samara hesitated to approach for a moment. This wasn't the way she wanted things to be left between them before the next time they would be able to see each other again.

Yes, he had a tendency to infuriate her, but those moments were few and far between. The last time they'd even had this type of an intense exchange was before he left Rio to go back to the States after he'd been able to help rescue his father when they were teens. She begged him to stay, but he felt differently.

"Dorian, I'm sorry if I assumed too much." Samara's expression softened as she moved into his space caressed his face, smiling when she felt the tension leave his body. "I know you have cultivated this persona that you're the most feared man on the planet and everything, but I wasn't scared of you when we were kids, and I'm not scared of you now. I didn't want to miss this shoot; a lot of eyes are on it for New York Fashion Week. Even as important as that was for me, I didn't want to miss *you*, either. It was an impossible situation to put me in, can't you see that?"

He looked up into her eyes, no longer holding on to the anger from moments earlier. He pulled her into his lap and kissed her like she was the most precious thing in the world to him.

"You'll never have to fear me, my darling. You weren't going to miss me. I'll always want you, Mara. And you're right; I shouldn't have placed you in that difficult position. Can you forgive me?"

"I can never be mad at you for long. There's nothing to forgive."

"Thank you, *querida*. I promise I will be more considerate next time I send for you." He moved to the edge of the mattress, gently sliding her from his lap. "Now, do me a favor and head into the closet so you can model the dresses I've picked for you to wear later tonight."

"God, I love when you take control of me, Daddy." She kissed him once more. "Will you molest me in it on the way to the gala and back?"

"I can't keep my hands off you as it is, so that isn't even a question. D'you want the driver to close the partition?"

"No, Daddy, it turns me on when she can watch."

Dorian shook his head as he chuckled over that thought. "You're such a naughty girl."

"I'm *your* naughty girl."

He gently swatted her butt, ushering her toward the closet. "Then get that ass in the dress you want me to molest you in so I can have it prepared. This gala is important to me."

Dorian picked up his smartphone again once Samara disappeared into the closet. He made a call to his pilot to alert him before he and his co-pilot began their pre-flight preparation. "Parker, there's been a slight change of plans."

"Yes, Mr. Nagi, is there something wrong?"

"Nothing's wrong, I'll be staying for a few more days. There's an important event I can't miss tonight. Take the next couple of days off and enjoy the sights, I'll want wheels up in seventy-two hours."

"Yes, sir. Enjoy the event. We'll see you in seventy-two hours, ready to fly."

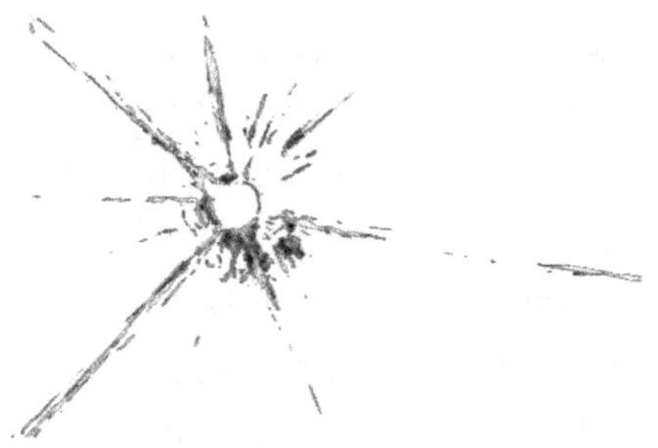

Chapter Six

Walking into his mother's latest art gallery opening should have felt familiar to him, but Dorian felt anything but familiar in the current surroundings he and Samara found themselves. The gallery where she was hosting her latest collection had the usual Bohemian feel to it, but there was something different this time. He couldn't put his finger on it, but he was certain that there was a different energy to the place.

His mother's collections had grown more provocative by the year, almost like she was having her own personal renaissance. She'd had Dorian at the tender age of twenty, putting a lot of her own dreams on hold while raising him. Once he'd gotten to college, she'd allowed the flood gates to open, unleashing a decades-long rush of creativity that seemed to have no end to its flow.

In the beginning, he'd done his best to not patronize his mother's talent and eye, but when the first series of buyers engaged in a bidding war for her whole collection, he had to change his tune. She'd become a near overnight sensation, going from Milan to Paris, to Barcelona, to hosting an opening in her native Brazil before heading to London and then to New York, all within a two-year period. He got caught up in the wave, too, buying several of the more sensual pieces to complement the other pieces in his primary residence in London.

Tonight, it would be yet another star-studded affair in North Africa.

He walked in with Samara, arm-in-arm as the other guests did their best to figure out who the stunning couple was, as though they were ripped from the latest fashion magazine. It was times like this that made him think about what the other side of the game would look like, how his "new normal" would manifest. They did as much as they could to be cordial to the other guests who were insistent that they were pretending to be regular people, despite Dorian's insistence to the contrary. All of that came to a full stop when the hostess of the event made it a point to begin her own personal inquisition.

"Well, well, well, my darling baby boy decided that he wasn't too good to make one of my glitzy affairs for once," Isabella Bentley, Dorian's mother, remarked as she placed her hand against his cheek. "I was beginning to think you were ashamed of being around your mother."

"No, Mami, I am never disappointed or ashamed of anything you do or have done. I love you too much for that, and you know I've never missed any of your events," he replied, patting Samara's hand as he began his own introductions. "Mami, I'd like for you to meet my date, Samara. Mara, this is my mother, renowned artist, Isabella Bentley."

"How splendid! And here I was thinking I would have to set you up with one of these eligible women in here, but since you have such an exquisite creature on your arm, I won't have to do any such thing."

"Mami!"

Samara giggled as she watched Dorian blush over his mother's fawning over her. "It's nice to meet you, Mrs. Bentley. You're too kind in your compliment. You look absolutely divine yourself, if you don't mind me saying so."

"Look at her, she's blushing. Don't mind me, lovely, I'm just friendly like that. He doesn't bring a lot of women home to see me, so I'm delighted that someone might have his attention for longer than a New York minute." Isabella took a long look at them for a moment, her eyebrow raised. "So, how long has this being going on? You look rather comfortable on my son's arm, and you look awfully familiar to me."

"Mami, I didn't bring her here to be on the receiving end of an inquisition."

"Well, it's too late for that. I noticed how you were looking at her, and that means that I need to find out more about her." Isabella took Samara from her son's arm. "Now, if you don't mind, I'm going to take this gorgeous girl away for a few moments. Go mingle, get someone to buy my pieces, make yourself useful."

The look on Dorian's face was priceless as he watched Samara disappear into the crowd, engaged in a very intimate conversation with his mother. He couldn't resist rolling his eyes; his mother could be the ultimate matchmaker at times, to the point to where she developed tunnel vision.

Realizing that he would not see either one of them for at least the next few minutes, he continued to look through his mother's collection, finding himself impressed with the breadth of the quality of the paintings she had on display.

"Well, well, well, I wouldn't have thought I would see you at one of your mom's events."

The unmistakable scent announced itself before she said another word. He knew it was her immediately; he'd purchased the intoxicating fragrance once for her birthday. What probably threw him off was why she'd managed to find herself halfway around the world on tonight of all nights.

"If I didn't know any better, I would say that I needed to ensure your Secret Service detail does not need to usher me away from you. I wouldn't want Terrell to get the wrong idea." Dorian couldn't contain his grin at the sight of the only other woman on the planet who he could never say no to—Lea McAvoy.

She looked as delectable as he'd remembered, and he'd sworn she'd grown more exquisite over time. He took a head-to-toe accounting of her assets, assets that had matured and become more pronounced since their college years.

They'd done nothing more than engage in clandestine flings over the years before she found herself in the employ of then-Senator Terrell Warren, the current Vice President of the United States. After that, their relationship took on a different dynamic, and while she went on to superstardom on the Hill and eventually the White House, he eventually became one of the biggest weapons dealers for the Department of Defense.

It didn't exactly stop their clandestine engagements, of course, but he was aware that Lea's attention and devotion remained with the distinguished gentleman from California. Dorian, some years later, would rekindle the passions with Samara, and Lea would be nothing more than a very close friend—one with connections that would come in handy if and when the situation called for her discretionary involvement.

"My Sir is always aware of where I am at all times, Dorian, and for the record, I'm not on as tight of a leash as you remember." Lea licked her lips as she closed the distance between them to give him a lingering hug and kiss on the cheek. "All it would take is a phone call to let him know there is some unfinished business that I need to attend to, and he'll simply reply that as long as that unfinished business doesn't damage what belongs to him, then … well, you know."

Dorian was taken aback by the sudden aggression that Lea showed after not seeing each other in person for nearly five years. It was like they'd only seen each other last week. "He's a better man than I am, I'll give him that. I would never let you out of my sight."

"And that's why things stayed the way they were between us, pretty boy," Lea replied. "But from what I observed earlier, you seem to have a wonderful woman to be for you what I couldn't be."

"Were you stalking me?"

"I always stalk my prey, even when they don't think they're being stalked."

Dorian smiled. It had been a while since he'd been put on the defensive, and Lea was always the one to have that ability. "So, does she meet to your satisfaction?"

"I'm not the one who needs to know that answer. The question is, does she meet to your satisfaction? If she does, then you need to do something about that, and soon. Women like her are very, very rare."

Dorian stared into Lea's eyes for a moment, watching them as they searched through his, nearly looking through to the deepest recesses of his psyche. She nodded with a wry smile, tracing his lips with her fingertips. "She does. She's the one."

"I know. It's written all over you, lover." Lea placed another kiss across his lips, wiping the remnants of her lipstick from his face. "I am very happy for you, truly. I would never want you to not be happy."

"For now, I am."

Lea raised her eyebrow at his response. "That doesn't sound like the Dorian Bentley I know. You sound like you're ready for a change of pace. Have things gotten too easy in the field?"

Dorian's eyes widened, but he didn't look away or sidestep the question. "I think there's more on the horizon. You might be right; it might be getting too easy out there."

"Well, honestly speaking, I don't think you were meant to do this long-term anyway," Lea opined. "Perhaps it is time to do what you told me you always wanted to do when we were in school. Your mind is in what you're doing right now, and you're damn good at it, but this was never your passion. Follow your passions, darling, and start with that beautiful creature your mother stole away from you to interrogate."

Dorian shook his head as he chuckled. "Even after all this time, you're still looking out for me."

"I always protect my assets, and you have been my longest and most desirable asset. If you ever need me for anything, always know that I will be there, with every resource I have available to ensure you're safe."

Lea turned to leave, stopping for a brief moment to take another look at Dorian before she disappeared into the crowd. "I'll say hello to mom before I leave. Do you have another piece that you could recommend for the house? My Sir has become quite the fan of her work."

Dorian grinned. "I'm standing in front of it."

"Consider it sold. Until the next time, my handsome one."

Dorian watched her head toward her detail, nodding as they pointed in his mother's direction. He searched the crowd to try to find Samara, his sudden apprehension catching him off guard when he couldn't find her immediately. He did his best to keep his emotions in check, but after dealing with Lea, he found himself unable to manage himself.

"Your mother is a riot. I haven't laughed so hard in a long time." Samara curled her arm inside of his, quelling the initial panic he felt. She was grinning from ear to ear. "I want to be like her when I grow up."

"I'm sorry, baby, I didn't expect her to pull that stunt."

"I'm okay, you're the one who looks like they need therapy." She snuggled close to kiss his lips. "She is definitely overprotective of her sexy ass son."

"Yeah, my mother is one of a kind."

"Yes, she is, but what I'm more interested in knowing is whether you were a good boy while I was gone or not?"

He raised an eyebrow. "Are you asking that as my date, or are you asking as someone who wants to be more than that?"

"I'm not answering your question until you answer mine."

Dorian threw his hands up. "Just evil for no reason."

"I just met your mother, sexy. From the way she was talking, I get to ask for and about anything I want to."

"Oh, my God, that woman is always trying to marry me off."

"Would it be a bad thing to be tied down? I mean, you've already tried to tie me down without the ring and legalities. Not that I'm complaining or anything."

Dorian pulled her close, his eyes piercing through her very being. Samara's legs weakened, causing her to tighten her grip to steady herself. She did her best to avoid his glance, but she found it impossible to tear herself away. He narrowed his eyes, intensifying his stare as his hands roamed in places that should have those around them uncomfortable.

He placed a small kiss across her lips, never leaving her eyes as he watched her surrender to his touch. "No, it wouldn't be a bad thing at all. If you're a good girl, maybe you might be the one to tie me down."

"You keep talking like that and we'll need to tell your mother that you won't be able to stay much longer."

"We can leave right now."

"What about your mom? Won't she miss you?"

"Mom will be fine, and I've done everything that I

needed to do here, including making her a few hundred thousand in sales of her paintings. The only thing left to do now … is you."

"Then you need to get the car, and be quick about it," Samara urged as she ushered him toward the door. "You can come collect me when you're ready."

As she leaned against the bar awaiting Dorian's return, Samara noticed a familiar figure approaching her. Her smile disappeared in an instant as the person closed the gap between them. She wanted to move from where she stood, but there wasn't much she could do in the crowded space, so she resigned herself to a conversation she didn't want to be bothered with.

"Well, hello, pretty girl. I was wondering when you would turn up again."

"Amelia, I don't have time for your drama right now. I'm here with my date, and you'll get your percentage, as always." Samara's body language stiffened, giving the distinct impression that she was uncomfortable.

"I already know who you're here with, and the fact that he happens to be one of my VIP clients is interesting in and of itself," Amelia replied. "I also know that he isn't paying you to be his escort tonight, otherwise Trinity would have alerted me. Have you forgotten your debt to me?"

"I haven't, Mommy, which is why I've been taking care of things on another front. You'll get what you want, as long as I get what I want."

"If I wasn't swamped with other issues that required my full attention, I would have what I want right now, and we wouldn't have need for this pointless conversation." Amelia slipped further inside Samara's personal space, a sneer spreading across her lips. "You're still mine; you can try to convince yourself otherwise, but we both know the truth. Better men have tried and failed to take you from me."

Samara's frustration only served to indulge Amelia's sadistic proclivities. Amelia's arousal was evident in the way she moved as she continued to agitate Samara by her presence alone. Samara closed her eyes for a few seconds to compose herself before she continued the conversation. "I will always be grateful to you for keeping me out of the Saudi prince's harem, but what you wanted from me after that, I couldn't give to you. My heart has always belonged to another."

"And he does nothing more than what the prince would have done, except for getting your ass beat if you didn't please him." Amelia frowned as she regarded Samara's indifference. "What could he possibly do that I can't? What makes this one so goddamned special?"

"You have no idea how deeply he and I feel for one another, the things we went through when we were younger." Samara did her best to sound confident, but her emotions were conflicted, and it was only a matter of time before Amelia would pick up on it. "Maybe you don't see it because you don't want to see it, but there has always been something special about him. Whether you like it or not, I never belonged to you, either."

"Mhm, and hopefully he will recognize what he has in you before it's too late," Amelia scoffed. "Where is your betrothed, anyway? That is your cover for this evening, right? I saw you cozying up to his mother earlier. Wonder how she'll react when she finds out who you really are? I wonder how he'll react when he finds out this *love* between you is nothing more than a figment of your imagination?"

"Sooner or later, you will have to let me go."

"I'm nowhere near done with you, Arianna. You can be certain of that. I'll expect you back at the house to collect your next assignment as soon as you're done here … and don't make me come for you, or you'll regret it."

Amelia left soon after, missing Dorian's arrival by seconds. Samara did her best to change her disposition before he took notice, grinning the minute he slipped into her space and grabbed her waist. "Ready to go?"

"Absolutely. Take me home."

"My chariot awaits."

CHAPTER SEVEN

Touching down at London City Airport, Dorian hit the ground running, getting into the Volvo S90 rental Ishmael procured for the day. The only thing on his mind was heading to his home in Kensington to set up the next transaction.

The private jet took off before they left the tarmac. There was never a need for the jet to remain stationed for longer than a day, but he also never wanted anyone to get a good look at it. As much as he changed the call letters on the jet to keep the law enforcement agencies off-balance, there was never a worry about someone reporting the jet or the flight patterns, but it was another aspect of his business practices. In his mind, one could never be too careful. He wasn't naïve; as much as he had certain protections Stateside, there was always a chance they could burn his whole operation and disavow all of them.

Ishmael was one of his young gunrunners who impersonated him while brokering smaller deals in Europe and South America. He was slowly becoming a jack of all trades; he was integral in his role when the whole thing in Cameroon went sideways. He pointed to the usual complement of products that awaited Dorian the moment he sat in the vehicle: *The Daily Telegraph* newspaper, coffee and doughnuts, a burner cellphone, and a throwaway gun in case something went awry while in transit.

The gun, of course, was sanitized, from the chamber and trigger to the bullets and the magazine. Ishmael knew his employer well, and took the liberty of running the instructions with such thoroughness that they were almost second nature when it was time to execute them at a moment's notice. Dorian took him under his wing, with the intention of possibly moving him up in the organization.

They moved with the flow of traffic, with Ishmael making sure he didn't draw too much attention to them, if at all. The more inconspicuous the better, especially by any law enforcement officers who might have wanted to tag along for the ride. Dorian was no fool. He knew certain law enforcement agencies—more specifically, agents of those agencies—didn't always want to play ball when it came to the business of funding and arming war efforts.

"We're coming up on Thames Street now, sir,"

Ishmael announced as he made the turn to the street that ran alongside the River Thames. Dorian took a look to his left, enjoying the view as the vessels made their way down the waterway. "JC said to make sure you called him the minute I picked you up."

He expected Juan Carlos to contact him, but Dorian didn't pay too much attention to it. He picked up the burner and held the number three key on the cell phone's keypad, automatically contacting the number to the other burner that Juan Carlos possessed.

"DK, I got Kale on the line, let me conference you in," Juan Carlos said. A few seconds later, Kale's voice could be heard before Juan Carlos spoke to let him know Dorian was online. "Okay, DK, what's this next score you texted us about?"

"Well, gentlemen, luck, as usual, favors the prepared," Dorian replied, getting ready to explain the situation to them. "We'll be heading down to Syria to help take care of the rebel forces down there. This job will take a few days to load up and deliver, so we'll need some additional help."

"Good, I was going to ask for some extra heat for this trip, sir," Kale stated. The background noise alerted the other two men that he was either in one of the rail stations or in a public space with a lot of people around. "After going through the last trip in Cameroon, we can't go in with a skeleton crew like that again unless we know the transaction is solid."

"He's right, DK," Juan Carlos interjected. "The last

thing we ever want to be is outgunned when we're delivering the ammunition and weaponry. We're going to need as many people involved as possible, including Harry."

The line got silent for a moment once Harry's name was mentioned, and it was not lost on Dorian over the reason why. The deal in Cameroon was on everyone's minds, and the fact that Harry wasn't conferenced in was a telltale sign of its own that something was amiss with his long-time bodyguard.

Kale broke the silence, trying to keep things on the level. "Harry has had his moments, sir, but you have to admit he has been a bit slower to react to the situations as they arise. He was contracted to be your muscle and protect you first, and lately JC has been the one pulling you out of harm's way."

Juan Carlos chimed in, "Kid, he's not the same man he was, and we have to find a way to figure out what is going on with him before something really bad happens. I'm not going to be around forever, either. I'd feel more comfortable with Ishmael covering you at this point."

"You both have a point, gentlemen, and for this particular job, we're going to need the extra personnel. The payday is huge." Dorian took a sip of his coffee as he left the phone's speaker open to keep his hands free. "I'll figure out what to do about Harry after we're done."

"Well, don't keep us in suspense, kid. What's the

score?" Juan Carlos asked.

"I'll get the confirmation from Locke when I get to the house, but the transaction is worth forty million dollars, and another thirty million euro. Do the math, gentlemen."

A collective whistle was heard over the speaker.

"Where did Locke get that kind of money from?" Juan Carlos's curiosity got the best of him. "For that matter, why are we going into Syria anyway? I thought the summit in Doha was supposed to yield munitions for the rebels?"

"That's the beauty of the ineptness of both the US Congress and British Parliament," Dorian laughed. "Thanks to both legislatures letting things die in committee, neither the US nor the UK can deliver on what they promised General Idriss."

"Well, I'm not about to complain. We handle this and I can really retire early, like next week," Juan Carlos remarked. "What do you suggest on the size of the team?"

"Well, as Kale suggested, we're going to need some extra eyes, three different vantage points, so we'll have better cover fire, just in case," Dorian told them. "JC, you'll be taking the point with me, but we'll be working with Lazarus this time. The Syrian rebels are expecting the Wraith to be there, but they are under the impression that he's either Syrian or Iranian, so he'll be a perfect stand-in."

Lazarus used that moniker to represent the Biblical

reference of the same name, the man who Jesus raised from the dead. In this updated case, Lazarus was clinically dead for about five minutes during a deal gone bad when he was in the weapons trade for himself decades ago. That was before Donovan began using him in the region as a liaison to help smooth over deals.

Dorian gave him a larger role once he took over, as he did with different associates who were native to the region. It was one of the reasons why no one, except those who needed to know, knew who the Wraith actually looked like.

Ishmael interrupted for a moment. "Sir, we'll be at the house in about ten minutes. Would you like for me to take the scenic route so you can finish your call?"

"No, Ishmael, there's no need. I believe everything is in order, and we can get the munitions and the hardware ready to go. Kale, get the people you need, and make sure the birds you use this time around are loaded with something special. Don't ask me why, just call it a hunch, especially when we'll be dealing with the Syrians in a hot zone. JC, make sure you make the calls to the Airbus crew and let them know we'll be flying heavier than usual this time around. Make it worth the trouble so they will commit to the job."

"Consider it done, DK." Kale cut his connection, leaving Dorian and Juan Carlos to finish the conversation. Juan Carlos cut straight to the chase. "Harry's a problem, kid, and you know it."

Dorian dismissed the concern. "You're imagining

things, Uncle JC. Harry just got caught slipping. It happens, even to you. Should I consider putting you on the sidelines, too?"

"Don't cloud the issue, this isn't about me. I've had your back for the past decade, remember?" Juan Carlos' tone changed. It was more animated than before, and his irritation was palpable. "What I am saying is that you need to get things under control with him before he puts us all in danger."

"Okay, I hear you, and you're right, you've never steered me wrong, which is why you've always been my right hand." Dorian paused for a moment to consider his next words. "Do you think we need to put a tail on him?"

"Not yet, but I'll keep an eye on him during this next score, to see what is really going on in his head," Juan Carlos replied. "I'm also serious about you needing to come up with an exit strategy, let the youngsters take things over and go from there."

"You're starting to sound like my father."

"Maybe he has a point, kid. We've had a good run, it's time to take the money and go legit," Juan Carlos suggested. "I've been thinking about going back home with my new-found wealth, maybe start a winery or something."

"Wait a minute, you never told me that." Dorian pondered his proposal for a few moments, sparking a bit of an epiphany of his own. "You might be on to something, but I'll have to think about it. Whatever I come up with, it won't happen any time soon. There are moves that have to be made to ensure seamless transition."

"I can get with that, but I want to make sure either Ishmael or Kale is ready to take over for me. I'm getting too old for this shit."

"Consider it done, I think Ishmael will be the one; Kale loves being in the gunner's chair too much to be on the ground." Dorian gave a nod to Ishmael as they pulled into the garage of his West London home. "Got to jet, Unc, I need to get everything ready for the deal tomorrow."

"Okay, we'll see you at the drop site."

Once Dorian disconnected the call, he turned his attention to Ishmael. "Thanks for the lift, I'm sure you heard most of the conversation. If I'm going to keep grooming you, you should be privy to more of these moves."

"Always a pleasure, sir, and I'll be ready when you're ready," Ishmael pulled to the curb to let Dorian out. "Oh, and I'll be flying out in the morning to take care of the smaller munitions transaction you sent me this morning before I picked you up."

"Good man." Dorian took notice of his surroundings, making sure nothing was out of place since the last time he'd been there. Most of his neighbors were still at work and rarely ever saw him, even when he lived in this house for the better part of a year. He then extended his fist to give Ishmael pound.

"Once you've taken care of that, take the rest of the month off. Oh, and enjoy Colombia. I'm sure the ladies will love you down there."

Ishmael couldn't wipe the smile from his face. "Yes, sir, I will enjoy myself. You will expect the block by courier once the transaction is completed."

The "block" Ishmael referred to was a microchip containing financial data that moved quicker and cleaner than stacks and racks of paper money. Once the transaction was completed, the block was taken to one of the South American banks that handled them and made sure the money was shifted to where it needed to go.

While the Africans still dealt in blood diamonds and stolen US dollars and Euros, most of the South American countries got with the rest of the 21st century, if for nothing else than survival. It was the only way they could compete with the rest of the civilized world, especially when a lot of their clientele were the cartels.

Once he was satisfied there were no eyes that needed to watch, Dorian walked inside of his five-bedroom home, securing the alarm system and firing up "The Cage" to get the communique from General Locke. "The Cage" was his self-contained unit inside the house where he wouldn't have to worry about outside eyes prying inside to see what he was up to. He learned how to do all that from his computer scientist and IT friends at Princeton who were always on a paranoia and conspiracy theory rant.

A text message came in on his personal cell phone, and he smiled when he saw the source of the text.

Art exhibition gala on Friday ... Art pieces and stock will be on full display for your perusal and purchase. We hope you can make it, sir, we know how busy you are.

That text came from the mysterious Trinity, his contact whenever he needed a top-notch escort for his more exotic needs. Of course, that was whenever he didn't want to make arrangements to bring Samara to wherever he was at that moment.

He texted Trinity back, letting her know he would be in attendance and to text him the particulars of the event so he could be ready when he got back to London.

For a few seconds, he felt like he was somehow being unfaithful to Samara by attending the gala, but he got over that feeling quickly when he reminded himself that he still wasn't exactly sure *what* he felt for Samara to even feel the guilt he thought he felt. Was he in love with her? He still wasn't sure how to answer that question. What he did know was that he would have to figure out the answer sooner than later.

Almost as soon as he flipped the switch inside of the room and began to make the sweep to make sure the lines were secured and no one could piggyback off the servers, Locke's information popped up on the computer screen. He looked at the information with a smile on his face. This would bring him closer to his endgame, and the rest of the team would be as happy as he was about the windfall that would soon come from it.

The block has been secured ... the eagles and chicks will be at the designated locale for acquisition, 1400hrs local time Wednesday. Ben made sure the block was loaded above and beyond for the short notice and inconvenience.

In other words, the weapons and the ammunition had been located and prepared for pickup, and the money had been confirmed from "Ben," or the benefactor who was funding the excursion into Damascus. Reading that the benefactor decided to up the payment for cutting into the usual window between transactions was unexpected, though. It was a pleasant surprise, but it kept his senses heightened.

Dorian picked up the voice-to-type headphones so he could verbally speak his response and multitask. *Will there be any interference from Big Brother?*

Negative. Big Brother's eyes are blind to the trip. You have a three-day window before their eyes are opened again. IP is dealing with a major issue near Russia, so attention is diverted. The moles are keeping things above-board.

That was all Dorian needed to know. No CIA, no Interpol. It should be a walk in the park. He never took that to heart, ever. Thinking like that usually got people killed, and he loved the way life was going at the moment. He wanted to be as prepared as he could be for anything to happen, and anything usually did happen.

Now that he had something to look forward to returning to the UK for, he wanted to get this done and have enough time to get back so he could get dolled up and see what Trinity and her employer had for display for the weekend. He normally took his time, but with the type of merchandise that Mommy had, if a client snoozed, they lost out on the premium pieces – pieces of art and pussy, to be exact.

He stepped out of The Cage to text Juan Carlos and Kale to accelerate the schedule so they could be on site to await the arrival of the package being delivered at the time the general specified, and he got with Lazarus to set up the meeting a day early.

The sooner, the better. He had more important—and pleasurable—things to do now.

Stepping back inside The Cage, Dorian made it clear to the general that the transactions would be completed ahead of schedule. *The transaction will be done in two. I'll expect the blocks to be couriered to the destination I specified. It's a pleasure working with you as always, sir.*

Good man, I knew I could count on you.

Now that he'd gotten business out of the way, he was ready to partake in more delectable endeavors, but not before he'd made a call home to ensure his mother had made it back home in one piece.

"Hi, Mami, I hope I didn't wake you."

"No, baby, I'm always up painting at such a god-awful time of morning. Where in the world are you today?"

"I'm back home in London, I just wanted to make sure you were home after your latest successful event."

"I've been home for the better part of a week," she replied. "I know you've been busy in the field, so I wasn't sure if the message I sent to you got through or not."

"It did, but I wanted to hear your voice. I'm planning to come home in the next few days before the next deal comes through and I have to take off again."

"I'd be happy to see you away from professional surroundings. I've missed you."

"I miss you, too. Will Dad be home?"

"You know your father, DK. He's more homebody nowadays. He's beginning to bore me. I may have to trade him in for a younger model, someone who can keep up with me."

Dorian chuckled. "You've said that every year since he's retired. You know you love that boring old man."

"Whatever, I'm not wasting my best years staying at home. If he doesn't want to come with, then that's on him. Maybe you can talk some sense into him when you come home, help him understand that his wife does not like to be home and staring at every news channel available to the free world twenty-four hours a day."

"Okay, Mami, I'll try when I get home. I love you."

"I love you, too, sweetheart. Please be safe out there, okay? I know you always are, you're so much like your grandfather."

"I will, Mami. See you in a few days."

CHAPTER EIGHT

Samara didn't want to return to the Gallery, but Amelia left her little choice but to comply. The look in her eyes was unmistakable, and she knew the freedom she'd enjoyed for the past year would disappear in an instant if she tried to defy the order. She needed to maintain as much of her autonomy as possible if she was going to find a way to remove herself from Amelia's calculations, which meant she needed to play the game—for now.

She padded down the main hallway, recognizing the familiar décor her employer had meticulously chosen. Memories flooded as she thought of the happier times, sighing over how things turned sour the minute she denied her employer's amorous claims to her. She couldn't do it then, and she was not about to change her mind now.

She stopped abruptly about halfway, chills running down her spine as she observed an explicitly erotic painting on the wall—of her. *What in the hell? She's gone too far!*

The more she took a look at the painting, the angrier she felt. In her mind, it was an invasion of privacy, taken from an intimate moment that was never supposed to see the light of day. She was more determined than ever to find the exit strategy she needed to rid herself of Amelia once and for all.

Her thoughts were interrupted by voices coming from the main reception area. The moans and banter drew her closer, her curiosity keeping her glued despite her clandestine positioning, out of the line of sight of the principal players for the evening's scene. She couldn't resist being a voyeur for a change, especially when it came to Amelia's favorite pet.

"So, what brings you to London?" Trinity inquired.

"I'm here on business, and hopefully a little pleasure while on business."

She nodded her head slightly. "I see. Well we can definitely help with that. Why don't I go ahead and show you to our parlor?"

He extended a hand. "After you my divine beauty queen." He bowed as she passed.

Trinity blushed at his pleasantries. Her fitted silk pencil skirt made her ample backside appear even more pronounced with every switch of her hips.

As she shifted her position to keep from being seen,

Samara continued to appreciate the overtly sensual movements in Trinity's gait. She'd forgotten how stunning, how beautiful she was, reminiscing over their own interludes during her stay as one of the gallery "pieces" to be selected. She shook from her thoughts to continue indulging in the scene as it played out in front of her.

"I heard from my colleague that you have an exotic selection of ladies. Is that true?" He seemed to be more anxious than the usual first-time customer, from what Samara could gather, but it could be more from being new to doing something like this. Trinity could smell the newness on him. "I want to have a good time, and I would love to be able to relax and unwind."

"I completely understand. After all, what's the point in coming this far if you can't indulge in a little innocent fun, eh?" Trinity smiled. The two of them surveyed the eleven available women who each wore sexy lingerie, high heels, and beautiful jewelry. They smelled delightful, their makeup was flawless, and not a strand of hair was out of place. He was getting the best money could buy.

"Have your pick," she smiled, as her girls vied for his attention. Trinity watched a look of lust wash over his face and his dark hooded eyes seemingly grew the size of gold balls. It was obvious he'd never seen anything like it before.

"Oooh, they're all so pretty!" His eyes moved around the delectable selections, looking like a kid in a candy store. "How many of them can I have? I mean, is there a limit to what I can choose?"

Trinity turned back to her customer. His pewter Armani suit, matching accessories, highly polished shoes and innate confidence, all exhibited a man of great taste and style. She gave the mayor a knowing look. "For you, I'll make an exception. You can have as many as you'd like."

He turned back to the bevy of beauties sitting on the plush velvet couches and chairs, all doing their best to win him over. He had a hard time trying to make up his mind. "I can't seem to decide. They're all so fucking beautiful."

He turned to Trinity, eyeing her along with the others. "Are you a part of the menu, too?"

Well, that depends, Mayor."

"Andrew. Just call me Andrew, darling."

"All right. Andrew. I'm not sure if you can handle what *I* have to offer."

"Oooh, I beg to differ, Trinity." He grinned as he tried to move his hands along her hips. He seemed to be warming up nicely, despite his initial hesitance. "I've had quite a lot of women during my political career, but to be honest, I've gotten bored with them, which is part of the reason I came to your fine establishment. I need a challenge."

Trinity was more than ready to be the challenge he was seeking. "You know the last man that said that went into cardiac arrest shortly after a blow job." She looked him over. "I would presume you're both around the same age."

"Well, I would imagine the gentleman you're referring to doesn't run five miles daily and still has enough energy to handle his executive assistant for lunch and the wife once he gets home." He licked his lips. "I think I'm more than up for whatever you think you can dish out."

Trinity was done talking. It was time he put his money where his mouth was. "Watch the floor," she called out to no one in particular.

Samara followed them, her curiosity getting the best of her. It had been some time since she'd watched a transaction in real time, and the anticipation of what was to come was too enticing to ignore.

Trinity began walking in the opposite direction, with Andrew following closely on her heels. Once they came to the stairwell, she said, "After this, you might want to consider early retirement."

"I like my women with a little mouth on them," he retorted, smacking her ass as she ascended the steps that led to the champagne room. "I wonder how well that mouth really works?"

"There's no reason to wonder my dear. You will soon find out the real reason as to why *my* services aren't listed. How do they say it in America? Never bite off more than you can chew?" She opened the door on the left and they walked in.

Unlike the rest of the spa, the cigar and champagne

room wasn't as elaborate but it was equally accommodating. The walls were draped in long dark curtains. Compared to the other brothels in the area, The Gallery was like a five-star resort. Each room had a big plush round bed hosted by chilled champagne and cigars, one chair, and a bedside dresser filled with extra linen, disposable cock rings, lubricants, condoms, and numbing gels.

Andrew eased off his suit coat as Trinity slowly slipped out of her clothes, all while knowing this wouldn't last five minutes. He admired her from behind.

"Why don't you hurry and find out how much of *this* you can chew on?" Andrew said. His erection was at full attention.

She turned to face him and took a casual stride over to where he stood. She cupped the sides of his clean-shaven face and then without warning, ripped his shirt open, causing its buttons to fly in every direction. He chortled at her sudden assertiveness.

"Such an aggressive little minx, aren't you?" He smirked. "That's all right. I was hoping you'd bring out the claws sooner or later. Show me what you got, sexy."

Trinity was never one to take a customer there to schmooze, so she figured the best way to prove her point was to show him. She shoved him onto the bed and commenced to unbuckling his belt. She yanked his pants and underwear clean off, then tossed them to the other side of the bed.

"Whoa, baby, easy on the material, now," he advised. "I didn't mind the shirt so much, but damn."

She disregarded his speech and climbed onto the bed, straddling him. Her silky tresses that she'd inherited from her Trinidadian mother spilled across his hairy chest as she leaned further into his body.

"You're a goddamned goddess, do you know that?"

His foul mouth was a complete turn off. It didn't matter so much when she focused on why she was there with him—money.

She stuffed all but her right thumb into his mouth and pressed her fingers firmly on his tongue. His eyes supplicated her for punishment while an inaudible moan escaped him. Controlling his head movements, she leaned further into him and drove the tip of her tongue along his left ear. Everything emitted from his mouth sounded like babble, but she was busy measuring the potential of his penis by the length of her left middle finger and found herself disappointed with her findings.

She began stroking his length to an even stronger erection, such as it was, enough to make the thrill ride down her throat worthwhile. She shifted her body sideways, never losing her grip on his mouth. As she snaked her tongue along his chest, her hardened nipples did the same. When she arrived at his midsection, she forced his head upward so that he could watch the show.

His slurred speech let her know he was exactly where he wanted her and she didn't waste any time. She was going to give him every bit of his money's worth. Her long tongue gradually wrapped around the thickness of his length. She watched him react to how well she handled his precious jewels with such precision and expertise.

Once it was wet and ripe enough to be consumed, she took it on a test drive so far down her esophagus she heard him squeal in delight.

Her fire engine red lacquered lips buffed his testicles with every downstroke, trying relentlessly to suck blood or cum out of him. Every time he squirmed, her jaws would only lock down even tighter, creating a virgin vagina with her mouth. She took her hand out of his mouth, freeing them both to massage his ever-tightening stones, feeling his hips clenching in anticipation of the eruption soon to follow.

"Oh, shit, you've got me ... fuck, I'm almost there!" He tried to regain control by grabbing for her head to slow her down, but she wasn't having any of that. He wanted a heart attack and she was going to give him one.

Samara continued watching until she felt a familiar pair of hands cup her breasts. The move startled her, but not enough to give herself away. One of the hands moved to cover her mouth, stifling any screams that would come out. The hands were more comfortable than usual, like they had traversed her body before.

That fact alone alerted her to who those hands belonged to.

"Hello, my exquisite doll. Enjoying the show?" Amelia whispered in her ear. "Don't bother lying to me, I can easily find out for myself. Keep watching, I love watching her work, too."

Trinity finally grabbed his hands and held them at his sides, sucking him down fervently.

Her head resembled a piston in an engine, bobbing up and down with the speed of a finely-tuned Maserati. He was obviously shocked at her strength in holding him in place, completely at her mercy as she pushed him past the point of no return.

The wave neared its crescent, and there was nothing left for him to do but wail and groan like an injured animal. The only question that remained was if when it was time to come whether he would sound like a man, or like a prepubescent teenager.

Amelia pulled Samara away, into one of the spare bedrooms so they could be alone, leaving Trinity to her client. "That was fun, huh? Seems like old times, doesn't it?"

"Those time are over, Mommy, and you know it."

"They don't have to be over, baby. You could have resisted me when I touched you, but you didn't. You're still into me; why do you continue to torture yourself?"

"You continue to torture me." Samara's attempts to keep her emotions in check were fading with each second that Amelia was in her space. "You're still torturing me as we speak, thinking that I would have consented to what you did to me back there. Why I decided to come back here like I'm still one of your pieces is beyond me, but I won't make that mistake again."

"What you fail to realize is that I can end you at any given moment," Amelia replied. "If I wanted you ended, I would have made a call a long time ago to have you exactly where you didn't want to be. That's what keeps you with me, and it would serve you to remember that."

Samara froze, the sheer panic in her body language evident to Amelia. She tried to regain her composure, but she also resigned herself to the bone-chilling fact that Amelia could, and would, make good on her promise to revoke her freedom at a moment's notice.

"I can see from your silence that you now remember your place. Now, go and wait for Trinity to let you know who your next client will be." Amelia showed no emotion at this point, no longer in the playful mood she was in a few moments ago. "And for your blatant disrespect, you'll be doing this one at your expense. Every dime you earn will belong to me."

Samara took her time walking to the reception area, slumping into one of the loungers to await her next client and location. The tears she tried to keep from falling matched the heat of anger in her heart. She was convinced more than ever that she needed to remove herself from Amelia's life, only this time, in her anger, she was able to figure out how she would accomplish it, and who would be able to help.

She resolved to keep being a "good girl" for now, starting with this next assignment. It would have to be her best performance yet, since she could no longer fake her interest during the date. Her heart, and now her body, belonged to the only one on the planet she would ever want to fully give herself to. She only hoped he could forgive her for who she needed to see to escape her own personal hell.

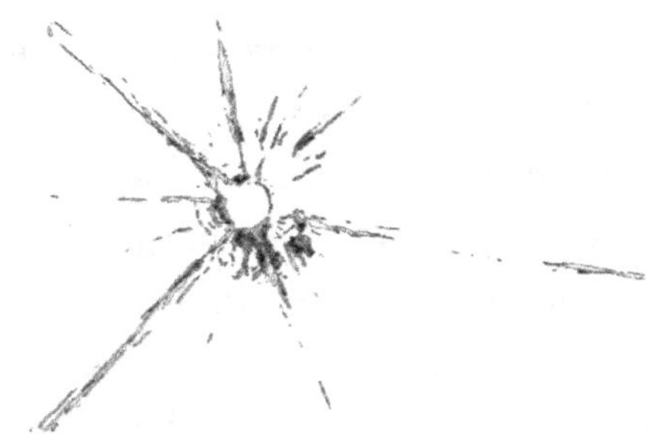

CHAPTER NINE

"I needed this more than I realized. Hopefully I can simply relax and indulge for a bit."

Juan Carlos sat in his hotel room at the Four Seasons Westcliff in Johannesburg, relaxing with his favorite brand of Scotch, a Hedonism Grain he picked up a few years ago that became his guiltiest pleasure. Nursing the glass in his hand, he thought back to the close call in Cameroon.

DK's gonna get us killed if he pulls another last-minute stunt like that again. He took another sip of the potent liquor, straight with no chaser. He wanted to sink into a deep sleep as quickly as possible, wondering if he'd finally gotten to the point to where he was too old to be gunrunning anymore.

He had to take some responsibility, though. He was

admittedly slow in reacting to the way things turned south on them, but he more than made up for it during their escape to the helicopter. If it weren't for Dorian's delayed instincts, the path would have been much clearer for them. He had always been a crack shot; he was his father's son, and he would dare say that the son was a better shot than his father. That was what gave him pause; something was off with his godson.

What he felt Dorian lacked in tactical ability, since he wasn't former military, he more than made up for in the analytical, especially when they were in high-pressure situations. It made Juan Carlos nervous, too. Donovan was never this edgy, and while his son's edge made him wealthier than he'd ever been during the Cold War in his younger days, he had to wonder if he would live long enough to enjoy his spoils.

Juan Carlos de Silva was a native son of Brazil, born of a second-generation Brazilian Navy engineer father and military wife mother. He joined the Brazilian Navy after secondary school, finding his calling as a part of the *Grupamento de Mergulhadores de Combate*, the Brazilian equivalent of the Navy SEALs. He discharged from the Brazilian Navy and hooked up with Interpol, which is how he ran into Donovan Bentley, who worked with the US Department of Defense at the time. Fast forward ten years, and the disillusioned colleagues left their respective agencies and began gun running at the height of the Cold War between Russia and the US.

Now in his late fifties, he could have retired a long time ago from being in the field, but he'd promised his long-time friend he would make sure his son was safe, until such time as he couldn't do it anymore. As Dorian's godfather, he felt it was his otherworldly duty to do so, but in his mind, that time was coming to where he would have to bow out.

He'd sacrificed a lot in fulfilling that promise. He lost his wife, who divorced him because she felt he'd abandoned her, and his family in Brazil disowned him the moment they found out he was involved in criminal activity after cultivating such a stellar military career.

For a man who valued family above almost everything, this was a blow his heart couldn't bear, so he locked it away and soldiered on, sending money back to them, whether they wanted him to or not.

He still felt he had it in him to eventually do things on his own, if only for a few years. His body had other ideas, despite his thinking that he was still the young and virile man he was thirty years ago. He was no fool, either; while he'd been with Dorian for the better part of five years, Juan Carlos was aware that there were replacements being trained up to replace him and Harry.

His emotions weren't as conflicted over his employer's contingency plans as he originally thought. On the one hand, he was relieved he wouldn't have to do this too much longer, as Dorian's replacement would want to have someone else as his second in command. On the other hand, he had a vested interest in keeping this going.

Although he'd survived the transition from father to son, he found peace in being able to transition into retiring with more money than he'd ever dreamed of. He even had ideas of possibly reconnecting with his wife, to possibly convince her that he wasn't as much of a deadbeat as she'd thought.

In the next moment, he'd had other, more pleasant thoughts. Thoughts of a woman who he'd give anything to turn back the clock and do everything over. The more he thought about her, the more he smiled. He reasoned out that trying to reconnect with his ex-wife would be disingenuous, when his heart still belonged to another.

He'd also compromised himself in ways that he wasn't proud of, thanks to a cruel twist of fate. He'd tried to resign himself to the fact that it was not meant to be, but he allowed his urges and his heart to reduce him to a man he barely recognized anymore. She was still his one weakness—the one he would never deny. Ever.

His cell phone rang, shaking him from his thoughts. Not too many had the new number, but he recognized the familiar area code coming from the States. "Yeah, Bentley, what is it?"

"JC, what's going on with Dorian?" Donovan's voice rang through the earpiece. "I thought you were going to keep him out of trouble. You two got caught in a fire fight in the CAR?"

"Your son is a grown man, Donovan. What did you want me to do? You asked me to make sure he doesn't get himself killed, and I've done that, and I've done it longer than I'd originally promised you." Juan Carlos was not in the mood to deal with Donovan, and that was putting it mildly.

Recently, Donovan had been nearly hounding Juan Carlos about his son's comings and goings. What once was a promise made to a friend had now become a chore he couldn't wait to be rid of once and for all. There were already strains on their friendship, and this was doing more damage.

"I know you have, my old friend, and I am grateful to you, but I have a feeling he's getting in over his head now." Donovan was undeterred in his inquiry, dismissing the irritated tone coming from Juan Carlos. "I think he's been working some of our old DoD contacts. Did you know he was talking with Locke?"

Juan Carlos raised an eyebrow. *How did Donovan find out about General Locke?* He felt the need to run smoke and mirrors. "Dorian has no reason to get in touch with Locke. We have enough weaponry to keep things flowing for at least another year without scraping the bottom of the barrel."

"Nevertheless, JC, the connection between my son and Locke was unmistakable when he came over earlier today." Donovan wasn't playing games, and he trusted his instincts, whether they were dulled from retirement or not. "I need you to find out if Locke has infiltrated the organization. If he has, it could get ugly. You remember what happened in Berlin, we don't want a repeat of that incident. That almost got us locked up. If it weren't for our collective quick thinking, God knows what would have happened to us."

Yeah, but the rules of the game have changed since then, Juan Carlos thought to himself as he listened to Donovan rant about past history. The old alliances and enemies were no longer what they were, and those who weren't in the know, wouldn't know. "I remember Berlin, and all the bullshit in the Czech Republic, too, and if my memory serves correctly, Interpol couldn't touch us then once Locke stepped in and bailed us out … *both* times. We both know that there was no way Interpol was going to do anything because they knew who we were. The agent who arrested us simply didn't get the memo."

The phone line got quiet. Juan Carlos knew he'd trumped Donovan on his romanticized version of the truth. Locke might have been an abstruse connection, but to paint him as anything other than the reality he represented would be doing a disservice to what they all were guilty of. Hindsight was always 20/20, but only when the person looking back didn't choose to see what they wanted to see. "Cat got your tongue, you smooth-talking son of a bitch? I don't think there is much more than what you're thinking there is. Locke is a step away from retirement, and you want to act like he's still deep in the game or something? What do you know that you're not saying?"

"JC, I'm asking you as a friend to check out this connection between Locke and Dorian." Donovan asked one final time, his obstinacy on full display. "You might think he has changed, but old dogs don't learn new tricks, I'm living proof of that."

Juan Carlos stared out into the stunning visuals of the Motherland, admiring the night lights and the beauty of the South African countryside. He wondered if this recent turn of events might put him in a compromising position that could cost him dearly. As with Berlin and Prague, in case the situation called for it, he was going to need an exit strategy. If he didn't develop one quickly, the wealth he'd built wouldn't be enjoyed into his golden years, and that he couldn't allow.

The first thing he needed to do was find out what exactly was going on with his boss and the general. He picked up his satellite phone, taking a long breath before exhaling as he dialed. "Harry, we need to talk, brother."

"What's the good word, brother?" Harry's voice rang through the earpiece. "I thought we weren't supposed to be doing another job for a couple of weeks."

"It isn't about that, although I wish it were." Juan Carlos tried to find a way to broach the conversation without triggering Harry's penchant for wanting to rage. "Have you noticed any changes in the transactions the past few deals we've been working? It's almost as though the contact has changed the protocols on us. What's your gut telling you?"

"Brother, I thought you would never ask!" Harry shouted. "I was trying to tell DK about it when it first happened, but this thing with Adam has me convinced that someone else is pulling the strings."

Harry's words caused Juan Carlos to take a pause. He wanted to take a pulse of the situation, and Harry sounded like he was dying to give him the smoking gun. "How did you know that the protocols have changed after the Adam deal? They couldn't have been that overt, could they?"

"I can't believe you can't see the old imprints on the communications from when we were dealing with DK's old man," Harry scoffed. "Are you getting slow in your old age, or are you that ready for retirement to see what's blatantly obvious?"

Juan Carlos wanted to reach through the phone and strangle him. "We promised Donovan that we would see things through with DK. Have you forgotten that?"

"And how much longer will that be, brother? Neither one of us is getting younger, and I'd rather spend my days with a young piece in my lap while I still have the ability to do something with it." Harry's laughter bellowed loud enough to cause Juan Carlos to pull the phone away from his ear. "You know he wasn't built for this life. I still don't know how he convinced his father to take things over."

"Well, he's been able to do pretty well for someone who wasn't built for this, Harry," Juan Carlos pointed out. "We've made more money and haven't had half the stress that Donovan used to put us through."

"And what do you call what the fuck happened in Cameroon? He's slipping, JC, and you know it," Harry deadpanned. "I know you got a soft spot for the kid, being his godfather and pseudo uncle and all, but face the facts, man."

"One mistake in five years, brother? Are you serious right now?"

"Deadly serious, brother. Mark my words, he will be our downfall before long. Things are getting just a bit too close for comfort lately, and I won't sit around and wait for it all to come crashing down."

"So, when the rest of the team agreed that you were the one slowing things down over the past few junkets, it was DK who made it clear that you were going to remain, but even he had to acknowledge he had to figure out what needed to be done soon." Juan Carlos felt the need to level with him. "That was how Ishmael even got brought on to begin with. If you'd been on your game, you would still be one of his lieutenants, helping to coordinate all this shit. He's loyal to you and you sound like you want to replace him at the top of the food chain. Is that how you repay loyalty?"

"DK's been loyal, I'll give you that. Okay, I'll trust

it because I trust you, but I'm serious. The minute something else goes down and our lives are put in danger, I'm jumping ship. I need to make amends for a lot of things before it's too late."

Juan Carlos disconnected the call, feeling more frustrated than ever. *I've got enough going on, and now I have to watch this hijo de puta.* The only thing he could do was stay focused and keep his wits about him. Dorian was family, and he would never turn his back on his family. Ever.

Chapter Ten

(Speaking Portuguese) "Hi, Mami, how was the rest of the art exhibition?"

Being at home and visiting with his parents always seemed to give Dorian a sense of balance after being on business for the past few weeks. Being out in the field was fun and exciting, but home was always where his heart was.

After Donovan turned the "family business" over to his son, they moved to an exclusive beach town in San Diego, California called Del Mar, settling on a quaint three-bedroom beach home where Donovan could relax and enjoy the ocean view from his front porch and his wife could paint to her heart's content, using the calming breeze and quiet surroundings to create.

Dorian walked into the converted bedroom his mother used to paint, slipping behind her to hug her neck and kiss her cheek. Despite the fear he inspired in others, at heart he was a mama's boy, always looking to please the one woman on the planet who truly understood him: Isabella Bentley. She was a strikingly beautiful woman in her mid-fifties, with a body that stood the test of time, putting women in their forties to shame whenever she took time out of her painting schedule to tan. It was a wonder in his mind how his father was able to keep her under wraps all these years.

(Speaking Portuguese) "Hi, baby, the art show was wonderful! Four of my pieces were purchased." She was in the middle of one of her creations, making sure it would be ready for yet another showing. "Thank you for helping with that effort, and I love that gorgeous girl you brought with you. Is she going to be around for a minute?"

Dorian groaned at the mere mention of his mother trying yet again to settle her son down. *Oh my God, here she goes again with this marriage argument. Why won't she let the subject rest, I'm almost forty, for crying out loud!* He had long grown weary of the constant questions from the both of them, and this latest invasion was unnerving.

For years, his mother tried to play matchmaker at nearly every exhibition she was featured in, introducing him to some of California's most eligible bachelorettes. Although she told her only child she made peace with his choice in occupation as she had with her husband's, it didn't stop her from holding out hope he would find a woman someday … even if she had to find that woman herself.

"Mami, you know how I feel about you trying to attach me to every woman who I happen to bring as a date to different events." Dorian observed the other pieces on the wall, admiring the distinctiveness of each piece when placed against the others. "It didn't work in high school when you tried it with Riley. It didn't work in college. Why do you insist on tormenting yourself?"

"Because you need to continue the family line, Dorian," Isabella replied, placing the paintbrush on the easel. She sighed as she looked at her son. "Your father and I had hoped by now we would have a grandchild to bounce around the house. At the very least, one, but we would have hoped for two in my wildest dreams."

He was set for a rebuttal when he looked into his mother's eyes. They were truly saddened, and it nearly broke his heart. He didn't like disappointing her, but while he was so busy running an empire and sticking to his rules, he neglected to take into account what his rules were doing to her.

"Dorian, we would never be the ones to tell you what to do with your life, but I also don't want you to get too old to enjoy your children one day." Isabella stood up from her chair and caressed his face. "The business you're in, it is not meant for you to be in until you're old and gray. Your father was fortunate to get out when he did without any real casualties, and I pray the same for you, my son."

He willed the tears from falling from his eyes, but he knew that wouldn't last long. His mother could see right through him, and there was nowhere to hide.

In times of stress or ecstasy, he always reverted back to his native Portuguese tongue. It was the language he learned along with English, thanks to his mother, and he fell back to it whenever he needed to get his true feelings across to her.

(Speaking in Portuguese) "Mami, I don't ever want to see you sad, but it is not easy to find a woman who can see the truth of me."

(Speaking in Portuguese) "You already have, my son, your stubbornness and greed in your business has blinded you. When the end comes, you will see who has been there and knows your heart. I only pray it won't be too late when you do." She wiped the tears streaking down his face. "Promise me you will heed my words?"

(Speaking in Portuguese) "Yes, Mami, I will."

She kissed him on both cheeks and gave him the onceover before turning and sitting back at her easel. She giggled to herself before changing the subject. "Your father should be in his office, talking to one of his old coworkers as usual."

He laughed as he thought about the way she said "his old coworkers" as he walked across the living room to the other part of the house, finding his father in the midst of a heated Skype conversation with one of his buddies at the Department of Defense.

"It's not my fault you can't keep a lid on this bullshit going on in Syria!" Donovan yelled at the screen at his buddy. For a moment, Dorian thought he would hurl a paperweight at the screen or something, as animated as his father was.

Some things never changed.

He allowed his father continue to try to work through his frustrations. His father wanted to get back into the mix, but Dorian was convinced that he was better off playing armchair quarterback than being in the field again. Their family had been put through a lot, including an incident that inadvertently became the catalyst for his current choice of career.

"Dad, can I talk to you for a minute? I promise it won't take long; I have to get back in the field soon." Dorian patted his father on the shoulder to get his attention as he recognized the man on the screen. "Hello, again, General Locke."

"Dorian! It's nice to see you again, son." General Locke greeted from the screen. "Business is still good, yes?"

"Business is always good, sir. It looks like the mess in Syria and Egypt is giving you guys the business, huh?" Dorian replied. He cut his eyes at his father, wondering why they were having such a heated conversation when the general was supposed to be making arrangements to retire soon. "You know the Israelis will be on high alert and ready to act."

"We're keeping an eye on the region, but it's nothing our boys and girls can't handle." The general laughed as he watched Donovan's face turn from anger over Syria to confusion over being left out of the loop with regard to the Gaza Strip. "Well, I'll let you gentlemen talk, father to son. Dorian, hope to see you when you hit the East Coast, and Donovan, we'll catch up tomorrow."

Donovan switched the Skype connection off, swiveling in his chair to face his son. "What was that about with you and the general?"

Dorian dismissed the question in his father's mind. "The general and I have been to some of the same parties in D.C., Dad, nothing more. Every so often I have dinner with him and his wife."

"Don't bullshit me, DK," Donovan replied. He got up from his chair with an accusatory tone in his voice. "General Locke is known in our world for going through back channels to get things done."

Dorian was not about to give him the satisfaction of being right about his suspicions. Besides, it wasn't the original reason he needed to talk to him. "I'm fully aware of his connections, Dad. In fact, I know he works with one of my chief rivals, Rainier. I haven't been able to make a dent in that connection for years. Hell, you can ask Uncle JC, if you have to be convinced."

He always threw Juan Carlos out there when he felt the desire to make his point clear.

Donovan backed down once Juan Carlos's name was mentioned. "Okay, DK, I'll lay off for now. And since the general is not privy to the answer, how is business going?"

"Adam tried to stiff us on this last run," Dorian recounted. "Things are getting desperate in Central Africa, but these new situations in Syria and Egypt promise to be lucrative, at least twenty million on both sides. You remember how it was in North Africa."

Donovan rubbed his chin, trying to make sense of what his son disclosed. After making up his mind before speaking, he clapped his hand on Dorian's shoulder. "Okay, but make sure you play both sides. The minute you choose sides, you end up dead."

"I know, dad, I've kept that to heart, but that wasn't the reason I came over to see you and Mami, though."

"Oh? So, you're finally telling me you've figured out an exit strategy so you can settle down and have us some grandkids?" Donovan asked.

The blunt force of the question should have knocked Dorian off his feet.

"No, I haven't figured out an exit strategy because I'm *not* ready to exit." Dorian stood his ground, knowing where this road would lead. "When I'm ready, I'll leave without any collateral damage in my wake. I can't say the same thing happened when you gave me the reins."

"You'll be mindful to watch your tone, Dorian." Donovan hardly ever called him by his legal name, always a nickname or term of endearment. As quiet as it was kept, he kept tabs on Dorian through his old business connections.

Despite the fact that no one in the Western Hemisphere knew what his son looked like, Donovan had grown increasingly concerned that the "Wraith" had developed more enemies than he could keep an eye on. "You're playing too fast and loose, taking your anonymity for granted. You'll make a mistake thinking you're untouchable, especially with the people involved in this game."

"Dad, I didn't come here to do this with you." Dorian sat down in the other chair, encouraging his father to join him. He rubbed his palms together, a tell-tale sign from his younger days when he wanted to broach a subject he was uncomfortable talking about with him. "When did you know mom was the 'one'?"

That question rocked the usually unflappable elder Bentley. "Wow, I guess I might have jumped the gun a little bit. You haven't ever asked me that question before."

"That's why I'm asking now," Dorian replied. "I … I think I … well, I'm not sure yet—"

"Hold on, DK, you either know or you don't know, okay?" Donovan leveled with him. "It's not a business transaction, there's no logic involved, nothing like that. If you're thinking about it, then you haven't found her yet. When I laid eyes on your mother for the first time, it hit me harder than any punch, any elbow, any kick could have ever hit me. Now, I'm not saying it's like that for everyone, son, but I'm saying that's what happened to me."

It was amazing whenever father and son chatted like that, there was more wisdom and information imparted than in an interrogation room. Dorian's logical side took heed to his father's words, and, at least for now, he realized what he had been feeling was more lust than love. The thing that scared him more than anything was he couldn't logically explain it away completely, either.

Dorian checked his timepiece and realized he needed to head to the airfield or he would miss his window to get back to his flat in London before noon the next day. He had an appointment he could not miss with another buyer in Ukraine, and he wanted to put make more headway into Rainier's territory by taking more buyers from him in the Slavic area.

He got up from the chair, rushing out the door. "Dad, I hear what you're saying, but I have to go. I love you, and I'll call you as soon as I land."

"Alright son, you make sure you take care of yourself and remember what I said." Donovan called after his son, shaking his head at his flightiness. As he stood in the doorway, watching Dorian peel out of the driveway like a bat out of hell, he couldn't stop laughing to himself. "That boy is going to realize that everything he needs was right there in front of him the entire time."

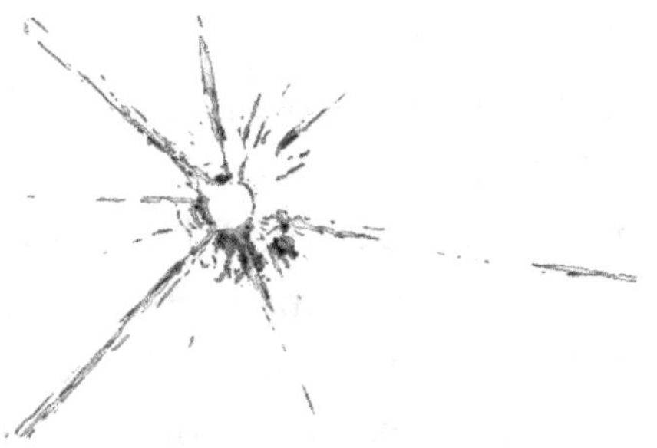

Chapter Eleven

Trinity was handling business as usual in The Gallery, watching as all of the different clients were being led to the different rooms that her girls had them procured for the evening. The smile that spread across her face was indicative of the lucrative evening that lay ahead for all involved.

She couldn't wait for the primetime showcase of the night to commence. Every piece available in the repertoire—except one—would be at the VIPs disposal. While she was personally disappointed in that aspect, she couldn't help but exhibit a little excitement over her employer's favorite client being among the attendees.

It was only after she processed the last of their transactions that she glanced over at the time and realized she had not checked in. She took a seat, picked up the phone, and when the other voice made its way into her ear, she squeezed her legs tight to keep from dripping onto the floor. "Hi, Mommy. Have you missed me?"

"Of course, I've missed my pretty girl," Amelia answered. "Are things prepared for our VIPs? I want to make sure the pieces are on full display."

"Yes, Mommy, everything is as you wanted."

"Good girl. I'll be there shortly."

"Yes, Mommy, how many of our VIPs will be arriving?"

"There should be the usual suspects, but there is one I want handled with special care … Mr. Nagi will be joining us."

"Understood. Should I ensure I'm the arm candy until you arrive, to keep the other VIPs from wanting to procure me?"

"Yes, I want you with Mr. Nagi until I arrive. Please let him know I will be there. We haven't been properly introduced and acquainted. That needs to change today."

"Thank you for attending our special VIP sneak peek, Mr. Nagi. It is our hope that the newest pieces in our collection are to your liking."

As directed, Trinity made sure that she was inappropriately dressed and attached at Dorian's hip during the duration of the showing. She grinned as he took long glances at each of the women, stroking his chin as he regarded each of their features. It was no secret as to why Amelia wanted him there; if he approved, the rest of the clientele would pay through the nose to have at any of them.

"Thank you for the invitation, Trinity. It was a welcome distraction from what I have had to deal with as of lately." Dorian continued to admire each woman, giving winks and blowing flirty kisses toward the ones who he knew would have his attention when he was ready to acquire for entertainment. "I may procure one for the evening if the mood strikes me."

"That's wonderful news to hear, sir. I believe you will find the selection to your liking. I know your palate is more discerning that the majority of our clientele. If you like our new additions, Mommy will be more than happy to keep them."

"Speaking of Mommy, will she be joining us this evening?" Dorian asked as he took an extended look at one particular woman with striking facial features and curves to die for.

"She should be here any moment, sir. She made it a point to ensure she was."

"Now, that's interesting."

"Why is that, sir?"

"As long as I've known her, she has never gone to such lengths for me," Dorian replied. "I've only seen pictures of her over the years, and while I would have pressed for a personal meet long before now, my professional pursuits and schedule never lined up with hers."

"Well, sir, you know Mommy; when she develops an affinity for a client, especially one who spends the type of money that you do, she makes sure they are handled properly, even if she has to take care of them personally."

"Remind me to express my gratitude when she arrives. By the looks of things, she has truly outdone herself."

"I'm pleased you approve, Mr. Nagi, but I'm more interested in this expression of gratitude you've mentioned. Does the lady of the house have the opportunity to choose the manner in which you get to express said gratitude?"

Dorian raised an eyebrow, intrigued by the sudden coquettish nature. "I thought the client chose their method of pleasure?"

"Not when I'm offering myself as the paramour, sir. However, for you, I'm more than willing to make the exception." Amelia met his gaze, emphasizing the intent of her comment. "You may want to take advantage while the offer is on the table. I don't afford anyone the luxury."

"And I assume you're offering, my dear? I was under the impression that I was choosing from this delectable gallery."

"You're more than welcome to do so, sir. In fact, she can assist me in whatever pleasures you would like to indulge, regardless of the depravity or your exquisite proclivities."

"My tastes are rather exotic, Ms. Emmerson."

"Call me Amelia."

"I see … Amelia, as you know, it is one of the reasons I've stayed as loyal as I have all these years. Your gallery is second to none, and they have been very acquiescent to my more sadistic pleasures."

"And in the interests of those pleasures, I believe that Hani would be perfect for what you have in mind tonight." Amelia licked her lips as she thought of the possibilities that would soon come to fruition.

"I believe you are spot on, Amelia. Outside of my favorite piece in your collection, I believe she will be able to handle what I have in store for you both. Shall we?"

Amelia smiled wide as she motioned for Hani to join them. Once she was at his side, Amelia motioned for Trinity to continue the collection presentation with the rest of the clientele. "Yes, let's. Hani, let's ensure that our premier client has a wonderful time."

Chapter Twelve

Dorian was in the midst of indulging a glass of Hennessy White while reviewing the information for the next transaction once the Syrian deal was done. He was a bit sore from the exploits a few hours earlier, smiling as he'd been able to keep up his energy despite two women who were quite insatiable. He made a mental note to keep Hani in his rotation for when his desires for inflicting sensual pain made its way to the forefront.

He was especially curious over why Amelia offered herself in the manner in which she did. He was convinced, from all of their interactions, that she was as much a dominant personality as he was, but the way she capitulated, the way she moved, it triggered everything within him to unleash every bit of aggression he had on her and Hani. He wondered if he had Amelia pegged wrong.

The sound of his cell phone interrupted his thoughts. He was confused as he looked at the screen, doing his best to wonder why anyone would be calling him in the early hours of the morning.

"Harry? Why are you calling at damn near five in the morning? Is something wrong?"

"I was about to ask you the same thing, DK," Harry replied. "Is there anything I need to know about? Ever since that madness in Cameroon, I've been wondering if things have changed at all."

"There is nothing you need to know about at this point, Harry. Things are flowing exactly as they should be. Idriss wants the next shipment sooner than expected, the tensions in the region have heightened and he wants to be as prepared as he can be at the moment." Dorian did his best to keep as much information as close to the vest as possible. Harry wasn't one of his lieutenants anymore, so he didn't need to be privy to every detail as he once was. "We will be getting with our distro in Kiev to ensure they are happy. Also, I need you to get in touch with our friends in Dublin; there are things we need to get to our domestic buyers."

"I thought we were done with Dublin?"

"You thought wrong," Dorian replied. "Our US connect wants to handle his buyers in Texas. The militias want to take care of some stuff at the southern border. Our Mexican connect also wants weaponry, so we need to take care of them to keep the tensions at a stalemate."

"DK, we can go through another distro. Dublin no longer needs to be involved."

"And why would we need to do that? They're taking all the risks, and all of our packages are legit and untraceable, there is no blow back if things go south between them. CIA is in the know, so is ATF. What's your problem?"

Harry rubbed his face over his hands, trying to keep the stress out of his voice. He hated being on the outside looking in, but he didn't have much choice in the matter. If he was honest with himself, he had only himself to blame for his diminished role within the operation. "It just isn't a good idea, kid. They could still burn us. The paper trail is too simple."

"I've done things a bit differently since the last you remember, Harry," Dorian pointed out. "I have things on lock, and there are no issues to worry over, unless there is something I need to know about?"

"I'm telling you, DK, I have a bad feeling about how things are going down. Have I ever steered you wrong?"

"No, you haven't, but there are things in play that you haven't been privy to for a while now. We need to chat about things once we're done in Syria. I may have something else I need you to do moving forward."

Harry paused when he heard that part of the conversation. "Are you cutting me out completely?"

"No, I'm not cutting you out. I need you to handle some things in the States for me. I'll enlighten you when we're done in Syria."

"Okay, DK, we will talk then. I guess I'll just sit here on my hands or something."

"I don't need you to understand what I'm doing and why I'm doing it, Harry. I just need you to trust that what I'm doing is benefiting everyone involved." Dorian picked up on the irritation in Harry's voice, and he was none too pleased about it. "If you can't rock with my program, let me know now and I can send you the money you asked me to keep safe for you and you can retire. No harm, no foul, no hard feelings. You've been loyal to my father, and to me, but I'm doing things my way for a reason."

"Okay, okay, DK, I'm still with you, kid. No need to get dramatic."

"I've told you before, and I'm telling you now, it's never personal, Harry. I consider you family away from the business, but no one will tell me how to run things, not even my father."

"Understood. I look forward to the call after the drop."

"Teams are in place, DK. We have a smaller window than usual, gotta make this count. Big Brother royally fucked us over."

The principal players in this transaction were

located in the Syrian town of Duma, which was far enough away from the Syrian capital that the transaction could be made with little incident. They had to move fast, as the decisions Stateside unexpectedly cast a sense of urgency over the transaction. The US-allied Kurdish forces would need some firepower to deal with the Turkish troops and their Syrian rebel allies who were slated to attack the northern borders.

Lazarus was front and center, with Dorian and Juan Carlos acting as his bodyguards, while Kale was hovering with the helicopter pilot at about five hundred feet, low enough to have a clean line of sight. The other two snipers hired for the job were at ground level, ready for evacuation procedures if the necessity arose.

General Idriss' captain, Captain Faroud, stepped out of the transport and walked over to where the three men stood. The cargo plane, an Airbus A330, was being unloaded as Faroud closed the gap between him and his men and Lazarus and his men. Faroud looked nervous as he regarded Lazarus, but he settled down after a few minutes so they could conduct their business.

(Speaking in Arabic) "I see you were able to get around your legislature after all, Wraith. Your reputation precedes you."

(Speaking in Arabic) "This was procured off the grid, compliments of a generous benefactor who wished to see the scales balanced."

(Speaking in Arabic) "The general will be pleased. He sends his regards, but he was unable to attend due to politicking on television."

Dorian wasn't tremendously concerned with the information Faroud spoke of. He'd gotten the intelligence from his trusted sources. He tapped Juan Carlos' shoulder and nodded silently that everything was still on the level.

Lazarus maintained his focus, playing his role to the hilt.

(Speaking in Arabic) "Do not worry, Captain, I believe everything will be to the general's specifications. He will not need to do much more politicking soon."

(Speaking in Arabic) "Thank you, Wraith. I believe this will conclude our business."

He pushed a button to trigger the wire transfer. Transaction completed.

Lazarus shook Faroud's hand, showing a slight smile from the transaction having gone off without major incident. That was before one of the rebel soldiers screamed out that a surface to air missile was in the air.

Juan Carlos and Dorian looked up in the direction of where the soldier pointed, and sure enough, not one, but two SAMs had hit the peak of their arc and were making their descent upon where they stood.

"Kale!" Juan Carlos shouted through his earpiece.

"Relax, fellas, the response is already on the way."

Kale's smirk could be felt through the earpiece as his gunship made its move toward the missiles. The second gunship took off and sped toward the other missile heading toward the cargo plane.

As the helicopters advanced, Lazarus and Faroud were in the midst of a heated argument in their native tongue. While Juan Carlos was confused as to what was being said, Dorian understood every word. Faroud was pissed.

Lazarus tried to convince him that this wasn't a double cross, but he was equally pissed that Faroud might have had something to do with the SAMs in the air, too. It wasn't uncommon for soldiers, even officers, to give themselves up for the sake of the cause in the region.

The argument paled in comparison to the imminent threat racing toward them.

The distance closed quickly between ground zero and the missiles and Juan Carlos grew more nervous by the second. "Kale, you think you might want to erase the threat, like, now?!"

"Hold your horses, old man! This actually *is* rocket science, dammit!" Kale said as the pilot tried to line up the gunship for an easy shot for him to take. "I got this, keep it together, boys."

An explosion boomed across the sky, alerting everyone to the destruction of the other SAM in mid-air by the other gunship.

"Tango down, sir." The other gunship's crew

radioed to Kale.

"A few more seconds is all I need." Kale got the line he wanted and fired off the rocket. Seconds later, the shockwave from the explosion could be felt from the ground as the shrapnel and sparks from the missile came crashing down, sending everyone fleeing for cover. "Tango down."

"It took your ass long enough!" Juan Carlos yelled through the earpiece. He checked around and saw Faroud and his men already at their transports and bugging out of the area, weapons in tow. "Some of us like living down here!"

"Chill out, JC, we got through this in one piece, alright?" Dorian began to wonder if his right-hand loved complaining in his old age. He called General Locke to inform him of the transaction completion. "Yes, sir, the eagles and chicks have been delivered … yes, sir, the extra turtles also, and we added some wheels to the order, for good measure … thank you, sir, I look forward to the next scenario."

Juan Carlos gave him a look as though he had lost his mind. "Please tell me we get to relax for a couple of weeks? I'm in need of some time off so I can recharge a bit. Something was off with this particular transaction. Is there something I should know about?"

"You're right, something isn't flowing right, and I'm just as confused as you are over the why of it all," Dorian replied. He pulled his smartphone from his pocket and dialed a number, waiting for the other party to answer. "I need to see you as soon as we land. Send me your location as soon as possible."

Juan Carlos kept his eyes focused on Dorian, waving his hands to get his attention. "Full disclosure, DK. We need to know what's going on."

"I know you do, but I don't have any answers, but I hope to have them soon," Dorian answered as his phone chimed, letting him know there was crypto-deposit sent to his bank in Brazil. He looked at the size of the transfer and smiled even more. *Hell yeah, this was exactly what I needed.* He would be able to keep his team happy, as he realized he would be able to send larger-than-usual percentages, which should keep things calm for a little while.

The second message upset him, considering he'd gotten off the phone with them only minutes earlier. He didn't hesitate, as the need for an on-the-spot contingency plan became immediate priority. "On second thought, take the next month off, and that goes for all of you. Kale, pick us up so we can get out of here. Wraith to Airbus crew, go to contingency plan Echo. Extract and meet at the secondary rendezvous point, ASAP."

The change of heart in Dorian perplexed Juan Carlos. In fact, it had Kale confused, too. All three men piled into the gunship and headed north, with Dorian giving instructions to the pilot to head out of Syrian air space with all due haste.

"I thought we were taking the Airbus out of the

country, sir?" Kale inquired. "I think it would be a less cramped flight, don't you think?"

The answer to his question came in the form of the Airbus exploding as they flew away.

The men turned to Dorian, who had a disturbed look on his face. Even Lazarus showed concern because he'd never seen Dorian so unnerved.

"Those SAMs were not an accident." Dorian's anger mounted. "Someone leaked our location for the drop, and I'm going to find out who it was and make sure they don't take another breath on this planet."

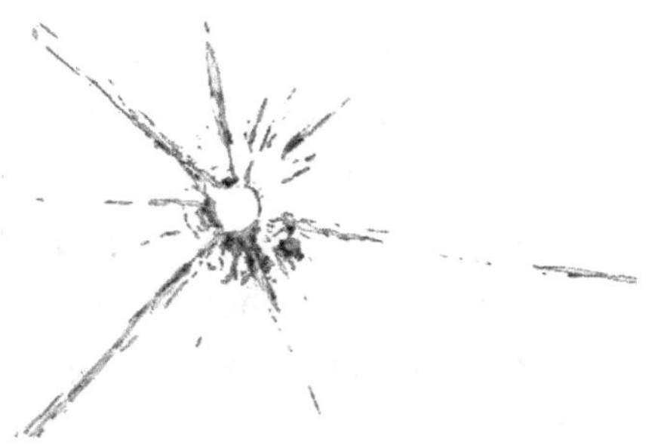

Chapter Thirteen

Whether Dorian wanted to admit it or not, he was shook.

This wasn't Cameroon. He could anticipate the alternative endings when everything went left during that campaign. This felt different on levels he couldn't put his finger on, and that made him nervous.

He sat in his living room with a glass of bourbon in hand, racking his brain over the different scenarios that led to the events from a couple days ago. He ran through every phone call in his mind, dissecting every text message with General Locke to find any possible deviation from their usual communications. He wanted to rule out every possibility so he could reach the most logical conclusion, but that would be a task in and of itself.

What he couldn't figure out was how he couldn't

see the double-cross coming with this particular transaction. He'd been meticulous in his normal protocol, took the normal contingencies needed for secondary evacuation. It was the reason he hardly ever planned transactions too close. He needed to look at every angle; ever the chess player, he needed to know where all the pieces were on the board. He couldn't fathom a scenario where there was an unknown variable that he couldn't account for, but he had to face the reality that could be the case.

The only real change in the protocol was not having Harry there with them, but he ruled that out entirely. Harry was not privy to any of the details with the Syria transaction; he made sure to feed him false information for his own protection. It was the first time he needed to employ that strategy, but he trusted no one more than Juan Carlos. If he said that Harry needed to be out of the loop this time, he followed that with every level of trust he could muster.

The more he tried to pull the right thread to unravel what might be happening to his organization, the more frustrated he became. He slowed down his rational process, attempting to keep his emotions from the equation, but to no avail. He treated the ones closest to him within the organization like they were brothers. Kale, Ishmael, Juan Carlos, Harry. They were all inner circle and damn near blood to him. He was convinced there was something that he was missing, that he couldn't see or assess to figure things out.

The follow-up call to his connect in the region went unanswered, which worried him further. He couldn't figure out whether they had been compromised or if they'd been turned against him. It wouldn't have surprised him if it were the latter; tensions were rising, and the bidding war became much more intense.

A call to Samara went to voicemail; he left a rambling message, irritated with himself that he was in such a vulnerable state. He rubbed his hands over his face several times over, needing to find his center the best way he could. As much as he needed her, he had to remind himself that she was not his, not completely.

It was usually in these spaces that he made the one call that always made him feel better. He hoped she would be at home by now, checking his calendar to trace her movements, thankful that she was between gallery showings at the time he needed her most.

"Hi, Mami, how are you doing?"

"Hi, baby, how are you doing?"

"I'm okay, just a rough day at the office. I needed to hear your voice. Is everything okay at the house? How's dad?"

"Yes, my sweetheart, things are okay. Your father has been a bit antsy with all of the stuff going on abroad, but I managed to convince him to head out to a party with me this weekend."

"Wow, how about that?" Hearing about his father's change of pace helped lift his spirits. "How did you pull that off?"

"Yep, I know, right? I'm happy that he's at least trying to get out more. It will be good for the two of us." Isabella paused in the middle of her thought as she shifted her vision. "You don't sound good, DK, are you sure you're okay?"

"I promise I'm okay. I needed to ground myself a bit. Hearing your voice helps more than you know."

"I'm worried about you, *pequeno*." Isabella paused again for effect. "You have me worried every time I hear about anything in the regions you are in, doing business. When are you going to turn things over to your lieutenants?"

"I have a little more time to groom them, maybe less than a year, tops. Then I can focus on other things."

"Have you figured out what those other things are yet?" For the first time since he got started in the business, Dorian heard the hopeful tone in his mother's voice. "I remember the dreams you had as a teenager. Maybe you can get back to that?"

"It is possible, mama. I just don't know if I'm built for a normal life anymore."

"There's nothing wrong with normal. You still have a lot to do and see in this world. Don't throw time away because you think you have more. Time is the one thing we cannot consistently earn; once it's gone, it's gone. Take what you have earned and use the time you have left to get to your happy ever after."

"As long as you get to spoil a few grandkids in the process, huh?"

"That's right! Rotten! I've earned the money to do it, and I'm going to!" Isabella's laughter caused him to smile wide. "And that gorgeous Samara would be a great woman to help make my dreams come true. I saw the way you looked at each other. That's a love you can't find anywhere else on this planet, sweetheart. She's your endgame."

"Okay, let me secure some loose ends and once I'm comfortable, I'll clear out and let my boys handle the rest. To be honest, I think they're ready, but I need to know that I'm ready to let go."

"You won't know until you do, baby. You won't know until you do."

His phone chimed almost as soon as he disconnected the call with his mother, a smile spreading across his face when he saw Samara's smiling face grace his screen. "I was just thinking about you. Where are you now?"

"I'm in Barcelona, escorting a client to one of his wine openings." Samara's tone struck Dorian as odd, and he could have sworn she sounded like she didn't want to be there. "I saw that you called, I excused myself from him so I could call my daddy."

He couldn't resist chuckling at that play on words, but it did not sway him from focusing on her demeanor. "What's wrong, Mara? You don't sound like yourself."

"I'm okay, Daddy, I promise. There's a lot of drugs and liquor flowing, and my date is being a bit more aggressive than usual," Samara replied. "It's almost like he wants to prove something to his younger subordinates who have been lusting over me all night."

Dorian found himself struggling with his emotions. On the one hand, his protective instincts would have him almost command her to leave her situation and scuttle her to a safe location. He realized the position it would put her in, and he didn't want to be a party to running afoul of her employer. On the other hand, if he didn't do anything and she found herself harmed or worse, he would never forgive himself.

In the end, he decided to trust her to find a way out of the situation without getting harmed. She was more resourceful than the average woman; if she could survive the favelas as a kid, high society should be a cake walk.

It still irritated him that she was still under Amelia's employ. "What does Mommy have on you, baby? I don't like the situations she places you in."

"It's complicated, DK, but I don't have time to get into it right now. My date is eyeing me as we speak, I need to get back to him," Samara paused like she wanted to say something else, but she decided against it. "When can I see you? I really need to see you. I'm trying not to sound like I'm craving you, but I don't care."

Hearing the yearning in her voice made him melt. "How soon can you finish things with your client?"

"I'll be done in the morning, if not sooner. I can

come to wherever you are, I don't care where it is. I need you."

"Meet me at my house in London as soon as you're able." The sense of urgency in his voice startled him, but it didn't scare him as much as it once did. "I'll have a few things I need to lock down and then I'm all yours. I'll have Ishmael bring you the minute you touch down."

"I can't wait, it will give me some time to work out a few things of my own. Can you give me a week?"

"I thought you needed me?" He couldn't resist teasing her, but he was a bit relieved that she asked for the time she needed. He still had to figure out the madness with Syria. "I mean, I can wait on you forever, so what's one more week?"

"Stop teasing me, baby, you know I need you more than you know, but we both have to clear out our entanglements and then we can enjoy each other," Samara giggled. "If everything goes according to plan, when I see you, we will have a lot to talk about."

"I'm looking forward to it. See you in a week, sexy." He wanted to ask about the plan she had, but he reminded himself that he wasn't entitled to those types of details—at least, not yet.

Chapter Fourteen

She shouldn't have been nervous, but she had every reason to be nervous. This would be the most important conversation she would have in her life to date. She knew the risks of what she was about to do and where she was about to go, but considering the personal purgatory she found herself in, she felt this would be paradise by comparison.

From the moment she touched down at Galeão International Airport and deplaned, she felt a sense of calm that she hadn't felt in some time. Being home had a tendency to do that for her. Still, she steeled herself against the dread that would soon wash over her as she traveled closer to her destination.

I hope he remembers me. It had been so long since the last time they'd seen each other, but he made it clear that he would never forget her. After what she'd done for his family, he told her that if she ever needed him, he would assist with everything in his power. She needed him more than she realized, and his power and influence would be more than enough for what she had in mind.

Samara did her best to enjoy the familiar sights and sounds of her home as she took the boats and ships in Guanabara Bay. As they turned onto Linha Vermelha highway, she settled into the seat a bit, focusing on what she would say and what she would request of one of the most powerful men on the South American continent. She would arrive there soon, so she had to prepare herself.

Passing by the shops along the highway felt like a dream sequence, taking her back to her youth when she worked for the Bread Maker with the hope of having enough money to move from the favelas. Her heart warmed as she thought of the chance meeting that led to her introduction to the man affectionately known as *El Jefe Supremo*—and the boy who made the introduction possible, while capturing her heart at the same time.

By the time the car reached the Jardim Botânico residential community, she was ready to have the conversation and comfortable with the way she wanted to dictate the flow of information. She looked at the massive homes and townhomes, her eyes widening at the spectacular view of Corcovado Mountain, host of the Christ the Redeemer statue. She closed her eyes for a moment, saying a silent prayer before exiting the vehicle and paying the driver.

She was immediately met by the security detail at the front gate of the palatial estate. She didn't flinch as she stated her reason for being there. She told them her name, waiting for the lead guard to radio to his detail inside the house. Within seconds, she was escorted up the driveway and to the front door, where she was transferred to the guards who would take her directly to where he was located.

Samara tried to stifle a giggle as Luciano de Souza gazed upon her and gave up the widest smile that she'd ever seen from him. In her mind, he hadn't aged a day, giving her chills as to the possibility of Dorian looking as devastatingly handsome at the same advanced age. He had his trademark Alonso Menendez Corona Mata Fina cigar between his fingers, a glass of cachaça on the rocks in his other hand.

She didn't recognize her voice when she finally spoke. "I wouldn't have come if I could find another way to deal with this. I need your help."

"And I told you if you ever needed anything, that you could always come to me, my dear." Luciano continued to pull on his cigar, tapping on the seating next to him for her to sit down. "What can I do to help you?"

Samara willed the tears from falling as she made herself comfortable, taking a water bottle that was offered to her. "I've found myself in a situation with someone who I cannot get away from, and I need to find a way to leverage my way out of the situation. To sever the connection once and for all."

"And what has this person done to you that requires the information you seek?"

"I don't know if I want to disclose that information."

Luciano rubbed his beard, regarding her suddenly sheepish body language. "I can't help you unless you can disclose the information, Samara."

Her eyes widened. The shock was evident. "I wasn't sure if you would have remembered me. It has been so long since we've seen each other. I simply assumed that you allowed me to enter because you wanted to know how I found you."

"I will always remember the girl who has my grandson's heart. You saved him and fell for him at the same time," Luciano replied. "There's nothing that you could do that could ever change the way I see you."

She couldn't understand why it was so difficult to explain to him, but she found the will to do so after she took a moment to compose herself. "I was an escort for a madam in the UK, and I no longer want to be under her employ. She won't let me leave, and has incriminating information that could ruin things with Dorian if he found out."

"It won't ruin anything. He loves you, just like I love you." Luciano's expression turned to concern as he took his finger to tilt her face toward his. "We all have things we are ashamed of doing, but it is the people who love us most that do not care about the things that are past. They only care about the future they build with you."

"I don't know if he loves me. How could you possibly know?" Samara's eyes met his, almost pleading for an answer that she wanted to hear. "He's been so hard to read lately."

"Because I know, and more importantly, his *abuela* knows, my dear." Luciano let out a laugh that seemed to vibrate the wooden bench they sat on. "She knew it when DK's father came around, and she knew it when she first saw you two together so long ago."

She didn't want to have this conversation with him in that moment. She wasn't ready to; her emotions were all over the place as it were, and the last thing she needed was to have her heart bleed all over the conversation. She needed to escape the chaos in her life before she could even think about a life with Dorian in any capacity.

She did her best to steer the conversation to where she needed it. "*Señor*, I need the information, and I hope you can help me get it. Can you help me get away from Amelia Escobar?"

Luciano's eyes narrowed as he regarded the name she mentioned. He nodded, leaning to kiss her forehead as an act of reassurance. "I have had dealings with your madam, and I don't like the way she conducts her business. I think I have something that will help you secure your release, but I will only give it to you under two conditions."

"Name them."

"First, take care of DK. He may be stubborn, and he gets it honestly, but he loves you more than anyone on this planet. He wouldn't have gone through so much not to have you in his life."

Samara nodded, despite her desire to protest his edict. "And the other?"

"Never call me *señor* again. You will be family soon, and you will call me *abuelo*, period."

"But what if he refuses me?"

"He won't because I've told him he won't. You are the one weakness he has in the world, the one he will never say no to. Ever. Do you understand me?"

The tears flowed freely this time, and she smiled as he hugged her tight and wiped the tears from her eyes. "Yes, abuelo, I understand."

"Good girl. Now, let's get this *puta engañosa* away from you for good."

Chapter Fifteen

"Does he know?"

Harry relaxed in his flat in downtown Glasgow, trying to figure out if what he was contemplating was the right move to make. An old Chinese proverb said that life is like a game of chess, it changes with each move. He remembered that proverb from his days in the Royal Navy. Taking the game up during those days, he began to understand the simplicity of the phrase. To be successful, you needed to be disciplined, assess resources, consider responsible choices and adjust when circumstances change. Either you made the right moves and checkmated your opponent, or you made the wrong moves and end up a pawn in someone else's game.

He wanted to make sure he was no one's pawn, but people in Hell wanted ice water.

"No, he doesn't know," he replied.

"Good, because we don't want him to know until he

can't do anything about it." The conversation was reminiscent of the old "cloak and dagger" of days gone by, but sometimes it was the old ways that flew under the radar in this technologically crazed world. "If you want to replace the Wraith, you will have to be able to play hard ball."

"I have no problems playing hard ball, as long as you keep up your end of the bargain, Rainier." If he was going to go through with this, he had to be given certain assurances. He'd already been outcast once by his blood. To be shunned by his second "family" would truly leave him alone in this world. No matter what, no man was an island.

"I figured your daughters would be your weakness. What has it been, fifteen years since you've seen them? They should be lovely, young and supple women by now."

"Leave them out of this. This is unnecessary, I'm doing everything I can to keep the Wraith from expanding. He has something else going that I'm not being looped in on." Harry rubbed his temples as the stress of the situation he found himself in began to wear on him.

"He's smart. He is his father's son."

"You were the one who put his father into retirement, remember? I helped you do that."

"And yet, our plans never came to fruition. The Wraith picked up where his father left off. I have a feeling you tried to cross me back then. Did you think

I wouldn't eventually find out?" Rainier's agitated tone worried Harry, but not enough to worry about whether he would do anything about his irritation.

"I didn't cross you. I did exactly what I was supposed to do."

"Do you want to place your daughters' lives on it?"

"Leave Angel and Jessi out of this, dammit! Let them go home!" Harry was besieged with sorrow. The last thing he wanted to have happen was for his children to be harmed. "They're babies, for God's sake!"

"They won't be by the time the French PM's son is done with them," Rainier replied, allowing a slight chuckle. "You have a choice to make McClellan, and this time, you have more to lose than your life."

"All right, all right. I'll take care of the Wraith, as we discussed. Once I do, will you keep your word?" Harry had no choice but to relent. Even though he wasn't on speaking terms with his daughters, he would rather die than see either of them harmed, or worse. "It will take some finesse to get it done. He has a protégé he is grooming."

"I'll pretend to care about problems that are not mine. If I have to intervene, none of you will be left alive long enough to matter," Rainier replied. "We will handle our end, and if things go the way they're supposed to, not only will you be richer, but we will be able to do something about your familial situation."

"That ship has sailed," Harry huffed. He nearly

regretted disclosing that information. "You can't do anything about that."

"Oh, I beg to differ."

"I'll believe it when I see it. My family considers me dead, and my wife and children want nothing to do with me."

"We don't make promises we can't keep, Mr. McClellan." Hearing those words and knowing what they'd already accomplished with the transaction in Syria had him convinced that maybe he might have a second chance at redemption. "You did your job, and now we'll do ours. In fact, that transaction should be done quite soon."

Harry hung up the phone, rubbing his face like he wanted to scrape it off his skull. Fifteen years he had been estranged from his family and they were supposed to make all of that go away in the blink of an eye?

He was dismissive about the whole thing, concentrating more on usurping power and influence from his employer and what it could mean for his future. No more outlandish jobs, no more fieldwork, either. He planned to work his team and be the kingpin he thought he would have been when Donovan decided to give the reins over to Dorian.

He should have campaigned harder that he was the better choice, opting to be the good soldier instead. Hindsight would show he'd made a calculated error, cleaning up the messes as Dorian went through his growing pains for a few years before he gained his foothold and became the Wraith.

I should be the rightful head of the organization, not him. The more Scotch he consumed, the more he was convinced that this was the right move. He simply needed to make sure the contingency plans were in place when it all went down.

He wouldn't need much to convince Kale to join in. While he was personally recruited by Dorian, he confided in Harry once that he had a problem with civilians working in a field that required military tactical savvy and precision. They were in agreement that while Dorian was smart, he didn't have what it took to handle himself if things really took a turn for the worse.

He knew that Juan Carlos would never go for the change in power, so he didn't think anything more bringing this to his attention. If anything, he would need to find a way to eliminate him from the equation to keep him from alerting Dorian to the potential coup.

The only other problem left to deal with was Dorian's protégé, Ishmael. He was ex-military like him and Kale, but his loyalty was unquestionably with Dorian. *He could pose a real threat, especially if he was DK's eyes and ears.*

He realized he needed to keep things extremely close to the vest if he wanted this to work in his favor. The only way to do that was to not say anything and not trust anyone, at least for the foreseeable future. He would have to live in a box until it was time to go rogue. But how would he be able to keep Dorian at bay until his co-conspirators were ready to drop the hammer?

His thoughts were interrupted by an unrecognizable number coming from what looked like Morocco. He wasn't sure why he needed to answer, but something in his gut told him that he needed to. He picked up the phone and the voice on the end startled him and shook him to his core.

"Dad? Dad, please help us. We're scared."

"Jessi? Baby, is that you? What's going on?"

"Daddy, these men came and took me and Angel. I don't know where we are right now. Please, Daddy, we need you, please help."

The phone line disconnected before Harry could answer his eldest daughter. He squeezed the phone so hard he nearly cracked the screen. How in the world did they get to his daughters? He was broken; his girls were his world, and there was nothing he wouldn't do to keep them safe. To hear the abject fear in her voice, it was unbearable to hear.

His phone rang again. "I take it we have your attention now."

"You son of a bitch!"

"What's with you mercs and your lack of vocabulary?"

"I'll show you more than a lack of a vocabulary if you don't release my daughters!"

"There's only one way to do that. I'll send you the location of where we need to meet and discuss how to negotiate the terms of your daughters' release."

Harry couldn't deny the demand; his girls were too important to act any differently. "Send the information, I'll be there."

"Very good. I will see you in a couple of days. Don't be late."

Chapter Sixteen

Dorian did his best to keep from feeling anxious about seeing Samara again. Things had changed so drastically in the span of a week's time that he wasn't sure how he could rationalize it all. All he knew was that he needed to simplify his life, and that started with Samara and coming to grips with how deeply he felt for her.

He realized that he couldn't think straight when it came to the issues swirling around the events in Syria because his mind was clouded. It sounded so juvenile, but it was the most logical conclusion he could draw. The minute that he saw his mother with her, it seemed to cause a shift inside him. He couldn't take anything—or anyone—for granted anymore.

He would have to come clean about everything. The true nature of his dealings, all of the distractions he put in his path to keep from dealing with his true feelings, all the time wasted because he was scared to have anyone close to him in an effort to keep them out of harm's way. He had to put all of that down and become the man he had always wanted to be for her.

The minute he laid all of those burdens down, he could see everything again. He saw what went down in Syria as though he were looking at it with a new pair of eyes, but what he saw unnerved him in ways he couldn't possibly imagine. He would deal with that later, but tonight, he wanted to get everything out, to finally get things aligned.

The knock on the door threw him off; he hadn't heard from Ishmael, letting him know that he'd dropped Samara off at the hotel. Considering he hadn't told anyone except Samara and Ishmael that he would be at this specific locale, he couldn't quite understand who would be knocking.

He opened the door, immediately irritated over who was standing in the threshold. "What are you doing here, Amelia? I don't remember calling your service in need of any entertainment."

"I thought we could finish what we started the other night during the Gallery showing." Amelia's lack of attire was nothing short of provocative, a hint of her nakedness underneath the trench coat she wore was a dead giveaway of her intentions in that moment. "I know I tapped out, but I wasn't prepared for you. I want another shot at taming you."

"No one can tame me any more than I can tame anyone. I'm not in the mood for the banter, I've got a lot on my mind."

"That's why you need me tonight, Mr. Bentley. To take your mind off things so you can think clearly."

"Oh, so we're gonna play those games now? Okay, since you've decided to take the mask off and deal like that, then let's deal like that." Dorian's anger rose to the surface; he'd ensured that no one knew his name, and for Amelia to flaunt like she knew the whole time was a betrayal he couldn't allow.

"Mmm, so aggressive. You've got me wet already."

"I don't care, you shouldn't be here. Being around you is more than dangerous right now."

Amelia licked her lips as she stepped through the door, amused by his stonewalling. "And why is that? I can tell from your body language that you want to see what's under this coat. Come on, open it up, see what I have waiting for you."

"No, that's not going to happen right now. You've already breached the confidentiality clause in the contract I have with your service, and that is already a problem for me." Dorian rubbed his temples, willing the headache to dissipate before it got started. "The second problem is that I only gave one person my hotel room number, so it makes me wonder how you got it."

"Mhm, and by one person, you mean one of my girls, the one you've been seeing off the books?"

"I have no idea what you're talking about."

"Oh, come now, no need in denying it, it's written all over your face. You've been seeing Arianna, or Samara, or whatever she wants to call herself these days."

Dorian was over this conversation already. "Fine, yes, I am, which is why you need to be gone."

Amelia took a step back, took another look at Dorian, and burst into laughter. "Oh, God, you're in love with her, too? You've got to be the fifth one this year. I need to start charging more. What's the going rate on marriage proposals these days?"

"You don't need to charge for anything when it comes to Samara anymore." Dorian kept his emotions in check, keeping his tone as even as possible. "Since you're not bothering to adhere to my request to leave, let's get the semantics of my request out of the way, shall we?"

"Okay, let's do that. I'll start by giving you the canned responses because these questions tend to get stale and redundant: one, her contract is not up for buyout; two, she is mine until I say she can leave me; and three, you're better off forgetting about her. She was specifically trained by me to seduce and give the illusion that she wants to be claimed."

"You don't know her the way I do."

"What you think you know is the girlfriend experience I instill in all my girls. But, go ahead, knock yourself out, keep believing she's in love with you."

A knock on the door interrupted the tense standoff

between them. Dorian rubbed his hand over his face to regain his composure as he opened the door to see who was there. To his surprise, and Amelia's amusement, Samara was standing in the doorway. Her initial shock in seeing Amelia in the room with Dorian turned to irritation in the next moment.

Amelia couldn't wait to start the next phase of the conversation. "Hi, pretty girl, nice of you to join us."

"Mommy, what are you doing here?" Samara's confusion continued to dominate her body language and facial expressions, turning to Dorian to offer an explanation.

"Helping you handle one of our VIP clients, of course. You sent me the information, remember?"

"I didn't send you anything. I don't know how you got here, or what type of game you're playing, but this whole situation has me more than uncomfortable right now."

Dorian leaned against the desk in the foyer. "That makes two of us."

Amelia continued to pour gas on the fire. "How else would you explain how I got here and how I knew when and where to be here?"

Samara's eyes snapped in his direction as she tried to make sense of the rising anger she saw in his eyes. She quickly realized that Amelia might have done something to manipulate the situation in her favor. She faced Amelia as she continued to make her case, dropping a bomb in the process. "It's quite simple, now that I think about it. I know you clone all of our phones in case you need information that we might not be forthcoming with. Trinity was more than willing to provide that information while we were … together … one night."

Amelia was taken aback by that comment, taking some time to figure out her response. "Hmm, I'll have to punish her for that lapse in judgment. No matter, even if that was how I got the information, it doesn't mean that we can't find a way to make this a memorable night."

Samara grabbed the door handle, opening the door to give Amelia a blatant hint. "It's time for you to leave, Amelia. Dorian and I have some things to discuss."

Amelia huffed as she sauntered out the door. "This isn't over, and don't even think about further negotiations. She belongs to me; you're leasing until I decide to revoke the privilege. Remember that."

The minute the door was closed, Dorian and Samara faced each other, a host of issues heaped on the ground between them. Dorian wasn't sure what he wanted to say, remaining quiet as Samara tried to close the distance between them.

"She's trying to poison you against me, baby. You do know that, don't you?"

"I don't know what to believe at this point. I'm not naïve about the things you have to do while you're employed by her. It's the reason I want you away from her."

"That will happen in time, but I need you to trust me. Please say you trust me."

"I trust you; I have always trusted you, but I didn't tell anyone else about this location except you and Ishmael." Dorian caressed her face, doing his best to calm his emotions. "Was it true about the cloning? I'm trying to make sense of this, baby. She knows my real name; she's somehow tracked my movements when it comes to you, Mara."

"Wait, she … *what*?" Samara scoffed. "She's got to go, period. This is getting to be too much. She's trying to rattle you."

"It's time for me to return the favor."

"Baby, that's what she wants. Don't fall for it, please."

"This was not at all how I wanted this night to go." Dorian shook his head, frustrated beyond measure. It wasn't the right time, but there would never be a right time. Before he could shift his thoughts to what he wanted to say, his cell phone rang. "Ishmael, what's up? A phone call about who? Okay, I'll deal with that in the morning, there's nothing we can do about it tonight. Pick me up at the usual time."

"DK, what were you talking about with tonight? Did you have something in mind?" Samara wanted to turn the evening around the best she could, but the tension she felt in his shoulders made it difficult to get through. "Tell me what you want, whatever it is, and we'll do it."

"I want to be alone right now."

"No, you don't. I know you, Dorian. You want to push everyone away when the world seems like it isn't making sense, but I'm not about to let you do that. You can push everyone else away, but I'm staying right here."

"Mara—"

"I don't remember saying that you had a choice in the matter, *querido*. Now, answer my question, and truthfully this time. Don't shut me out."

Dorian's shoulders slumped as he sank into the desk chair. For the first time in a while, he didn't feel like the persona that everyone feared. He felt … human. "Mara, I just want to take my mind off tonight and forget the bullshit with Amelia even happened. I'm exhausted from everything that has happened over the past week, and I need to just be. Can we do that tonight?"

"I thought you'd never ask. I have just the thing in mind."

Chapter Seventeen

"Kale, I need to see you and Ishmael. There are some things we need to discuss. Where are you now?"

"I'm in Accra, taking things easy for a couple of days. I can set up a secure video link within the hour. Have you hit Ishmael?"

"Yeah, he's in Paris, and he said the same as you. I'll set up the link so we can talk now. We need to prepare for some things, ASAP."

Juan Carlos was a creature of habit, and today was no different. He'd been down this road with Dorian enough times to know that when the standard protocol deviated by even the smallest minutiae, there would be reason to be concerned. That meant, for him, the need to get everyone inside the circle together and figuring out what happens next.

Although Kale and Ishmael had not been with

Dorian as long as he had, Juan Carlos had come to intrinsically trust each man like they were extended family. He took that seriously; hence the reason they needed to tighten things up moving forward. The only missing variable in the equation was not having Harry in the mix.

Over the past couple of transactions, he'd noticed a slight change in Harry. He remembered it well while in military service; the soldiers who progressively got sloppier before discharge from service because they were looking forward to life on the other side. He did his best to protect himself against it, then and now, and he swore that if it crept up into his psyche, he would walk away before jeopardizing the lives of his family.

Harry needed to be cut from the scenario and he knew that was the prudent move to make; the trick was to make the move and get Kale and Ishmael on board. He was convinced they were silently wondering on their own whether Harry needed to be coerced into retirement or not, but he wanted to put it on the table, full disclosure and transparency ruling the day.

He set up the equipment to establish the secured link to connect the three of them, despite their considerable distances from each other. He chuckled at the technological advancements that he could only dream about as a child.

There were a lot of things he'd dreamt of when he was a child—and as a younger adult—that he never thought he would have access to. Now, it was only a matter of time before he would be able to retire to more pleasant and elaborate surroundings—and hopefully with the one who had always possessed his heart.

If only she was available to be possessed.

"You okay, JC? You look like you have a lot on your mind." Ishmael's inquiry seemed to jolt JC out of his musings, but not enough to keep from sparking the question. "I know we've had a lot to digest since Syria, but you're more solemn than usual."

"Ishmael's right, JC. Something's off with you. What's the trouble?" Kale inquired.

Juan Carlos rubbed his hands over his face a couple of times before he cut to the chase. "Gentlemen, there's no easy way to say this, but there are a few things that we need to get into and come to a consensus over before I bring this to DK."

"Such as?" Ishmael asked.

"Retiring Harry."

"I guess I shouldn't have been surprised at that response," Kale replied. "It was becoming a near forgone conclusion to draw based on the boss's movements as of late."

"I thought Harry was the boss's right hand outside of you, JC?" Ishmael's confused expression was palpable. "Has something else happened that we're not aware of?"

"No, but I have my suspicions over where his loyalties are starting to fall," Juan Carlos remarked. "He has been distracted since the job in Cameroon, and

I'm worried that it will put the whole operation in danger. I don't know why I feel this way, but I can't shake the feeling."

"There's no question that it the case, but the question is why that is the case?" Kale threw the question that might not have been posed. "Do you think he's gotten to the point to where he's no longer about this life? It wouldn't be surprising, we've all seen it during our tours of duty."

Juan Carlos regarded Kale's question, nodding at the distinct possibility. "Here's the plan: I'll find out where Harry is so that he and I can have a one-on-one conversation and I can read him to see where his state of mind may be. If he is where you think he is, then I'm going to try to nudge him in the direction of cashing out."

"Do you think that's wise, JC?" Ishmael asked. "I feel like I need to be with you, or at least put one of DK's assets on you wherever you may end up. I mean, you're asking an OG to walk away, there's no telling what type of response you'll get."

Juan Carlos paused for a moment as he took in Ishmael's assessment. His eyes shifted from Ishmael to Kale and back to Ishmael before shaking his head. "I've known Harry a long time, gentlemen. I think he will take the suggestion better from me because, let's face it, this life isn't for either of us anymore. This is a young man's game; it's built for the two of you."

Kale shook his head in response to Juan Carlos.

"Look, old man, you're nowhere near done yet, and neither is Harry, but I get the sentiment. We'll back you with whatever you need, even if you say you don't need any backup. That's not how Ishmael and I work, and you know that."

"Well, I'm telling you to stand down. The last thing I want is for him to feel like he's being forced out," Juan Carlos replied. After getting the nod from both men, he continued. "Since we truly don't know his state of mind, I'm going with standard protocol when we're in downtime. Besides, I can bring his favorite bottle and, if I'm lucky, a few sources of entertainment to help keep things on the level."

Kale and Ishmael laughed at the intimation. Kale continued his attempts to stifle his laughter as he responded to Juan Carlos. "Remind me to employ that same tactic when it's time for you to cash out, okay? Hell, I might even make that standard protocol when it's time for us to do the same."

"Okay, gentlemen, I think we have a plan."

"JC, I'm serious, you need a shadow." Ishmael was dogged in his attempts to protect him. "I know why you wanna do this, but I need you to take my offer."

"If it were a known hostile, then cool, I'd take it in a heartbeat, Ishmael, but this is family. You don't turn your back on family, even if it looks like they're going in a direction that you're not comfortable with."

"I'm not treating him like he's a hostile, though," Ishmael retorted. "One of the reasons you and DK brought me on was that you trusted my security assessments when the situations presented themselves. I'm asking you to trust my judgment on this."

Juan Carlos kept his own emotions in check as best he could. While he understood where Ishmael was coming from, he had his own instincts that he trusted, too. After a few more moments, he finally proposed a compromise. "I'll send a text to you once I touch down, and once I'm at his location, I'll send another text—let's say, I send the number 8103—if I need the asset quickly. Deal?"

"Deal. I'd prefer it my way, but I know how you OG's like to roll." Ishmael picked up his phone while he was in the midst of talking, reading a text that made him grin. "Okay, gentlemen, I have some business to attend to, so, I'll be looking for that text, JC, and Kale, I'll get at you later in the week. Be easy."

"Yeah, I'll be relaxing as usual, taking a look at the cryptocurrency mining since I have some down time to get some real work in," Kale remarked. "Be safe, as always, gentlemen, and I'll catch you in the next few days."

Juan Carlos switched off the feed, taking some time to himself to figure out his next moves. How would he bring up the subject of cashing out? Was Ishmael right over whether Harry would react negatively over the idea of being retired?

He didn't have the answers, and he wouldn't have the answers until he sat down with him. Until then, the only thing he could do was get his affairs in order until he was able to get in touch with Harry.

An unexpected phone call jolted him from his thoughts, and from the minute he saw her exquisite smile on his screen, he knew the day was about to get more complicated. "I thought we weren't supposed to be keeping in contact. Why are you calling?"

"I need to see you. Things have changed drastically in the last couple of weeks. I'll be heading to Johannesburg in the next 24 hours."

"That isn't a good idea. You can't be here."

"No, it isn't, but I need you, Juan Carlos. I can't do this anymore."

He wanted to say no and mean it, but he couldn't do it, either, if he was honest with himself. He was always the release valve when things got too tight. He allowed himself to be that. The only thing he couldn't figure out was whether he wanted to continue doing so anymore.

Hearing her voice made the decision all the more difficult. In the end, he couldn't tell her no. "Let me know when you're in Joburg. I'll have the car bring you here."

"No, I won't be here that long. Can you meet me at the airport? I'm taking a private charter so I can say what I need to say."

Juan Carlos shook his head, wondering why he was allowing her to dictate the terms of their meeting. He closed his eyes, willing himself to have the strength to work through this situation. "I still don't think this is a good idea that we meet at soft location, but I understand if you're not going to be here that long. I'll meet you at the airport."

"Thank you. I'll explain everything when I get there. Once I do, I know you'll understand why I have to do what I'm about to do."

Juan Carlos disconnected the call before she said anything more. The less he knew, the better. Plausible deniability was best in these situations, although he was fully aware that they would be linked forever by a decision he made with his heart. A decision that could cost everyone dearly.

Chapter Eighteen

"I thought we were supposed to be meeting at this location? What kind of game are you playing, Rainier?"

Harry gave a lot of leeway while he was transported to the location coordinates given to him. He allowed the blindfold and the hood covering. He allowed the no weapons stipulation. He even allowed the burner phone instead of his personal cell phone to keep in contact. But once they were at their destination, to be told that he would be meeting Rainier at the prearranged location, only to then be told that the meeting would be via secured video link, it was a bit more than he could deal with in that moment.

To say he was livid was an understatement.

His adversary was undeterred and unconcerned with his plight. "I unfortunately had to make other arrangements. I can't be entirely certain that I can trust you to keep your word."

"You have my daughters, you son of a bitch! Why in the bloody hell would I endanger their lives? Are you fucking daft?" Harry couldn't keep his emotions under control any longer. He was being toyed with; if he'd known he was going to be playing a shell game, he would have tried to find his girls himself. "You must be an idiot or something, or you've been watching too many fucking action movies."

"While I understand your frustration, there is no need for the conversation to devolve in such a manner." Rainier's face and voice were both hidden and distorted, which only served to infuriate Harry even further. "You want what you want, and I want what I want. This should be a simple transaction."

"Then, why hide your face and your voice? Are you afraid I might recognize either and figure all this shite out on my own?" Harry queried. "There must be something that is spooking you to go through all of this old-school, cloak-and-dagger bullshit."

"I take these measures for obvious reasons, much like your current employer, yes?"

"I don't give a fuck at this point. At least I know the identity of my current employer. You say you want to make me a partner in your organization, yeah? Transparency and trust are the pillars of a good business relationship."

"And what assurances do I have if I do decide to

honor your request?"

"You want what you want, and I want what I want, remember?"

"You are correct, so, I guess this is the part to where I make my request, is that about right?"

"You're catching on."

Rainier let out a chuckle. "Fine, then let's get to it. I want the Wraith erased from the landscape."

"That isn't simple."

"Neither is extracting your daughters from their current situation."

"*You* put them there."

"Semantics, Harry. Focus on the task at hand."

Harry's frustration continued to mount. He needed to figure out how to balance the scales. "I want proof of life before I do anything whatsoever. There is no guarantee that they are even alive and that you will have me on a suicide mission."

"Is my word not enough?"

Harry scoffed and laughed at the implication. "Nope, I can't be entirely certain that I can trust you to keep your word. Trust begets trust."

"Touché. Check the phone; this is from thirty seconds ago."

Harry picked up the burner phone, almost frantic to see his girls. The images he saw nearly made him sick to his stomach. Both of his daughters—Jessilyn was in her teens and Angelica was just turning twenty—were in next to nothing, catering to the whims of grown men.

He couldn't make out the dialect, but it was distinctly French being spoken. The things he heard them say as they approached each man with different drinks on the trays were enough to make him go nuclear.

He threw the phone toward the ground with such force that the device shattered into pieces. "What kind of sick and twisted shite is this? Those are my babies, you lunatic!"

"You asked for proof of life, Harry. You should be more careful of what you ask for."

"I swear, when this is over—"

"You will be the biggest weapons dealer on the planet, with my various connections at your disposal." Rainier interrupted Harry's veiled threat with his own continuation of the statement. "At the end of the day, that is the only thing that matters."

"Even if I'm able to take out the Wraith, I have to deal with his lieutenants, JC and Ishmael. They'll be out for blood once they find out what happened to him."

"Then, you'll have to get rid of them, too."

"The price is too steep."

"I thought nothing was too steep to see your daughters returned safe and sound."

"Won't matter if I'm dead, will it?"

Rainier paused for a moment. "Name your terms."

"I take out JC, you release Jessilyn."

"The price is too steep."

Harry laughed it off. "You're asking for a three-for-two deal, and you need me to get close enough to do it, otherwise, you would have done it already. Those are my terms, take them or leave them, it makes no never mind to me. You want what you want, and I want what I want."

"Noted. Done. You drive a hard bargain, Mr. McClellan."

"You're asking me to betray one family to keep another family whole. If I was a different man, I would be coming for you, regardless of what you've done with my girls."

"We both know you're not doing that. You're a businessman and a mercenary now, so take the deal and let's make some money when the dust settles." Rainier was surprisingly lighthearted before ending the call. "You're not that man anymore, so, let's not have delusions of grandeur. You get what you want, and I get what I want. After that, you become a rich man and worthy of being both feared and respected. Enjoy your trip home, you have a lot on your plate."

Once the link was disconnected, Harry let out a frustrated howl. He didn't care that Rainier's goons were still around him; if he wanted to, he could have taken them both out. It wouldn't have made him feel any better, and he was acutely aware of that fact. The only thing that he could do was play the game to its final conclusion. If that meant he would die in the process, then he was willing to accept that fate.

For now, he had to figure out what to do about the

situation at hand.

He quickly punched in Juan Carlos' number, doing his best to keep the urgency out of the tone in his voice. He needed to make it sound like a routine check in as best as he could, or he could tip his hand and spook his longtime friend and colleague. He had to do this right; his daughters' lives were at stake.

"Harry, what's the word, brother?"

"So far, so good, brother. Did everything go smoothly in Syria? I heard the region was starting to get a bit dicey out there."

"Nothing we couldn't handle, but we definitely need to see about some other interests that don't place us in hot zones, that's for sure." The jovial tone didn't make things easier for Harry as the wheels continued to turn in his head. "What about you, Harry? I know we had to keep you on the sidelines for this round, but it was DK's call."

The mere mention of being cut out of the last transaction stirred the anger he'd thought he'd forgotten about. "That isn't a worry. I know he had his reasons for doing it. It wasn't the first time he's made decisions like that; it's just been some years since the last time he's done it to me."

"Well, that's part of the reason I wanted to get with you, so it was fortunate that you ended up calling me," Juan Carlos replied. "We need to sit down so we can talk about the other things that we can set you up for moving forward."

Harry did his best to keep his anger in check for a little while longer. "Sure, brother, I can come to you. I need some time away from the UK anyway. I can catch the next flight in the morning and see you in Joburg."

"That will work, brother. I'll see you tomorrow."

Harry disconnected the call, seething as he considered his options once he touched down in South Africa. He made another call to one of his clandestine connections to set him up with everything he needed for his meeting with Juan Carlos. If he planned it right, he would be able to be one day gone before anyone knew what happened.

This was the point of no return, only this time, he had no qualms about passing it. Some things were more important.

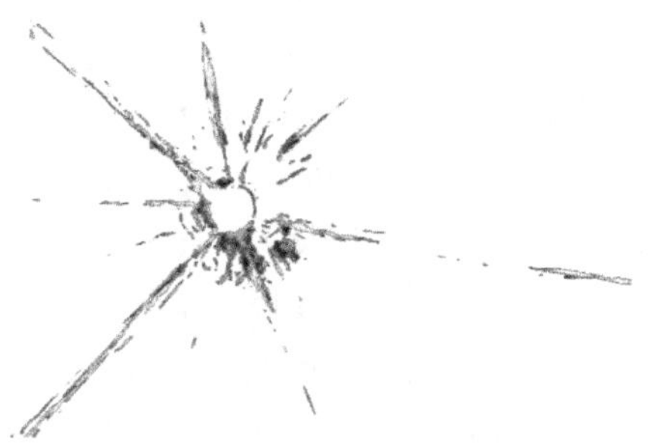

Chapter Nineteen

The past few days had been nothing short of maddening for Samara, and the unfortunate part was that she knew the source of her frustration. She couldn't reach her betrothed, which served to amplify her irritation, and she was going to do something about it, whether he liked it or not.

She thought things were solid between her and Dorian when she left him last, but when she tried to call him the next day to check on him, the call went straight to voicemail. A second time, voicemail. Secondary number, disconnected. *Something isn't right; he never cuts connections without giving me the numbers.*

Every deduction she could draw led to one simple solution: Amelia still found a way to get to him. The thought of that possibility angered and terrified her.

She was getting closer to freeing herself from Amelia, and yet, Dorian was starting to slip away from her. There was no way she could allow that to happen.

She found herself inside the Gallery for a second time in less than a month. The mere prospect of having to deal with either Amelia or Trinity was enough to induce nausea, but she needed to figure out why Dorian wasn't responding. If anything, Amelia would be smug enough to offer enough candor in the answers to her questions that Samara would know what to do next.

She found her and Trinity in Amelia's office, and from Trinity's body language, things were looking very good. Samara took a deep breath before she walked through the door. Sure enough, Amelia's face lit up the moment Samara stepped into their space, while Trinity's body language resembled that of a jealous girlfriend.

"Well, well, well, this is a lovely surprise. To what do we owe the honor of a second visit in such a short period of time? Did you miss me after all?" Amelia inquired.

Samara got right to the point, realizing that her patience was thinner than she'd given herself credit for. "What did you do to my man, Mommy?"

Amelia scoffed, holding her palm flat against her chest in mock anger. "Your what? I have no idea what you're talking about, or who you're talking about, for that matter. The last time I checked, you have about three different men trying to claim you. So, which pitiful fucker did you convince to be in a relationship with you?"

"Mommy, stop your game-playing now. What did you do to Dorian?"

"Oh, you mean the talented Mr. Bentley? Is he not answering your phone calls at the moment?"

Samara took a couple of steps toward Amelia, only to be intercepted by Trinity within seconds. A quick stare-down between them ensued, eliciting a series of giggles from Amelia at the spectacle of it all. "Trinity, step away now, I don't think you want to go down this road with me."

"Try me." Trinity's sneer made it clear she was not as mesmerized by Samara as her employer was. "Take another step toward her, and you'll find out if I'm ready to go down this road."

"Mmm, this whole situation is making me horny. Damn, keep it up, you two, I may orgasm spontaneously over this."

"Do you think this is a game?"

"And then some, but why bother going through the madness with you, all this is going to do is cause you pain, and I don't want that," Amelia replied as she pulled Trinity back to her side. "I simply sent him proof of who you *really* are, nothing more. He's probably trying to process everything for himself."

"He'd never believe anything you sent him."

"Oh, but I didn't send him anything … one of your other gentlemen, the one who proposed to you earlier in the year—I think his name was Forsythe, the one in Istanbul—was more than happy to prove everything that needed to be proven."

Samara's eyes widened at that revelation. She dissolved her relationship with Forsythe when he made the proposal—the one she rejected because she wasn't in love with him. She let out a low growl in frustration. "Are there no levels that you would sink to in order to get what you think you want?"

"You're the one who keeps forgetting her place, whore. That is what you have been, for me, for Dorian, and all the other clients I allowed you to have." Amelia's eyes narrowed. "It's time I stopped giving you such a long leash and bring your sexy ass back to heel."

"And what do you think you're gonna do? I'm not some bottom bitch off the streets. You made sure of that."

"And I can unmake you with one fucking phone call."

"Try it, and I'll fuck up your whole universe with one of my own."

Amelia never flinched, dismissing Samara's threat as quickly as she'd heard it. She tossed her cellphone in Samara's direction, crossing her arms before she spoke again. "You don't have the juice you think you have. Maybe I should prove my point. Call your alleged betrothed, let's see what he has to say about it."

Samara was confused over why Amelia had his

number, but she called anyway, if only to hear his voice so she could at least know that he was safe.

"Why are you calling me, Amelia?" Dorian's voice was as cold as she'd ever heard him. "Our business is done; don't you get that?"

"Baby … baby, it's me." Samara hesitated; she wasn't sure how he would receive her voice based on the tone she'd already heard. "I'm calling from Amelia's phone."

Dorian never changed his cadence or his tone. "Mara, I don't have time for you right now, either. I've got a lot on my plate right now. I'll call you when things calm down."

"No, tell me where you are. I know she sent one of my former clients to try to poison you against me." She didn't care that she sounded so desperate in front of them; she didn't like how he sounded, and she needed to do something to try to soothe him. "Tell me where you are, please?"

"I said I'll call you when things have calmed down."

Dorian disconnected the call before Samara could respond. She didn't bother to call back; the call would roll to voicemail, and she knew it.

"So, I'm assuming your man is a bit indisposed at the moment? Could he be mulling over the authentic video evidence of you saying a lot of the same things to another man … while trying to escape me?"

Samara lunged for Amelia, intercepted again by

Trinity. Trinity's fist connected with Samara's cheek, dropping her to the ground. Trinity stood over her for a few moments before she heard Amelia command her to come back to her. Samara remained on the hardwood flooring, nursing the bruise as Amelia continued her ranting.

"You were supposed to on to bigger and better things here at the Gallery. You were supposed to help run a cache of Gallery pieces for yourself, the same as Trinity, but no, you wanted to go and fall in love with someone who couldn't do half of what we can do for you."

"What you wanted I couldn't give you, Mommy, but you didn't want to see that," Samara retorted. "What you were offering came with strings that I didn't want. I don't belong to you, I never belonged to you. Everything you're doing is making things worse. What about Trinity? Have you even thought about what this is doing to her?"

"She has never been this much of an issue. Besides, she doesn't want to leave me, and she knows that I am who I am and I get what I want."

Samara's eyes turned to Trinity, recognizing the rage that filled her eyes. "Trinity wants you to herself, and you know it. Each time you try to grind against that truth, bad things happen. Pay attention for once in your life. People are not property to collect and trade."

"God, is this what good dick does to a woman? You really are delusional."

"I'm not delusional, but you need to wake the fuck up." Samara finally rose to her feet in an attempt to leave the office. "This will blow up in your face if you don't adjust and take care of the ones who truly love and care about you."

"You sound like a bad *Lifetime* movie." Amelia slammed a file against Samara's chest. "Here's your next client. Go make me some fucking money, since that's all you're good for now."

"That's not going to happen."

"You might want to rethink your words."

"What I'm going to do is find a way to extract myself from you. It's the only way I'll ever be at peace."

"You will never be able to leave me. If I decide it's time for you to go, then that will be the only way you'll ever be free of me." Amelia kissed Trinity as she waved her hand. "Now, be a good bitch and do as I told you before I decide that you need to be put back in the Gallery full time."

Samara left the office without the folio, willing the tears from falling until she left the building. The moment she sat in her rental car, she screamed as she repeatedly struck the steering wheel. Amelia forced her hand, leaving her no choice but to make the phone call she warned her about. She closed her eyes and silently thanked Luciano—*abuelo*—for giving her the ammunition she needed to get away from this life, forever.

There was still one thing she needed to do, and there was only one person who would be able to help her with that. It was a long shot, but she managed to keep his number during one of her excursions to see Dorian.

"This is Ishmael, what can I do for you, Ms. Acosta?"

Samara was taken aback by the instant familiarity in his voice. "I didn't think you would recognize my number, Ishmael."

"It's part of my job to ensure that you are taken care of, when I'm not helping to make sure your boyfriend is out of harm's way." Ishmael referencing Dorian the way he did brought a small smile to her face. "I assume you're wanting to make this a surprise visit this time, my lady?"

Samara nodded before she realized she wasn't on a video call nor was she talking to him in person. She was also acutely aware that Ishmael wasn't aware of what was going on with her and Dorian yet. "Yes, I want to make this one very special. I know he's been under some stress. Can you take me to him?"

"Yes, my lady, it would be an honor to do so. You caught him at a decent time; he asked me to run interference for a couple of days while he sorted out some personal matters, but I think he would be more than thrilled to see you. I know I would be."

"Okay, where is he now? I'm currently still in London, and I was hoping he would be, too, so this would be a short trip."

Ishmael laughed. "He is rarely ever in London when he needs to decompress, but since you're in London, this will be a quick trip for you. How soon can you get a flight to Barcelona?"

"Within the hour."

"Call me when you touch down, I'll bring you to him."

Samara smiled as she picked up her smartphone to make the flight reservations. "Thank you, Ishmael. I'll take full responsibility if he gets mad at you for bringing me to him. I know how he gets when he wants to be alone sometimes, but this is too important for him to be alone right now."

"Understood, my lady. I'll see you in a few hours."

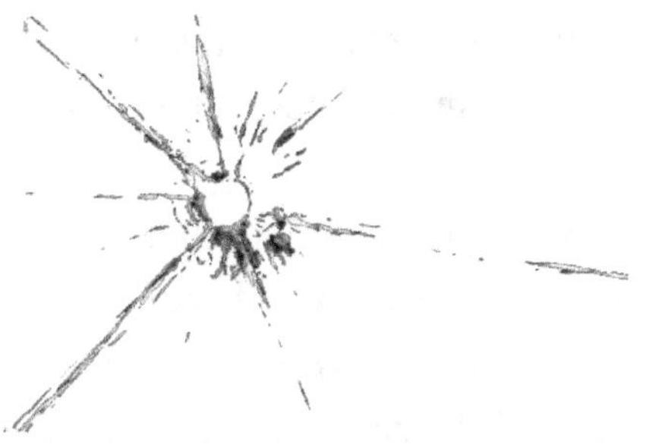

Chapter Twenty

Juan Carlos didn't want to deal with the emotions swirling through him, but there was no other choice in the matter. This was a long time coming, and he had to face them or else it could cause him to lose focus on what he had to deal with later in the day with Harry. In a way, he felt relieved; he wouldn't have to pretend anymore, but the consequences could be more than problematic. He had to be ready for whatever would come next.

Seeing Isabella Bentley and pretending that he wasn't in love with her for nearly forty years had been the most excruciating experience of his life. They'd met when they were teenagers when they were both in Rio, falling in love almost at first sight. They had a heated, blossoming romance for the better part of a year before Juan Carlos made the decision to enlist in the military, convinced that it would be the one path he could take to provide the type of lifestyle that Isabella had been used to, since she was one of the daughters of *El Jefe Supremo*. Isabella understood why he enlisted, and promised that she would wait for him to come back to her.

During that same time, another man had eyes on Isabella, too. No one knew where the smooth-talking American came from, or how even managed to have a conversation with Luciano, but he won an audience— along with an offer that, at the time, could not be refused. Everyone in the city was shocked, including the woman who'd promised her heart to another.

By the time Juan Carlos had gotten back to Rio on his first leave, he'd received word that Isabella was set to be married. The anger and betrayal he felt was enough for him to want to take drastic steps to exact revenge on both of them. He made the decision to confront Isabella first, and if he didn't like what he heard from her, he would kill her on the spot. He couldn't believe she didn't keep her promise to him.

The moment he saw her, every ounce of hatred he felt melted away in an instant. Her eyes were sad; as it turned out, her persuasive suitor had managed to sway her father, but her heart still belonged to Juan Carlos. Luciano arranged the marriage on the premise that the union would give Luciano access to Europe, based on his connections. It was a ruse that no one saw coming, and it wasn't until they were married and living in the

States that the deception was revealed.

That suitor—Donovan Bentley.

She did her best to convince Juan Carlos that he was always the one for her, that she was in love with him. Despite the fact that she would run the risk of angering her family, she dropped off the grid for two days, confining herself to a small cottage in Colombia with him. To this day, for him, it was the most magical time of his life. Isabella married Donovan a week later and moved to the States, while Juan Carlos went on to serve in the military.

All of this would come full circle in a few minutes when the love of his life—the woman he did his best to avoid at every opportunity for the past two years— stepped off the private jet and headed in his direction with the biggest smile he'd ever seen on her face. He braced himself the best way he could, realizing the emotions and urges would rush to the surface and any defenses he'd built up would crumble as soon as she slipped into his personal space.

He did what he could to keep the greeting as innocuous as possible, offering a hug as she approached. "Hello, Isabella. I trust the flight was smooth?"

The scent of her perfume dulled his senses before she ever spoke a word. "Hello, my darling Carlito. Yes, the flight was fine. It gave me some time to think about things. How are you doing? You look well, considering I haven't seen you in person in about a year."

Juan Carlos dismissed the quip. "You're looking very well yourself, young lady. The artist life agrees with you."

"So, now that we've gotten the simple pleasantries out of the way—" Isabella cupped her hands around his face and planted a kiss on his lips before he had a chance to resist. "I've been wanting to do that for at least the last year … and probably longer than that."

Juan Carlos ripped her hands from his face. "Are you trying to get us killed, Bella?"

"I've been dying a little for at least the past thirty-five years because I've had to do what I thought was right and live without you, my darling." Isabella's body language was relaxed, like she had a heavy weight lifted from her shoulders. She was the carefree, light and airy teenaged girl he fell in love with so long ago. "I want to spend the rest of my life with you, and I'm no longer ashamed to say it. I should have done this so long ago; it hasn't been fair to either of us to be away all this time."

"We didn't have a choice, Bella. We still don't have a choice. The only way that we can be together is if you tell him that you're no longer happy being with him."

"I was never happy, Carlito. I have been lying to myself this entire time," Isabella admitted. "I had to keep up pretenses the best I could, for the sake of appearances. He was high in the Defense Department, and the minute he started weapons dealing, the nights were lonely. Every time you and I were together was torture, but I couldn't wait for the next time we could, even if it was only for a few days. It kept me sane, kept me going this whole time."

Hearing those words felt like his heart was being gauged from his chest. He had told himself for so long that she was better off without him that it felt more fact than fiction. Even their indiscretions when Dorian was growing up—he chalked that up to a woman who was in need of comfort at a very stressful time when her husband was constantly in the field, trying to earn a living.

He tried to keep from resenting Donovan for abandoning his family, but he couldn't avoid it. In his heart, he knew he could treat Isabella better, and after running weapons and making a lot of money from it all these years, he felt emboldened enough to try to convince the love of his life to finally be with him.

Being asked to stick with Dorian when the transition was made for him to take over the weapons dealing from Donovan was both a blessing and a curse. He could keep an eye on Dorian as his godfather, but it kept Donovan at home full-time, which made it more difficult to see Isabella as often as they had been when he was managing the operations.

Against his better judgment, he let his heart override his logic. He couldn't continue the way they were any longer. "If you don't want to be with him anymore, you need to tell him. I can't be a party to adultery anymore; I did the best I could to convince myself that I could be that for you for as long as I could. I have never stopped loving you, but if we're going to be together again, it has to be done right."

He took a risk by saying that, but it was the only way he could live with what could only be a betrayal of a decades-long association, despite his underlying feelings. He lowered his head for a moment, doing his best to stay patient while awaiting her answer to his request.

"I needed to hear you say the words in person, my darling one." Isabella smiled as she caressed his face. "I can face him knowing that you'll be waiting for me. I love you, Juan Carlos de Silva."

Juan Carlos blinked a few times, trying to understand why she was leaving in a flash. He grabbed her arm, stopping her in her tracks. "Wait, you're leaving already? You just got here. The pilots must be tired from the flight, they need some rest."

"Yes, beloved, and the pilots were aware of the quick turnaround. I have a showing in a few hours in Morocco." Isabella's eyes were filled with hope and optimism, never once leaving his. "I came for what I wanted, and I have your heart, although I know I've always had it. I promise that I will return to you in a few days, and we can figure out the rest of our lives then, okay?"

Juan Carlos took her hands in his, kissing each fingertip as his eyes never left hers. "I'll be waiting. I promise.”

She kissed his lips once more, tracing her fingers along his jawline before she turned on her heel and headed back to the jet. She stole looks at him as she made her way up the stairs, blowing a final kiss before disappearing into the plane.

Juan Carlos waited against his vehicle until the jet took off again; Morocco was only a few hours' flight time, so he was sure the pilots would not be too fatigued to get her there safely. He was so enthralled with what had transpired in such a short moment of time that he didn't realize that Harry was standing behind him.

“Wow, I wonder what Donovan would think about what I just witnessed?” Harry's anger was on full display, and Juan Carlos was caught dead to rights. “And here I thought this meeting would be awkward.”

“Harry … it wasn't what you thought it was.” Juan Carlos was in damage control mode. He paused for a moment, confused as to how Harry happened to be at the airport to begin with. “How in the world did you know I would be here?”

“Because I followed you here, that's why.” Harry kept his distance as he continued to feed on the anger of what he saw. “I had been planning for the right time to erase you from the playing field, but I never expected to see what I've seen. How could you betray Donovan like that?”

“Wait a fucking minute! Donovan betrayed me,

dammit!" Juan Carlos couldn't believe what he was hearing. "Who put you up to this? It couldn't have been Donovan; he doesn't know anything is going on."

"That's not what it looked like from my vantage point, *brother*." Harry wiped the tears from his eyes as the weight of the catch-22 crushed him, but he had to see it through. "It doesn't matter what I saw, I don't have a choice in what I have to do here and now."

Juan Carlos's eyes widened as he saw Harry pull a handgun from behind his back. The way his eyes focused on him as he raised the weapon, Juan Carlos held his hands in the air. "What do you think you're doing, man? I'm unarmed, for God's sake! You're gonna kill me here in cold blood and in broad daylight? What's possessed you to do this?"

"I'm doing this to protect my family. You couldn't understand that since you're betraying yours. You're betraying Donovan. What would DK think about all of this? He is your family, too."

"That's not true, Harry, you don't understand what's really going on. Don't do this. Whoever is making you do this … we can find a way to keep this from happening." Juan Carlos inched his way to the wheel well of his car, hoping to get a chance to reach for the handgun he had lodged underneath. "You said you're trying to protect your family. Did someone do something to your daughters? Look, we can get DK and find them. You don't have to do this!"

Harry wanted to yell as the conflicting emotions

burned through him, threatening to rip him apart. He realized what Juan Carlos was doing, and he couldn't allow it to happen. "Stop trying to stall, JC. I know where you keep your throwaway. I have to take you out. It has to be done."

"No, you don't. Tell me what's going on, we can find a way to fix this."

"I'm sorry, JC. There's no turning back for me."

Harry squeezed off several rounds before Juan Carlos could get to his gun, hitting him in the shoulder, the lower abdomen and lower leg. Juan Carlos dropped to the ground near the door to his car, struggling to breathe, as Harry approached him for the potential kill shot. Harry saw the look of anger in Juan Carlos' eyes, almost like he dared him to take him out. That look soon turned to confusion as he continued to fight for his life.

Before Harry could get the final shot off, sirens sounded off in the distance. He was stuck in a conundrum of whether to be seen killing Juan Carlos or to let the authorities try to figure it out. He finally reasoned that the spots he hit would be enough to kill Juan Carlos. It would be a slow death, but by the time the authorities would be able to catch up to him, he would be clear across the planet and in a non-extradition country.

Harry ran to his car, nearly stomping on the accelerator to get out of the area before the airport police would be able to make out his vehicle. He constantly looked in the rear-view mirror to see if anyone was following him, relieved to see the units stopping at Juan Carlos's car to administer aid.

He cursed as his mind raced, trying to figure out the best way to prove that he killed Juan Carlos. His daughters' lives depended on it. There was still a possibility that Juan Carlos could have survived the attack. He couldn't chance it, so he decided to stay in the city to find out where they might take him—and if he survived. One way or another, he would get his proof.

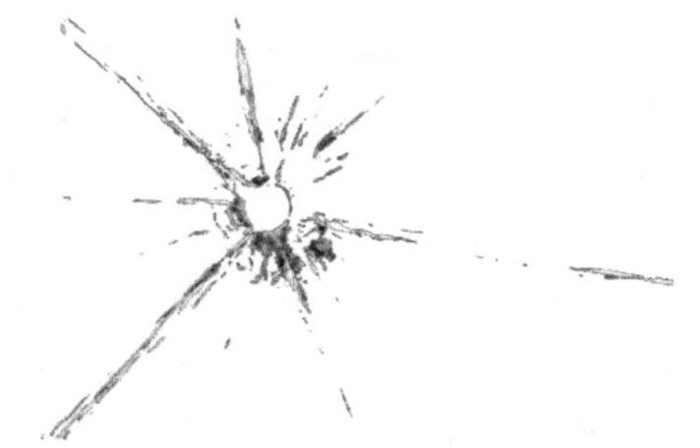

Chapter Twenty-One

Dorian did his best to sort through his feelings while in his beach home in Barcelona, unable to get through the rage he felt over the conversation he had with a man who, as far as he knew, had no axe to grind with him. The fact that he was also one of Amelia's clients became a point of contention, until the gentleman explained that he had become enamored with the love of his life, too, and wanted nothing more than what Dorian wanted: to claim Samara for himself.

What started as a conversation worthy of a bad romance novel eventually grew into an earnest confession and undisputable proof that the Samara he knew and the woman he saw in the video that was sent to him were not one and the same. He did his best to sound like Samara wasn't anything like what was being told to him, but deep inside, his heart was on the verge of shattering beyond repair.

By the time they were done speaking, he literally threw the phone against the wall, watching it settle onto the freshly waxed hardwood flooring. If he was a weaker man, he would be distraught; he reasoned with himself that he wasn't anywhere near that weak. However, he cut himself off from the world, ignoring every call for the better part of forty-eight hours.

He wanted to reach out to his father, but he thought better of it. He'd been married to his mother the whole time, and Donovan might not have been able to relate to Dorian's cavalier outlook on dating. He didn't want to reach out to his mother, either; she would have read him the riot act for not giving Samara a chance to explain herself, and he didn't need to hear that at the moment. Whether he wanted to admit it or not, he was hurting, and there wasn't much anyone could do about it.

He continued to think too much, consider every angle that didn't need to be considered, nearly driving himself into madness. Before long, anger turned to indifference, and indifference turned into logical reasoning. But no matter how much he tried to tell himself that he didn't need Samara in his life anymore, there was one fact that he could not deny: he was, and always would be, in love with her.

Before he could get up and head to the bathroom so he could take a long, hot shower to wash away as much of the despair in his heart as he could, his cell phone rang yet again. This time, he decided to pick up the call. He needed to get back to the real world; work would be the best medicine to mask the hurt he felt.

"Hello, who is this?"

"Good afternoon, Mr. Bentley."

"Who is this, and how did you get this number?"

"You'd be amazed at what can be procured with the proper motivation, sir."

It took him a minute to recognize the distinct tone in her voice, and it served to put him in an even worse mood than he was in for the past two days. "This is becoming more and more frustrating with each passing day. I need to purge a few things from my life. What do you want, Trinity?"

"There's no need for that tone of voice, sir. This is not what you think it might be. I need to pass on some valuable information that you will need. It could be a matter of life and death." Her voice was even, business-like. "I will admit, I'm pleasantly surprised that you remembered what my voice sounds like. I'm impressed."

"Spare me the hollow compliments and get to the point, you and your employer are the last people I want to speak to right now."

"Sir, I admit that what she did to try to sway your opinion of Arianna was beyond unnecessary, and what I want right now is to save the one I love most in this world by protecting her from herself."

"How do you hope to accomplish that? I'm of the

mind to let all of you go on about your business and leave me the fuck alone."

"That would be unwise, sir. Arianna is madly in love with you."

"She has a funny way of showing it."

Trinity paused for a moment. "That video must have really gotten to you. That is unfortunate, but it was a performance for him, and nothing more. She got what was asked of her to get, and she didn't pay him another thought."

"Okay, say that I believe what you're saying right now. Amelia will erase you for what you're thinking about doing."

"You don't know her like I do, sir. She likes to self-destruct until I remind her who and what is real in her life. This time will be no different."

Dorian was a bit perturbed with the whole conversation, but if it meant he didn't have to deal with Amelia anymore, he was willing to listen a little while longer. "So, how will you be saving her this time? Indulge me."

"I'll tell you exactly what you need to do and say to release your betrothed from her employ." Trinity was never one to mince words, and when it came to what she wanted to get done, she was very adept at doing so with blinding speed. "If you're able to get this done, it will sufficiently kill two birds with one stone, as you Americans love to quip."

He sobered up in seconds. "You have my attention."

"I thought I might. Mommy was a legitimate madame when we first got involved. It wasn't until recently that she started falling for dirty money."

"I don't think I'm gonna like where this is going." Dorian's memory darted back to a time that he would rather forget.

"You might not like it, but it will keep you alive."

"No more riddles, dammit. Tell me what I don't know."

Trinity paused again, measuring her words carefully. "One of your men has been compromised. He had something precious taken from him in order to compel him to betray you."

Dorian's heart stopped at the prospect of what Trinity was alluding to. "There's no way that could happen, unless—"

"Unless what, sir?"

"Where are his daughters? The only thing that would make Harry betray me is if something has happened to his daughters. Where the fuck are they?"

"How did you know it was him? It could have been any one in your inner circle who could have betrayed you."

"I know my men, that's how." Dorian's tone began to take on a hurried, frantic tone. He envisioned the domino effect that could happen before he had a chance to stop it. "The only one of my men who has anything worth betraying the rest of us is Harry. I don't like repeating myself; where are his daughters?"

"They're with the French Prime Minister's son." Trinity didn't hesitate with the information. "They were procured over a week or so ago."

Dorian clenched his teeth to keep from growling, but he was still confused. "How did he end up getting them? Who even knew where they were?"

"Mommy facilitated the acquisition, a man called Rainier dropped the information. He managed to find out where they were and had them picked up. It was done to ensure ... protections and assurances."

"You both have fucked with the wrong family." Dorian was at critical mass, on the verge of an explosion. "Rainier is about to find out what happens to people who have my full attention."

"I'm telling you this information so that we will no longer have your full attention, sir," Trinity replied. "Mommy isn't perfect, but I don't think she would have agreed to this quid pro quo if she'd known that his children were that close to you. If you keep her out of the equation when you extract your family, you can use that leverage to have your betrothed released, too."

"And you really believe that Amelia will just let Mara go without a fight?"

Trinity let out a soft giggle. "I have made the necessary provisions to withstand the fallout. Mommy always has her tendencies, but she will be fine. It's business, never personal."

"So, what happens now? You have to know that it will take more to get your mistress to relinquish control. She's stubborn to a fault."

"I did everything that was needed to get to this conversation, and I have gone as far as I'm willing to go to ensure that things are back in balance. The rest is up to you, but I am earnestly asking that you leave Mommy out of the collateral damage you plan to inflict." Trinity's voice softened as she finished her thought. "Goodbye, Mr. Bentley. For what it's worth, you were our best and most favored client. It's a shame that our relationship will not be able to continue."

Trinity disconnected the call before Dorian could retort, causing him to bang his hand against the tabletop. He took some time to calm himself, realizing that the situation in front of him was where his focus was needed. He would have to deal with Amelia and Trinity later.

He grabbed one of the burner phones he had earmarked for his French connections and dialed the preprogrammed number in the phone. Before the call connected, he switched on the trace equipment, as a contingency plan in case things got a bit ugly.

He didn't bother to wait for the other person to acknowledge him before he got straight to the point. "You have some precious cargo that I need to reacquire from you as soon as possible."

"And what precious cargo would that be, Wraith?" The man on the other side of the line asked. "I don't recall having any cargo that belongs to you at this moment."

"I didn't say that the precious cargo belonged to me, Mr. Deputy Prime Minister, but since you want to play those games, then we'll get right to it: there are two pieces of cargo that I know you are in possession of, and one of those pieces is underage. Those two pieces happen to be family, and they were procured under questionable circumstances."

"That's unfortunate, but I need to understand what that has to do with our current business arrangement."

"Our current business arrangement will be considered null and void, and I would divulge sensitive locations and the inventory within those locations to interested parties that would love to get their hands on them to cause some strife in the region, which would make things a bit tenuous for you," Dorian replied. "The last thing you want is for Turkey to turn to Russia for assistance with what is going on over there at the moment, and with Brexit happening and the US having other things that need their immediate attention at the moment. Let's just say, you may need the pipeline that I'm still offering to you at this moment to keep things balanced."

"You're bluffing. You wouldn't burn the bridge of one of your biggest clients over two pieces of ass."

"I'll burn the whole of France down, city by city, over my family, starting with your boss's son's proclivities that his father insists on covering up and enabling at every turn," Dorian barked. "So, you will remove those pieces from the board or I will commence with following through on my bluff, as you call it. I'm sure the media fallout would do wonders for his reelection interests."

"There is no need for such extreme measures. The PM, as you have stated, does not need to be burdened with such matters, but there is going to be a price for replacing the pieces that you mention."

"But I thought you didn't know what I was talking about?" Dorian chuckled through clenched teeth. "The fact that you want to continue playing games means I need to hang up this phone and roll up the chain of command."

"You're the one playing the dangerous game, Wraith. Don't think for a minute that we can't find out who you are on a moment's notice." The voice on the other line was getting agitated, which was what Dorian wanted the entire time. "You're lucky I don't disconnect this call and see what kind of power you think you have. You don't even know where they are, let alone find where I am."

"You're currently with your mistress at her residence in Saint-Nom-La-Bretèche … or should I say, your residence, since you paid for it to keep her away from your wife." Dorian's voice was as monotoned as he could muster as he rattled off the information. "I imagine if I tap into the Defense Ministry database to pull up the GPS coordinates, I would find your security detail is sitting right outside of the house, waiting for you to get your rocks off.

Need I go on?"

There was silence on the other end for several moments. "It is safe to say you're serious about your demands. How would we explain the disappearance? They have become favorites of his."

"Comatose patients who did not make it to the emergency room after ingesting poison."

"This is going to take time."

"You have forty-eight hours."

"That is not enough time."

"Forty-eight hours, or you'll be explaining to your boss and the Minister of the Armed Forces as to why the military doesn't have the specific weaponry that has been of such optimal use to you the past couple of years. Hesitate further, and you'll be explaining to your wife as to why your mistress is the same age as your eldest daughter and that you've been financing her university ambitions."

"These threats aren't going to go over well. We can, and we will, find out who you are."

Dorian furiously worked on his laptop while they were talking, picking up every piece of information he needed to keep the pressure firmly applied. The more information he found out about his current adversary, the more he smiled at how stupid powerful men could be when it came to a nubile woman willing to do whatever it took to level up.

"You haven't, and you won't, because your superiors like it that way," Dorian explained. "There is nothing more beautiful than the words plausible deniability. As long as I'm keeping their interests at the heart of the matter, there is no need for them to sever my relationship with them … as long as specific lines are not crossed. They are aware of this balance, and the fact that you aren't lets me know that you haven't been in your position very long. Don't worry, you'll find out how this all works very soon."

"I still say you're bluffing, Wraith."

"Wanna bet your political and personal life on it?" Dorian inquired. "Your wife's mobile number is +33 86 27 18 97, and I can send the pictures off your phone to her of your exploits that are sitting on the iCloud for anyone to see for themselves. My, my, sir, you've been rather busy lately. I wonder if your mistress even knows that she isn't the only one."

Dorian wanted to break into full-throated laughter when he heard an exasperated yell come from the other side of the call. "All right, you win. They will be released in forty-eight hours. You have my word; we will figure out the replacement pieces."

"Pleasure doing business with you, Deputy Prime Minister. My regards to your boss and your wife."

Dorian disconnected the call quickly so he could get the laughter out of his system before he angered the Deputy PM any more than he already had. He felt a weight lift from him as he took a deep breath to take care of another piece of unfinished business that he needed to settle. He was in the middle of dialing the number when the doorbell rang.

Ishmael is the only one who knows I'm here. Confusion washed over his face as he headed toward the front door to greet him, not understanding why he would arrive unannounced. He opened the door, only to see Ishmael, as he expected—and Samara, standing next to him.

"Surprise, boss! Look who I managed to smuggle to you!"

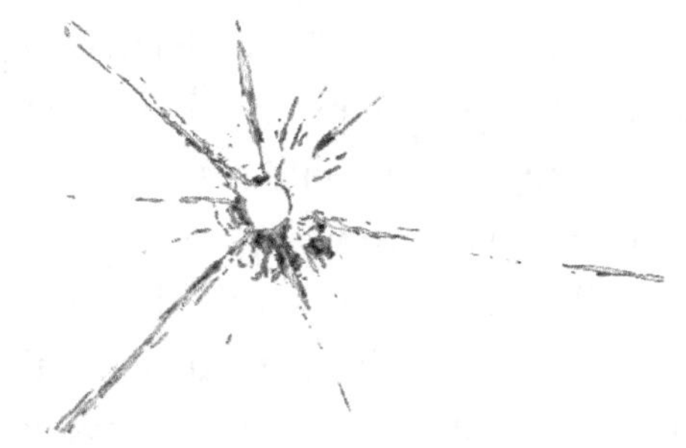

CHAPTER TWENTY-TWO

Ishmael tried to keep the moment light by presenting Samara like she was a surprise gift on a game show, but he quickly realized he might have gotten himself caught up in an awkward reunion moment.

Dorian tried to look amused, but he wasn't sure how to feel in that moment. He was happy to see her, ecstatic that she was there, but he was still trying to figure out the words he needed to say to her.

Samara's sheepish expression combined with Dorian's confusion was enough to throw Ishmael off completely. "Wait, this was not the reaction I expected out of either of you. Here I am, all hyped up to see an epic PDA moment and y'all acting like you're in the midst of a divorce proceeding."

Dorian shook off his emotions to address Ishmael

directly. "No worries, kid, you weren't operating with the full complement of information, or you wouldn't look as confused as you are right now. Mara and I have a few things to discuss, and I'd hoped to set up the time and place myself, but it seems she beat me to it."

"It was the only way I could get to you without you telling me not to come, baby."

"Okay, well, check this out, this ain't about me, and I'm not about to make it that right here in this moment, so, the fact that I was able to get you two in the same space to work things out works for me, too." Ishmael turned on his heel to head back to his rental car. "So, I'm about to go back into the city and get back to the two lovely creatures I left in bed to make this happen, okay?"

"Thank you again, Ishmael, and I hope you aren't mad at me."

"I could never be mad at you, my lady … unless you did something to upset my boss, then I'd have to reevaluate my words."

Dorian closed the door as Ishmael pulled out of the driveway, staring at Samara like he hadn't seen her in years. He did his best to contain his emotions so he didn't sound like he was angry about the conversation he had days ago that put them in this awkward predicament in the first place.

He wanted to start off by saying something else, but one look at her and the words escaped him. "Hi, baby."

Samara gave up a half smile, not sure how to

approach him. "Hey, baby. Ishmael said you were trying to work through some personal things on the way over here. Can you tell me what's going on? Maybe I can help clear things up?"

"I don't want to talk to you about it because I don't want to be mad at you, Mara."

"There's nothing for you to be mad about, sweetheart. I haven't done anything wrong."

"You can tell that to your client, Forsythe. He was the one who sent me the videos of you and him and the words that I thought were only reserved for me."

Samara closed her eyes and cursed under her breath. The look she saw on his face was enough to break her heart. "Amelia was behind this nonsense. I haven't seen Forsythe in over a year. I don't know what he said to you, but it was nothing more than a performance for me. She wants you poisoned against me so I can go crawling back to her. My heart is with you, it has always belonged to you. You have always known that."

"I don't know what to believe, Mara. We aren't those kids anymore. How do I know you truly love me after what I saw and heard?"

"What kind of question is that?"

"A blunt one in need of an answer." Dorian narrowed his gaze as he crossed his arms.

"You've been acting strange around me ever since your mother's art show, when she took me away from you to have a chat. What is going on with you?"

"Nothing is going on with me. I'm trying to figure things out before I consider what's in my mind."

Samara walked up to him, uncrossed his arms, and was within inches of his face. "Like what, DK? I know you love me, there's nothing else to consider or figure out."

"What are you talking about? You still haven't answered my question, and you don't get to answer mine by asking one of your own."

"I'm standing here, in front of you, and I'm telling you that I love you. What I'm wondering is whether or not you're going to stop denying the fact that you love me, no matter what you saw."

"I'm not denying it."

"Yes, you are. Everyone can see how you feel about me. Ishmael sees it, your mother saw it. Hell, your abuelo saw it, for God's sake."

Dorian made a move to push Samara away, but he found it difficult to lift his arms. The mere mention of his grandfather stole every ounce of strength from him. "Wait, how do you know that?"

"I went to see him about something, and he told me how you feel about me and to never give up on you," Samara replied. She took his hands and brought them to her lips to kiss them. "He gave us his blessing; even said he would trigger your trust fund so that we can get away from all of this."

Dorian was still in shock from the knowledge that Samara had a full conversation with his grandfather.

"Abuelo doesn't talk to anyone outside of the family unless it's business. How did you … Mara, I'm not deflecting my feelings for you. No woman outside of mom is more important to me than you are. Look at things from my side and tell me you wouldn't feel a little betrayed by what I saw?"

"Baby, consider the source of the information. I told you that Amelia was manipulative; look at what she did to you over the last couple of days." Samara caressed his cheek, feeling him begin to relax against her touch. "I am yours, always."

"That was why I continued to deal with Amelia. I needed to find a way to get you away from her." Dorian kept his eyes fixed on her face. "I can't let her get away with what she's done to the woman I—"

Samara's eyes widened as his voice trailed off. "That you, what, Dorian? After all this time, we've had this thing between us, pretending that we aren't in love with each other, and now you've been acting like a jealous teenager. Say it, baby, stop holding back."

"I'm in love with you, Mara. Ever since that night in Rio when we first met, while trying to rescue my father, I've been in love with you." Dorian sighed as he gripped her hands. "I'm deeply, hopelessly, in love with you."

Samara froze in the space she stood. Since they were teens, she'd been waiting for him to say those words again. Now that she'd heard them, she reacted like she was dreaming. "Wait … what?"

Dorian felt like he was purging every thought, every emotion left inside him. "No one else has my heart. *Eres mi amor. Mi corazón siempre te pertenecerá.* I know that I have been acting like you aren't important, but I don't make any major decisions without figuring out how you fit into those plans. You are the primary reason I want Amelia to disappear. You are the reason I'm getting out of weapons dealing. It has always been you."

Samara stood speechless for what seemed like forever to them. "DK, I … baby, I love you, too. I need you to trust me when I say that I have Amelia handled, and this time, for good. Abuelo gave me everything I needed to make her disappear."

"You know I can't do that. I don't want you in the same room with her."

"Yes, you will, because it will be the best way to keep us both out of harm's way. Her one weakness is that she won't ever harm me. If she sees you, she'll want you dead on sight."

"Mara, no."

"You don't have a choice in the matter, *querido*."

"I'm sending Ishmael with you."

"You will do no such thing. I'm still the girl who got you out of the favelas, remember?" Samara scolded. "You trusted me then, you can trust me now."

"God, you're never gonna let me live that down, are you?"

Samara smiled before kissing his lips. "Nope … and

our grandchildren are gonna hear all about it one day."

"Okay. When you're done, call Ishmael; he will take you somewhere safe until I finish up things here."

"I will, baby, and you better come back to me in one piece, too. You can't just reveal your true feelings after all this time and die on me."

Dorian wrapped his arms around her and pulled her close, his eyes never wavering from hers. "I will return for you. Promise. Abuelo will kill me all over again if I don't."

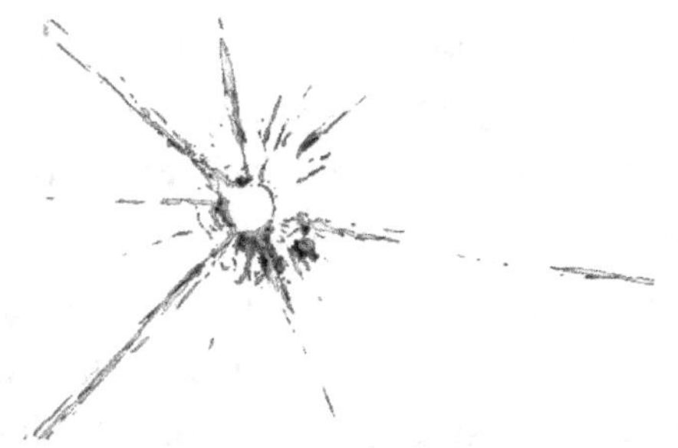

CHAPTER TWENTY-THREE

Samara didn't waste any time in finishing things with Amelia, hopping on the first available flight back to London. When she called her to ask if she could see her, Samara put on the performance of her life, making it sound like she was desperate to see her. Amelia fell for the distressed act, giving her the address to her private penthouse in Camden. It was the opportunity she needed to permanently remove herself from Amelia's world.

She laid it on thick, donning her svelte frame in her soon-to-be former employer's favorite outfit, ensuring that every asset was on display. The lilac and rosemary scented mixture that graced her neck and wrists were meant for one specific purpose: seduction and coercion. Even with all of these measures at her employ, she kept something special tucked away once she revealed her true intentions for her visit.

Amelia opened the door, taking in the striking visuals that stood present before her. A short inhale roused her senses, eliciting a smile across her face. Samara returned a grin in return as she entered into the foyer, realizing that her approach was working in her favor—so far.

"I honestly didn't think you were serious, and yet, here you are." Amelia continued to linger over Samara's frame from head to toe. "A visit to my house? You must be ready to come back to me to make such an intimate gesture."

"As I told you over the phone, I needed to talk to you about something important. Is Trinity here?"

"No, she's running an errand for me in Paris. She won't be home for a few days. That gives us plenty of time to work through the details of our reconciliation."

Samara gave up an actress' smile, despite the indignation she felt deep inside her core.

She wanted to keep up the charade for a little while longer, but her ability to deflect and ignore a person who now repulsed her was no longer there. She was already pushing her luck by being in an enclosed area with her. "Don't get your hopes up, Amelia. What I needed to talk to you about has nothing to do with us."

"You can stop the act, Samara. You're wearing my favorite scents on your skin; you're wearing my favorite outfit," Amelia scoffed. "I know you're still into me, despite your infatuation with your so-called betrothed."

"Things with Dorian are fine now, I'm not worried about that anymore," Samara shot back. "This is nothing more than me tying up loose ends so I can go on with my life."

Amelia slipped inside Samara's personal space, getting another whiff of the intoxicating mixture emanating from her skin. She laughed as Samara extended her arm to create some space between them. "Mhm, that was something we never got around to doing. Why don't we head upstairs so I can cross that off my fuck-it list?"

"That's not happening. I don't want you anymore. You're really obtuse about how things are now between us." Samara never once budged from where she stood, almost daring Amelia to try to be the aggressor. "I left Interpol before I came over here. I turned over evidence of your *other* endeavors. I only came over here to inform you and to warn you to lawyer up while you still have time."

"You didn't know enough about my alleged other endeavors to be able to turn over anything to anyone, much less those inept wankers." Amelia crossed her arms over her chest, regarding Samara's power stance. "You're bluffing."

"He said you would say that."

"And who would that be?"

"Luciano de Souza … *El Jefe Supremo*."

Samara was surprised by the sudden pause and lack

of response from Amelia. The mere mention of his name tended to have that effect on even the most hardened criminal element. She watched as Amelia did her best to maintain as expressionless as possible while contemplating the next words to say.

"Now I know you're bluffing. You have no way to get to *El Jefe Supremo.* You don't have that kind of influence." Amelia frowned as she tried to sort through Samara's body language. "Oh, my God, you really think you're on top like that, huh?"

"Do you want to take that chance, or do you want to lawyer up like I suggested earlier?" Samara sneered at her, resting her hand against her neck. "If you'd done your homework like you normally would do, then you would have known that he is Dorian's grandfather. But I guess that pretty package had you dickmatized, too, huh?"

Amelia sneered. "I should kill you where you stand, whore."

"You won't do that. Despite your manufactured reputation, you don't have it in you."

Amelia glared at Samara, cutting her eyes in the direction of the desk toward her right side. She refocused her attention back to Samara, a smirk spreading across her face. "Don't mistake my affinity for you with my ability to end your life. If what you've said is remotely true, I have no reason to want you take another breath on this planet."

"Don't mistake my coming here as naïveté, either. I

assure you, everything I've said is true."

"So, what's stopping me from grabbing a piece and pulling the trigger instead of having this rather pointless conversation?" Amelia mused. "This is not exactly the way I envisioned things happening when you first arrived."

Samara continued to trace her fingers against the lining of her top. She continued to keep a sharp eye on any sudden movements. "Despite my disdain for the new direction you've taken, I don't want to see you harmed. This is bigger than your desire to get back at me now."

"And that's your problem, pretty girl. You think you have it all figured out. While I'm touched by your compassion, I'm not worried about anyone coming for me. I guess I can kill you now."

Samara took that moment to pull the Ruger LCP .380 from the holster attached to her bra and point it at Amelia's chest. "Not if I take you out first, bitch."

Amelia froze in place, unprepared for this turn of events. "Well, this is new. I guess fucking a weapons dealer does have its perks. You look sexy with it, but can you do something with it?"

Samara squeezed the trigger, barely missing Amelia's left ear. The bullet lodged itself in the mirror hanging against the wall, leaving a shatter pattern in its wake. "I've had some time to practice. After all, fucking a weapons dealer does have its perks."

"No more foreplay, trick. Just do what you came

here to do and be done with it, I don't have time for this madness anymore."

"Give it up, Amelia. The CIA will be on to you soon once Interpol gets done with the information that I gave them. They'll come with the heat and turn everything around you to ash. Think about Trinity and the rest of the girls, for fuck's sake."

"The CIA won't do anything, not with the current administration in place. Now, if you said that fine ass VP was the one bringing the rain, I'd be worried, but that puppet in the Oval Office won't lift a finger to worry about what I'm doing." Amelia kept a wary eye on Samara as she continued pouring on the bravado. "My Saudi benefactors will ensure that anyone who tries to touch a hair on my head is handled."

"I swear, you are unbelievable. This is the endgame for you, take what you have stashed away and disappear. This heat is not what you want in your life."

Amelia took a quick glance down before their eyes met again. "I'd rather feel the heat between your legs, but I guess I'll have to settle for this misplaced concern."

Samara lowered her gun for a moment. "This is not a game. For once in your life, do what you need to do and disappear. All of this is as real as it can get."

"None of this has been a game, but you should know that I always land on my feet. Since it's obvious that this is no longer a thing, do me a favor, yeah?"

"Do I even want to know what the favor is?"

Amelia shook her head, motioning for Samara to lower her gun. "If you're so intent on this happy ever after madness with Dorian, make sure that he puts down the Wraith. He doesn't have it in him to be that man anymore. He will break your heart if he continues down that path."

A smile spread across her face as she kept her gun trained on Amelia. "You don't have to worry about Dorian, or me, anymore. Besides … I have one damn good reason for him to leave that life behind. Now, since we're talking favors, indulge me, okay?"

"Depends on the favor."

"Disappear from our lives. If we so much as hear a whisper that you're even breathing in our direction again, certain persons will hear about it, and they won't be as forgiving as I am."

Amelia shrugged her shoulders, resigning herself to the inevitable. "Well, I guess that's that. Goodbye, pretty girl, it was a good ride while it lasted. Now, get out of here before things get messy."

Samara turned on her heels as she walked out the door. "It's been a pleasure doing business with you. My regards to Trinity."

The minute she slipped into her rental car, she took a deep breath and exhaled, allowing the sense of relief to course through her. She closed her eyes for a few more moments, thanking God for the ability to finally free herself from her situation. She mouthed her thanks to Luciano for providing earthly protection and giving her the ability to do what she needed to do to extract herself from Amelia.

She turned on her Bluetooth to get in touch with the love of her life. Hearing his voice only enhanced the euphoria she felt, realizing that her path was cleared. "It's done, baby. I'm ready to be yours now."

"Thank goodness you're safe. Did she harm you?"

"Nope. Got the drop on her before she could get to it. She's got no choice but to disappear. The information from abuelo is enough to keep her out of our lives for good."

"Good. Meet Ishmael at the airport, he will have the plane ready to go. I need you to stay there until I'm done with all of this unfinished business, okay?"

"I'd rather be with you to help you finish all of this."

"I know you can handle yourself, but I'm worried about me right now. If I know you're safe, I can focus on what I need to do. Can you do that for me, sweetheart, please?"

"You know I can't say no to you."

"Neither can I when it comes to you, *querida*. I promise this will be handled quickly, then you have me for the rest of our lives."

"I'm going to hold you to that. We have a lot to make up for."

"I know. Once this is all done, we will take all the time necessary to do what we need to do."

"Okay. I'll be waiting for you. I love you."

"I love you, too."

Chapter Twenty-Four

Dorian sat in his chartered jet while it taxied down the runway to prepare for takeoff, taking in everything that transpired over the past few days. He was beyond elated that soon he and Samara would be able to find a way to each other after all these years.

If he was honest with himself, he should have claimed her long ago, before their paths diverged, but he was too immersed in getting things off the ground to worry about any entanglements at the time. Whether he wanted to avoid the truth or not, hindsight was cruel, and if they'd gotten together sooner, she might not have fallen under the employ of Amelia in the first place.

It was in his best interest to not beat himself up for playing revisionist history with his own timeline. It was liable to drive him insane, and he needed his mind to be clear of distractions, not when things were finally falling into place. The only thing that was left to do was to facilitate the transition of power so that he could move on to the next phase of life. He'd managed his holdings well enough to be able to maintain his lifestyle for the rest of his life, and with the knowledge that his abuelo was releasing the money to his trust, life could begin anew on various levels.

Seeing his father's phone number pop up on his smartphone was the icing on the cake. He wanted to tell his mother first, but this time, his father would be the beneficiary of great timing. "Dad, hey, what's going on? I have so much to talk to you about."

"Hi, son." Donovan's tone was subdued, even more than what Dorian was used to.

"Dad, what is it? Is everything okay?"

"I wish I could say they are, DK, but I would be lying to you."

Dorian paused for a few moments while the jet took off and began its ascent. Once the jet leveled off, he continued his conversation. "You rarely ever call me son, so, what's happened? What's going on?"

"There was a hit put out on JC. He's been shot. He's hurt pretty bad from last I heard," Donovan replied. "He's down in Johannesburg in the hospital being treated. Had surgery that lasted over eight hours."

Dorian felt like he couldn't breathe in that moment. "What the fuck? How? Who did it?"

"I don't have those details, DK. I can't go to see about him, either, I don't want to take the chance that the man who tried to kill him might be waiting for me."

"I need to get down there," Dorian barked. "If you can't see about him, then I will and let you know what's going on."

"I don't want you down there, either, kid."

"You didn't have a choice back then, and you don't have a choice now, Dad."

"Stubborn as ever."

"Yep, and that's not ever going to change." Dorian managed a chuckle before switching his focus. "Are you and Mami okay? Could this be someone holding a grudge, coming for payback for something? I need to know what to do to keep you safe."

"No, I can't think of anything. The only person who it could have been has been dead for nearly twenty-five years," Donovan mused. "I know I can't convince you to stay out of this, son, so, just be careful when you get down there, okay?"

"I will, and I need you and Mami to go to my safehouse in Southampton. The address is in the safe in your office." Dorian wasn't taking any chances, and he was already in his personal protocol over who he needed to contact next.

"DK, is there anything I can do to help? I can call a few people and see if I can get a detail for your mother while we see what's the trouble in South Africa."

Dorian shook his head, not realizing that his father couldn't see his nonverbal response. "Do what you need to do to keep the both of you safe. It will be one less thing for me to worry over. I know who might have been behind this, but I need to move quick. Call me when you're in the UK. Don't argue with me on this one, please, Dad."

"I gave up arguing with you or your mother a long time ago." Donovan managed a hearty laugh that eased the stress levels a bit in his son. "Do what you need to do. We will be fine."

Dorian disconnected the call, immediately grabbing one of his burner phones to text Kale, Harry, and Ishmael to relay the same news: he needed them in Johannesburg within the next 24 hours.

Kale responded seconds later. Dorian explained the situation and that they would need assistance once they were on the ground.

Ishmael called within minutes. After he explained to Dorian that he was awaiting Samara so he could ensure she was at the prearranged location, as they'd agreed, Dorian told him that he needed to secure someone who could be trusted to keep Samara safe so he could join them in South Africa.

Harry had yet to respond.

Dorian wasn't sure what to make of the lack of response from his father's oldest friend, but he wasn't in a space to do a deep dive over why he hadn't. He had to figure out what happened to his uncle and, more importantly, how to find and eliminate the person responsible for what he felt was a clear and imminent threat toward everything and everyone he held dear.

Chapter Twenty-Five

Dorian wasn't in Johannesburg for more than a few hours and he'd already turned over nearly every stone he could find in order to find the person responsible for the attempted murder of Juan Carlos. He'd moved through Soweto, speaking with as many of the locals as he could, using the word of mouth to get closer to who might have known about what went down at the airport. He knew that if anyone would know anything about what happened, it would be either there or in Cape Town.

While he relied on the streets to get the word out, he made the stop through to the hospital where Juan Carlos was being treated. He wasn't sure how he would feel when he saw him, but the moment he stepped into the suite that he'd arranged for Juan Carlos until he recovered, he nearly fell apart.

The nurse stayed with Dorian until he was able to

get himself together, letting him know that it was best to try to talk to Juan Carlos, despite his comatose stasis. She was insistent that patients can hear their loved ones, bringing them back from the darkness. Dorian hoped that would be true, but he didn't hold out much hope. All he knew was that he couldn't lose Juan Carlos. That would take a piece of his heart away that he wasn't ready to give up yet.

He sat down next to Juan Carlos, doing his best to ignore all of the tubes and monitors, searching for the words that he could say that would bring him back. The silence, save for the noise of the equipment keeping him breathing, was enough to drive Dorian crazy. A few moments later, the words seemed to flow from almost nowhere, speaking from the depths that he didn't realize existed.

"I guess I'm trying to figure out how to say the right things to bring you back to this side of consciousness," Dorian began, wiping the tears from his eyes. "I've taken advantage of the fact that you've been damn near bulletproof all this time, and here you are, fighting for your life when we have so many things that need to get done."

He leaned forward in the chair, taking a deep breath so he could get his thoughts straight. "You've been around for as long as I can remember, and even though I knew you wanted to roll into retirement once Dad got out, you stuck with me anyway. You've been like a father to me in so many ways that I don't know what I would do if I lost you."

He sat in silence again, closing his eyes for what he felt was a few minutes, allowing his mind to travel to a warm and tropical locale, indulging in doing nothing for the foreseeable future. Lying next to him was Samara, in a bikini that left so little to the imagination that he almost forgot he was in the hospital room.

When he awoke, he took a look at the clock and realized two hours had passed. He cleared his throat and stood to wake himself up. He looked over at Juan Carlos, who looked like he was resting comfortably at that point. "We will find out who tried to take you out, and that motherfucker will pay dearly with their life."

He headed out of the room and immediately headed to the nurse's station. The nurse who assisted him was busy with work when he walked up to the counter. "Thank you for looking after him. It means more than you know."

"I heard what you were saying to him. I hope you don't mind me prying," she stated. "I was worried that he didn't have a next of kin. He was in pretty bad shape when we received him. I'm happy that he has someone to look after him when he wakes up."

Dorian smiled, slipping an envelope into her hands. "This man is not being treated here, okay? It is imperative that no one knows that he is here. Can I count on you to deflect any conversations that are routed in his direction?"

The young woman smiled as she opened the

envelope, her eyes widening in surprise at the contents of the package. "Yes, sir, no one will know he is here. By the way, my name is Iminathi. If you need anything at all, please let me know, even if I'm off shift."

Some leads turned into short chases that didn't give him much to go on, but he was able to get to the person who inexplicably needed to take a few days off before the hit was made. In order for him to get close, Dorian dropped nearly 25,000 Rand to pull off a bait and switch to gain an audience. His Xhosa dialect was rusty, but he was willing to brush up quickly in order to find out who got close enough to try to take his godfather out.

He was led by one of the locals to a shanty inside the infamous Diepsloot slums, which became infamous for the kidnapping and murders of children during a crime wave nearly a decade ago. Despite Ishmael's protestations to the contrary, Dorian trusted his instincts to not have any muscle with him to get the answers he needed. He only hoped he would live to not regret that tactic.

He was introduced to a young man by the name of Ako; he was one of the up-and-coming artists in the area who happened to be working at the airport the day that Juan Carlos was hit. Word spread at a lightning-quick pace of the money being offered for the information; Dorian was a bit surprised that he didn't attract more attention when he arrived. He didn't see a lot of vehicles in the area, and the motorcycle he rode on was likely to not be there once he'd finished conducting his business there.

Ako was in the midst of finishing a painting of Akon City, its stunning design and landscaping and the lighting from the African sun from overhead nearly making Dorian wish the city existed now instead of waiting for its completion in the next decade. He was so enamored with the panoramic view that he initially didn't hear Ako greet him.

(Speaking Xhosa) "You must not fear much to come down here by yourself, my friend. Either that, or others must have a reason to fear you."

(Speaking Xhosa) "My security detail would agree with you. There is no reason for me to fear much, especially when we deal in these areas throughout the continent on a regular basis."

Ako never turned to face Dorian as he continued to put the finishing accents on the painting. He was keenly aware of his guest, despite his lack of eye contact in the moment. *(Speaking Xhosa)* "That explains your comfort zone. That's fair. More should be like you, then maybe we might have more than a fighting chance to be more like the northern suburbs."

Dorian nodded, then got to the point of his need to visit. *(Speaking Xhosa)* "Since word has gotten to you as quickly as it has, then you know that my time is valuable and short. There is a man I need to track down before he leaves the country, and I've been told that you got a good look at him."

Ako placed his paintbrush in a can of water, taking one more good look at his work before turning to face Dorian to respond to his assertion. *(Speaking Xhosa)* "Yes, I got a look at the *khaki* when he snuck up on him. Plugged him a few times; surprised my man survived the hit."

Dorian frowned when he heard a specific word, but he wanted clarification. *(Speaking Xhosa)* "Are you sure it wasn't a yarpie trying to get rich quick?"

Ako broke out into a laugh that threw Dorian off balance. When he finally settled down to catch his breath, he soon recognized from Dorian's facial expression the gravity of the query. *(Speaking Xhosa)* "He didn't move like a yarpie; it was too rigid, too uniform. I know ex-military when I see it. They looked at each other like they knew each other, too. Would hate to have a friend like that in my world."

Whether Ako realized it or not, he'd inadvertently confirmed Dorian's worst fears. Dorian didn't want to believe that Harry was the triggerman, but the facts were cold and unadulterated. The only thing he couldn't understand was why Harry would do such a thing, and he wouldn't get that answer until he tracked him down and got the answers for himself.

Ako regarded his guest with a curious expression on his face. *(Speaking Xhosa)* "You look like you've just been hit with a terrible truth, my friend. I take it the information I provided was worth the trip after all."

Dorian shook from his thoughts, nodding in

acknowledgement to Ako's assessment. In the next moment, he was already plotting his next chess move to keep them both out of any trouble. *(Speaking Xhosa)* "Yes, unfortunate, but yes. Now, I have a question about your newly finished piece right there."

Ako raised an eyebrow, trying to figure out where the conversation was heading. *(Speaking Xhosa)* "It was a vanity piece, nothing more. I was not looking to sell it to anyone."

Dorian shook his head, dropping a bag on the coffee table in front of him. *(Speaking Xhosa)* "Well, I'm purchasing it from you. That painting will do quite well in my mother's collection, and she has connections to see that Akon sees such a beautiful rendition of the city he is soon to build."

Ako's eyes widened as he opened the zipper and took a look inside. He immediately collapsed on the couch, trying to grasp the reality of the current situation. He looked skyward, whispering something before he refocused his gaze toward his unexpected benefactor. *(Speaking Xhosa)* "This is too much for such worthless information. You could have gotten that by other means."

Dorian grinned, sitting down with Ako to place a reassuring hand on his shoulder. *(Speaking Xhosa)* "This is not for the information. This is paying your worth for the talent that God has bestowed upon you, my friend. Our paths were meant to cross, though it was for another purpose altogether. I have the ability to give you the tools and to do what you want to do for your community to make it better."

Dorian rose from the couch, preparing to leave the residence. Ako walked him to the door, still wiping the tears from his eyes over his new-found small fortune. The two men shook hands as Dorian took out his cell phone to call Ishmael to come and retrieve him from the area. He was surprised to see that the motorcycle was still outside of Ako's home. He turned to Ako, silently requesting an explanation over why his transportation had not disappeared within the first sixty seconds of his arrival.

Ako shrugged his shoulders, as he could offer no rational response for his inquiry. *(Speaking Xhosa)* "You were right, perhaps our paths were meant to cross, and it was also meant for you to exit in the same manner as how you entered, my friend. This area does not deserve its former reputation, and thanks to you, perhaps I might have a hand in giving it a newer, more reputable perspective for the world to see. I wish you peace in your journey to extract the truth you have learned this night."

Dorian nodded as he made his way to the motorcycle, breathing deeply as he started the engine. His mother would always say while he was growing up that there were never any mistakes made in the universe, and that the way things were supposed to happen would happen, no matter what one tried to do to affect the outcome. He rode the manifestation of that belief out of the area, armed with information that would help him unravel more of the mystery surrounding the attack. He wasn't ready to concede that Harry was the man that Ako saw that day, but he needed to hear the truth from his mouth. Only then would he deal with the aftermath.

Once he was back on the north side of Johannesburg, he made the call to both Kale and Ishmael, trying to get a location check from both of them. He didn't waste words, putting them on alert with one cryptic phrase. "The game may have changed on us, gentlemen. I'll explain when the car drops you off at the house. See you in a bit."

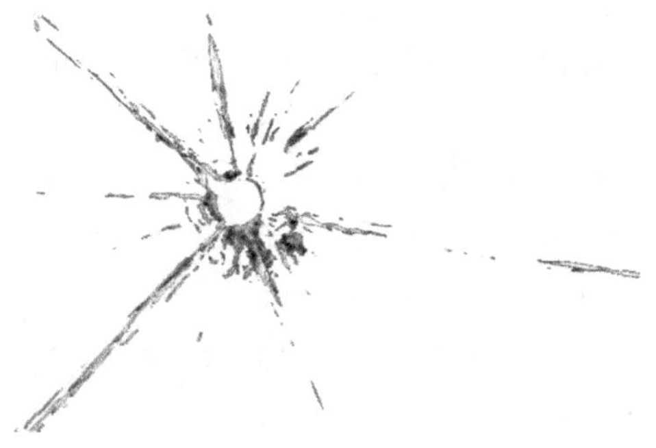

Chapter Twenty-Six

Ishmael and Kale were taken aback by the stately home that would be the destination to their somewhat long journey. It didn't look much larger than the estate homes that they'd purchased or resided in Stateside, but they also knew their boss had a penchant for being both subtle and opulent. Considering they were in the affluent suburb of Morningside, it was only a matter of time before they would find out how deceptively massive the estate was.

They were not disappointed once they were greeted by a lovely young woman at the door, who guided them to where they would house their bags and explained to them that "Master Bentley" would like for them to join him in the gazebo in the back yard.

Ishmael could only laugh at the over-the-top manner of everything happening around them, but he appreciated all the eye candy on display as there were more in the kitchen preparing dinner as the young woman escorted them to the gazebo inside of a backyard that seemed to track as far as the eyes could see.

Kale shook his head, focusing his attention to where Dorian sat, looking like he was in deep thought, pen in hand and scribbling notes on a legal pad. He didn't want to waste any time, either, wanting as much information as Dorian was willing to give. "Okay, sir, what's with the secrecy, and why are we in Joburg?"

Dorian picked up a Mombacho Liga Maestro Gordo cigar, taking his time to light and even out the ash with a few pulls of the stick. He turned his attention to his two lieutenants, a pensive expression awash over his face. "I needed to have back up for what we're about to deal with. JC was hit. It's bad."

The space got quiet for more than a few moments as the startling news hit the men hard.

Ishmael was the first to respond, the aggression in his voice evident. "How bad, and who needs to bleed?"

"Bad enough for me to want to string up whoever is responsible. If they hit him, my father could be on the hit list."

Ishmael shook his head, showing the thumbs down signal. "Your father has been done for a dime, DK, why on earth would anyone want to come for him now?"

Dorian continued to indulge in his cigar as he listened to the logic play out. "My father had more enemies than I ever realized growing up. Hell, for a time, he went under an assumed name while my mom went back to her maiden name. That's why I've made my own decision: I'm putting things in place for you two to run things from now on."

Kale and Ishmael gave each other incredulous looks before they turned and nearly in unison asked for clarification. "Wait … what?"

"I'm not out of my mind, I've thought this through for some time. It's your time, gentlemen," Dorian stated. "I'm not built for this life anymore."

"Look, DK, you know that's not my flow. My place is in the air. I have no problems backing Ishmael, not a single one." Kale looked over at Ishmael, who looked a bit shellshocked himself. "I will admit, this is coming from left field. Did JC getting hit shake you up that badly?"

Dorian leaned back in his chair, nodding as he considered his answer. "It wasn't the catalyst to what I've been considering, but to be real, it shook me up. I respect your decision to stay airborne. What do you think, kid? Are you ready for this? Do you have anyone you can roll with?"

Ishmael leaned against the edge of the railing, taking some time to consider his response. He grinned to himself, nodding as though he'd made up his mind in that moment. "Yeah, I got someone who can cover my six while Kale handles the aerial support."

"Can you trust them with your life the way I've

trusted you with mine?"

"More than you know, DK. He's like family; I'd give my life for them, and vice versa."

"Good man, because I want you to set up the meet so I can see them for myself," Dorian replied. "The last thing I want to do is complete the transition and things are not on solid ground. I have something on the horizon that will have my attention for the foreseeable future."

"Yeah, I know, and she's about 5-foot-6 and a handful." Ishmael laughed as he remembered the last time he'd left Samara and Dorian together. "Seriously, it's time. You said it yourself: better to get out on your own terms than to be taken out."

Kale still pondered the inexplicable absence that hadn't been addressed. "Where's Harry, sir? He should be here to help with this hunt."

Dorian sighed, exhaling slow as he considered his words. "Harry won't be helping with the hunt."

"Why not? He'd want to do the guy that tried to take JC out as badly as we do."

Kale closed his eyes for a moment, struggling to find the words to convey his thoughts. "Harry is the hunt, am I right?"

Ishmael scoffed. "Nah, that's some bullshit. Harry's not the mark. Come on, DK, tell him Harry's not the mark."

"Yeah, DK, tell me I'm wrong. I really, really want to be wrong right now." Kale rarely showed any emotion; it was one of the things that kept him sharp while sitting in the sniper's perch.

Dorian's silence was more than any of them could handle. He did his best to try to verbalize his response, but he was reduced to nothing more than a slow nod of his head.

Ishmael was beside himself. "Why the fuck would Harry try to take JC out? That makes no sense."

"Only Harry can answer that question, boys." Dorian wanted to remain calm, but inside, he was raging. He needed to believe for himself that Harry would never betray his family. "For now, we have to figure out where he is, and once we have him, then we snatch and put him in the box. If he doesn't answer questions, we erase him."

A few seconds later, Dorian's phone rang, the number showing as unknown. "Hello? Who is this?"

"DK, it's Harry. I heard about what happened to JC. Where are you?"

Dorian did his best to suppress the rising anger, but Ishmael and Kale saw him stiffen up, alerting them to who was on the other line. He pulled a few more times on his cigar, slowly blowing the smoke into the air. "We're in Joburg, bruv, where are you?"

"I just got down here, I took the first flight I could get once I got word."

"And who did you get word from, Harry? I tried to call you on the burner I gave you. Why didn't you call back?"

There was a pregnant pause over the line, which further stoked the fires inside Dorian, lending more credence to the possibility that Ako did positively identify Harry, even if he didn't know his name. "I … I must have misplaced it or something. Your father gave me the head's up, thought it might have been one of our old enemies coming back to take us out."

Dorian wanted desperately to believe him, but there was a sickening feeling in his gut that Harry had been in Johannesburg the entire time. "I was thinking the same thing. You know where my house is in Joburg, you can meet us here."

Another pause threatened to infuriate him to the point of calling him out over what he knew of the situation. "Sure … yeah, I'll be there. I can shoot down in the next thirty, just need to grab a car."

"Good man. We will see you then."

The men sat in silence as Dorian contemplated the next move to make, working through the plans swirling around in his head. He glanced in Kale's direction, a silent nod over what needed to be done, but unsure over whether it needed to be done.

"This is going to be tough sledding over the next few hours, DK." Kale felt the need to state the obvious, but there wasn't much else that could be said. "Once he gets here, if he has the balls to show up, it's going to get real."

"It got real the minute he tried to tap dance around my questions, Kale," Dorian responded, still doing his best to try to keep his emotions in check. "I've known him since I was a teenager. He helped me rescue my father all those years ago, and now he chooses to turn on us like this?"

"I understand this has to be difficult, but he made the decision to try to kill JC. That makes him radioactive in my book at this point, DK," Ishmael remarked. "He's gonna get all the smoke on this one, whether he meant to do it or not. Some things are difficult to come back from."

"I hear you both, and you're both right. We will have to see how this all plays out once he gets here. That's all we can do."

"So, what's the next move, boss?" Ishmael asked. "This next hour is going to feel like an eternity. Anticipation is its own form of torture."

"Now, we wait. Get everything prepared in case we have to interrogate."

Chapter Twenty-Seven

The moment Harry stepped through the door he immediately regretted his decision to meet Dorian in hostile territory. While taking the thirty-minute ride down to the estate from his hotel room, he might have changed his mind a half-dozen times over whether he would meet or not.

His instincts told him that Dorian probably already knew about his part in Juan Carlos' attack, but at that point, he no longer cared what happened to him. All he needed to know was whether his precious girls were out of harm's way, and he would meet whatever end awaited him.

Staring down the business end of Ishmael's gun didn't help matters, either.

The look in Ishmael's eyes all but confirmed that Dorian shared his suspicions about Harry, and he knew how loyal Ishmael was to Dorian. He never flinched when the hammer cocked back. "So, are you taking me to the boss so I can explain myself, or are you under orders to drop me on sight?"

Ishmael sneered as he kept his gun trained on Harry's temple. "DK said he wanted to see you first before I put you down, although Kale could have dropped you at the driveway. The way I see it, why not add a little drama to the situation. It's bad enough you killed a man you considered your brother, there's no coming back from that. I'll give you credit, though; coming here was not the move I thought you'd make. I was ready to go on the hunt."

"Let's get this over with. If any of you had any shred of compassion for me, you'll drop me quick."

"That's not my call, that's DK's. But like you said, let's get this over with."

Ishmael led him into the basement of the estate, and from first glance, Harry could tell that the area was soundproofed and insulated. A lesser man would have panicked, but Harry felt the need to allow things to play out. If anything, he could get Dorian to help with the situation that caused him to betray everyone he loved in the first place.

Dorian sat in a nondescript folding chair, lending to the no-nonsense tone of the situation at hand. His eyes were cold, a Poker face that would make even the most seasoned Texas Hold'em player flinch. Harry couldn't read his body language, and for the first time in his life, he was ready to panic. They sat, face to face, within a foot of each other, close enough for them to shake hands, if the atmosphere were not so acrimonious.

Dorian's voice inflections were even-keeled, almost monotone. There was no emotion to find in anything he said. "This is one of those times where you need to be very careful about the answers you give to my questions."

Harry leaned forward in the chair, searching for anything that he could grasp to gain traction in this discourse. "After all that I have done for you and your father? Why are you questioning my loyalty now?"

"I don't have much of a choice in the matter. You killed JC. What could possibly have compelled you to take your family out? You hand-picked him when you were running with my father. Help me understand, because none of this makes sense."

"Come on, DK, let me ice him. He killed JC; he probably would have tried to kill you. I can't let that happen." Ishmael still had his gun in hand, itching to be let loose. "This can't go without a response."

Kale, who'd managed to enter the room as Ishmael made the request, chimed in with his opinion. "Ishmael has a point, sir. If JC could get shot without a moment's hesitation, then we're all expendable at this point. Who's to say he wasn't supposed to gun us down, one by one, until he was left to pick up the pieces and start over?"

"Do you hear them? Is there any reason why I shouldn't let him put two in the chest and one in the dome?"

Harry kept his emotions in check. He already knew where this was going, it was simply a matter of getting there. "I'm in a no-win scenario, kid. Do what you have to do."

Dorian raised an eyebrow, finally allowing his anger to erupt. "I shouldn't have to! You were inner circle, dammit!"

"I didn't have a fucking choice!"

Dorian took a beat, breathing a couple of times to keep from letting his emotions get the best of him again. "So, since you seem to fear whoever you're protecting more than you fear what we will do to you, let's get right to it. Why did you betray us?"

"You were never meant for this life. Even when you were younger, I knew you were meant for more. Your father wanted more for you, not this bullshit life." Harry seemed to be steadfast in his assessment.

"So, you decided that I was done, right? Did your new partner convince you of that?"

Harry shook his head. "You were supposed to cash out and disappear, for fuck's sake! Once JC and the rest of the crew was out of the picture, you were supposed to fade out. I tried to persuade you, but your stubborn ass wouldn't take the hint."

Kale swung at Harry with a left hook that struck blood the minute he connected. "You wouldn't have been able to get close enough to get to the rest of us once we found out about JC. I'm beginning to think that you didn't think this whole situation through."

"If I could have, I would have tried to get everyone in one place so I could have made this easier on myself, but the clock was ticking, and I had to improvise. Cutting the head off the snake was my only option."

Dorian got closer into Harry's space, to make his next statement clearly. "You knew there would be a reckoning, regardless of whether you succeeded or failed. You may have thought that I was that kid you remembered and that I didn't have safeguards in place, but I'm not as sloppy as you think I am."

"He had my kids, DK!"

"And we could have kept them safe!" Dorian shouted. "Did you think I wouldn't be able to find out they were taken? I love those girls like they were my own blood."

"And I'm their father! I was supposed to keep them safe, not you!"

Ishmael was at his breaking point, pointing the gun at the back of Harry's head. "DK, give the word and he's done. There's nothing more left to learn, he's already confessed."

"Not yet, kid, I have one more question to ask." Dorian sat down, crossing his arms as he leaned against the back of the chair. "Was it worth it?"

"It doesn't matter anymore, I failed. My girls are probably dead by now anyway, I couldn't provide proof of death. You say JC is dead, but I can't prove it."

In the next few seconds, Dorian's satellite phone rang, causing a pause among the men in the room. Kale walked over to pick it up, requesting the person to identify themselves. He flinched for a moment, turning the phone over to Dorian for confirmation.

Dorian took the phone, speaking a few words to determine who was on the line. A small smile spread across his lips, but not long enough for anyone to notice. He then handed the phone to Kale, who placed the phone in front of Harry, engaging the speakerphone. "It's for you."

Harry's confusion was evident as he took the phone from Dorian. "Hello?"

"Dad? Is that you?"

Harry wanted to cry out, but he simply mouthed "Thank you, God" before answering his oldest daughter's question. "Angelica, it's me, baby. Are you and your sister safe?"

"Yes, DK's man just dropped us off with Mom. We're okay. How did you find us? Where are you now?"

He looked up at Dorian for a moment, willing the tears from falling. "I'm with DK now, baby."

"Will we get to see you soon? We convinced Mom to let you come home to see us."

Ishmael pulled Dorian to the side, trying his best to whisper so Angelica wouldn't hear their sidebar. "DK, we can't let this ride."

"Ishmael, trust me on this one. I got this handled."

"I trust you, but he could have killed us all."

"And we will ice the man responsible, I promise. He will die, you have my word."

"The man responsible is sitting right there."

"Chess, not checkers, Ishmael. You don't take out a pawn when you can use it to take a shot at the king. I need you to trust the moves on the board, even if you don't see them yourself."

Ishmael nodded, holstering his gun so they could return to the conversation at hand.

"Baby, I have to have a long talk with DK, but I hope I can see you soon. We have so much to catch up on."

"Well, tell big brother he can come, too. He's family, after all, and we haven't seen him in person in almost two years." Angelica's smile could be felt through her tone.

"I will, baby … I need to go. I love you so much."

"We love you, too, Dad. See you soon."

Kale disconnected the call, watching as Harry burst into tears. He recovered a few moments later, straightening himself in the chair, resigning himself to the inevitable. "I'm ready. Thank you for at least allowing me to talk to them one last time."

Dorian waved off that sentiment. "There are three reasons you are still breathing right now."

Harry's eyes narrowed for a second, his face showing the understanding and confusion over the riddle. "I know two of the reasons, but I'm confused on the third."

"JC is not dead."

Harry gasped, the shock of the news taking his breath away. "He's … he's still alive?"

"Yes, and at a secured location. Now, I can only imagine the person who put you in such a bind to be able to turn on us without a moment's hesitation."

Kale snapped his fingers as the lightbulb went off. "Rainier."

Ishmael scoffed. "Do we even know who this motherfucker is at all? How does he have this much intel on any of us?"

"We don't … but Harry does, whether he wants to divulge the man behind the moniker or not. And whether Harry likes it or not, he's going to set up the meet so we can end this once and for all."

Harry sighed. "DK, you don't want to go down this road. You're not going to like where it ends."

"It won't end any other way at this point. We are taking the fight to him. Now, set up the meet, let him know you have proof of death."

"Dorian, I'm serious. You don't want to know what I know. Please believe me when I tell you that I'm doing this to protect you."

Dorian pulled his gun from his shoulder harness and pressed the barrel against his temple. "I'm about thirty seconds from reneging on my initial promise not to kill you. I'm not a patient man, so, pretend I'm not family and tell me what the fuck I want to know so I can end this."

Harry took one look into Dorian's eyes and realized that the threat was real and he could die in that moment. He thought about his daughters and the second chance that he'd been given and decided that whether the pain would be too much for Dorian or not was no longer in his control.

He let out a heavy sigh and nodded, causing Dorian to lower the gun. "Yes, I know who Rainier is, and it's going to piss you off once you find out he is."

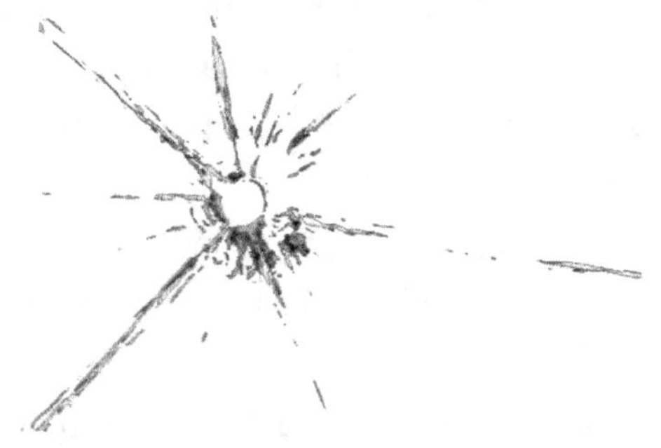

CHAPTER TWENTY-EIGHT

A lot of things swirled through Dorian's mind as he awaited the details of the meet from Harry. As he told Ishmael earlier in the night, chess moves outpace checkers moves any day of the week. He had to wonder if he had been making chess moves throughout this whole situation.

He moved into the safe room in his home, similar to The Cage he has at his primary residence in the States, and made a phone call to the one person who might provide the missing piece to this whole situation. He knew it was a risk due to his connections, but in order for them to be able to move forward in their continuing relationship, there were answers he needed.

"General Locke, I hope I wasn't disturbing you on an off day." Dorian took into account the seven-hour time difference from DC, so he knew it wouldn't be an odd hour for his clandestine partner. "There are some things we need to discuss."

"Dorian, this must be important for you to break protocol like this. Is this line secured?"

"Always, and ghost servers have been deployed. We're safe."

"So, what can I do for you, son?"

"I need to know what you know with regard to my chief rival, Rainier."

"What makes you think I know anything?"

"Because I know I'm not the only supplier for the DoD, sir." Dorian kept his tone smooth and casual, not wanting to tip his hand yet. "I know your people know who Rainier is, and I wanted to avoid having this conversation. The playing field has changed, and one of my men was nearly killed due to that change in the landscape."

"Even if my people knew who Rainier was, and I'm not saying if they do or don't, why would I be expected to betray that confidence? If that happens, I can't be expected to keep your confidence, either." The general was playing the usual shell game, which was to be expected. "There are things in play that you might not be aware of, and I'm urging caution before you decide to upset the balance."

"I can't be expected to sit by and allow this to happen against my team. A response is expected, and a response will happen. The only way to stop that from happening is to tell me who Rainier is so we can have a sit down and negotiate."

"Dorian, this isn't like you. You're acting like a common thug trying to settle a turf war. There are other ways to handle things."

"Dubya tried to take out a whole country because hostiles came to New York and dismantled the towers almost twenty years ago. I don't think you're in any position to lecture me about turf wars."

General Locke paused for a moment, leaving dead space on the call. "It is not the policy of the DoD to get involved with tensions between contractors. I'm not about to open the Department up for reprisal, especially when it isn't in our best interest. You know how this works."

"Yes, I do, and when that tension is eliminated, I don't want any issues on the back end. Sounds like a winner?" Dorian wasn't about to compromise his position, but he wanted to ensure that Locke knew that there would be some drama before things settled back down. "I'm going to need you to understand that whatever happens in the next few days, it will happen with or without consent."

"I understand. I hope you have considered the aftermath of that decision."

"I have."

"Fair enough. I look forward to our next conversation, through the usual channels, of course."

"Of course, General. Until the re-up."

Locke is hiding something; I know he is. Dorian tried to place the puzzle pieces together to make them fit and show a different picture. The information Harry divulged nearly rocked him to his core, to the point to where he outright called Harry a liar to save his own skin. He went through the paces of deducing all the possibilities that could lead to someone else being Rainier, but as he eliminated those possibilities, the only thing that remained was the cold, hard truth.

Kale entered into the room, a concerned look on his face. He gave Dorian the satellite phone, hesitant to give him the news. "Your mother is on the phone. Something bad happened Stateside."

Dorian couldn't take the phone from Kale fast enough. The panic that raced through him was nearly debilitating as he raised the phone to his ear to hear his mother's voice. "Mami? What's happened?"

"I still don't know, baby, it all happened so fast. There was an explosion and I barely got out of there, and the only thing I could think to do was come to Papi's house, and I—"

"Mami, I need you to try to slow down." Dorian felt as panicked as his mother sounded, but he needed to find out some information to help him figure this new twist in the way things were going. "Why are you in Rio? Where's Dad?"

"Baby, I don't know. One minute I was on the phone with him, and then the line went dead in the middle of the conversation. I thought I heard someone in the house, which scared me because your father wasn't home." Isabella rattled off as much information as she could in rapid-fire succession. "By the time I made it outside to our neighbor's house, Ms. Cora, the house blew up. It still feels so unreal. Everything is gone, DK."

Dorian punched the wall so hard he left a hole in the drywall. There was no doubt in his mind that Rainier, and someone who knew his family and connections, was behind this assault. Coming after his parents was the final straw. "I'm coming to you now. I'll be there in the next few hours. We'll find Dad, okay?"

"Okay, DK. My God, this feels like the same madness all over again."

"It will be fine, just stay at Abuelo's house, you'll be safe there until I get there." Dorian disconnected the call, letting out a frustrated scream that got Kale's and Ishmael's attention.

They rushed into the room, guns drawn, wondering what they needed to prepare for. Ishmael noticed the pained look on Dorian's face and went into protective mode. "What happened, DK? Kale said your mom was on the phone. Say the word, we'll be wherever you need us to be to crack some skulls."

Dorian couldn't think, all he cared about was getting to Rio. "Keep an eye on Harry, make sure that meet gets set up. When you get the location, let me know."

"DK, I understand that you are emotional right now, I'd be burning down a few cities over my mom, too, but is this the right move to make right now?" Kale tried to get his boss to see things as clearly as he could. "Maybe this was Rainier, maybe this wasn't, but he wants you distracted so you can make a mistake. Think this through."

Dorian glared at Kale for a moment before checking his emotions. He took a deep breath, closing his eyes to figure out what the next move needed to be. "Kale, I don't know if this is the right move or not, not this time. I want you and Ishmael to stick to the primary plan of attack for now, but I need to see what's going on with my parents. With my father missing, I'm convinced that this has something to do with him."

Kale pressed his hand against Dorian's shoulder, nodding in agreement. "Do what you need to do. We got your six."

"There is something else I need you to do." Dorian thought about it for a moment, nodding to himself when he made up his mind. "I need you to get in touch with our IT connect in Dubai, Yaya. Call it a hunch, but I don't want to leave anything to chance. When Harry makes contact, I need her in place to find out where Rainier is."

"Consider it done. As soon as we link up, we'll have her on it. What are you thinking?"

"I have a feeling he thinks that we are one step behind him. He might have been right for a good minute, but he has my full attention now," Dorian replied. "Time to play catch up, and that phone call will be exactly what we need to catch him slipping."

"You know he might try some other bullshit while we're trying to lock him down," Kale mentioned. "We might need to check all available connections to ensure no one else is caught up like Harry did."

Ishmael snapped his fingers like a light bulb went off in his head, pulled out his phone, keying in a number to call. "Bro, tell me the precious cargo is still secured? Good man … DK, Samara is okay where she is. Had to make sure the queen was still protected on the board. Your knights are in the best position possible, so make sure that home is handled. We got this."

Dorian nodded as he headed out of the house and mounted his motorcycle. Before he turned on the engine, he made the call to see about his beloved. "I miss you, *querida*. How are you holding up?"

"I'd be doing much better when I can be with you again. I miss you so much." Hearing Samara's voice seemed to ground him, settle him down. Her presence was soothing to him, helped him focus on what was most important to him. "Is it almost over? I should be out there helping you finish this."

Dorian chuckled, knowing that nothing would make him happier than having her by his side. "I know, and it will be over soon. I need a couple of days, and then I will send for you. For now, I need you in a safe location."

"I'm safer than I've ever felt, *mi amor*. I'm trying to avoid cabin fever. As soon as this is over and we can start our life together, I want to travel for at least a month. I'm not used to being still when I know I can handle myself."

"That's a promise, *querida*. I'll check on you once I've gotten to Abuelo & Abuela's house to check on Mami. I love you."

"I love you, too. Be safe out there and come home to me."

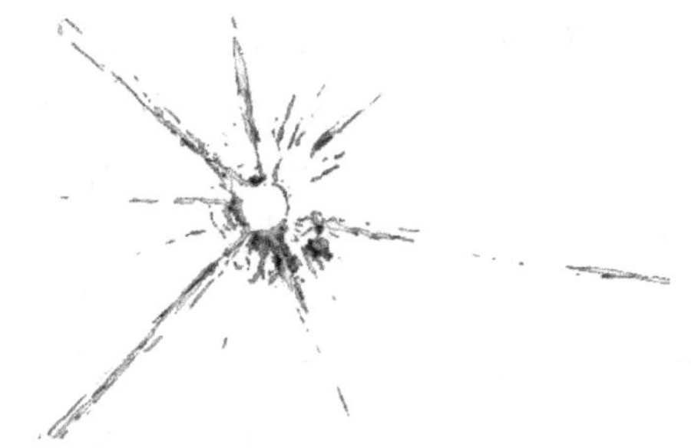

CHAPTER TWENTY-NINE

It took Samara a while to keep her body from tingling after she'd finished her call with Dorian. She couldn't resist how he made her feel, and now that things were starting to fall into place again, it intensified the visceral reaction she had to something as simple as his voice in her ear. She needed him there with her, but she understood that he had something that needed to be done so they could start their new life away from the craziness they'd both known for too long.

With Ishmael in the condo that Dorian had them stay in for what seemed to be forever—if she could call the past few days forever—and her penchant for developing cabin fever in less than a day or two, it was only a matter of time before she would begin to start acting out. She wandered toward the bedroom to change into something that would keep her in the sensual mood she felt, holding on to the heat coursing through her body for as long as she could.

Ishmael will have to get over it tonight. I need to feel Daddy so badly my body is liable to explode. She wandered into the bathroom to run a hot bath, preparing to welcome the soothing sting of the heat to match the insatiable hunger deep in her core. She stepped out into the bedroom while the tub filled, pulling the wine from the mini fridge so she could indulge further inside of her wanton state.

She didn't mind her protector's company; he'd been an excellent conversationalist since the first day they'd gotten acclimated to their temporary residence. Had it been anyone else, she probably would have tried to find different ways to escape, if only for a few hours to keep from driving herself crazy. If anything, he'd been the perfect gentleman, taking great care to not be pervasive or creepy in any manner.

It wasn't for a lack of her trying to tease him. In her mind, it made the time flow faster, and that's what she needed more than anything in the world. It impressed her that she couldn't get a rise out of him—or at least, he never gave an overt sign that she was getting to him. Tonight, however, she was close to throwing caution to the wind and swearing him to secrecy if she were to place him in a compromising position.

Samara quickly put those thoughts out of her head as she set her nearly empty wine glass on the side of the tub, sinking into the water, hoping that she could at least loosen the tension she felt in her muscles. The water enveloped her like a fluid blanket as she slowly slipped her body further below the water line. It was so hot, it was almost painful, but it felt so wonderful against her skin, her muscles, that she no longer cared about which she felt more, the pain or the pleasure.

The minute she rose from the tub, she reached for the first lotions she could find, a silken blend of almond oil, mango butter, vitamin E oil and lavender oils that she purchased from one of her clients. As she caressed her skin with the lotion, she couldn't stop imagining her hands were his, threatening to arouse her senses all over again. She grabbed her satin robe, padding out to the deck outside of the bedroom, noticing that the sky had darkened quite a bit while she indulged in her bath.

Looking out over the landscaped back yard, she observed the roiling clouds in the sky. The branches of the trees whipped back and forth, bending to the will of the gusts of wind that developed. She always loved summer storms. There was something erotic about the unbridled energy of the wind and rain. The rain and wind, the flashes of lightning and rumbling thunder, it was all enough to work her into a frenzy.

The lightning was still off in the distance, far enough to enjoy its splendor, and since she could enjoy a measure of privacy, she left her robe open, allowing the mist of the rain to kiss every inch of her body. The water trickling down felt so delicious to her that she removed her robe, exposing her naked form to whatever the elements had to offer. Her body trembled, and she felt her heartbeat quicken. She closed her eyes, embracing every one of her senses as she took her hands and roamed over her curves, praying that she could survive the energy the storm continued to surge through her.

She lost herself in the storm, moaning softly against the rumble of the thunder. In the next instant, she swore she felt another pair of hands against her hips, holding them in place to stop her from swaying. She blamed it on the wine and her overheated state; Ishmael was downstairs and never so much as disturbed her once she'd retired for the evening.

"You smell succulent, *querida*. Inhaling your scent made it worth the trip all worthwhile."

Samara flinched for a moment before she realized the surprise presence behind her. "Mmm, I thought I was dreaming. I wanted to feel you so badly, Papi. I missed you terribly."

"I didn't want to keep you waiting too much longer. It has been torture being away from you for so long."

"It's only been a week, darling."

"It shouldn't have been that long."

"Once you take care of what you need to do over the next day or so, I'll be yours forever."

"Is that a threat or a promise?"

"I don't make threats, *mi guapo*. You should know

that by now."

The thunder rumbled closer to them, but neither of them cared. Nothing else, and no one else, mattered in that moment between them. The rain began to fall harder, the warmth of the water mixing in with the thunder and flashes of lightning, creating a symphony that they didn't want to end.

Samara lost herself in the moment, welcoming Dorian to come inside and unleash the storm she felt within him, a storm that rivaled the one swirling above and around them. The louder the thunder cracked, the louder she screamed from his maddening strokes, acting as though they would never have another moment like this in their lives. She encouraged his release, begging him to let everything go, to be the sounding board to everything that he needed to clear from his mind and body, and letting loose a delicious grin when she felt him erupt.

They never moved from their space on the deck as Samara closed her legs around his waist, silently willing him to stay with her for as long as possible. The rain, relentless in its downpour, served as the soothing shower that they both needed to refocus. She felt him shudder, a telltale sign he was regaining his energy.

"I can't wait for nights like this again," she purred.

"Soon, *querida*, soon. I promise. This nightmare will be over, and the next phase of our lives will begin. Are you ready for that?"

"More than you know. More than you know."

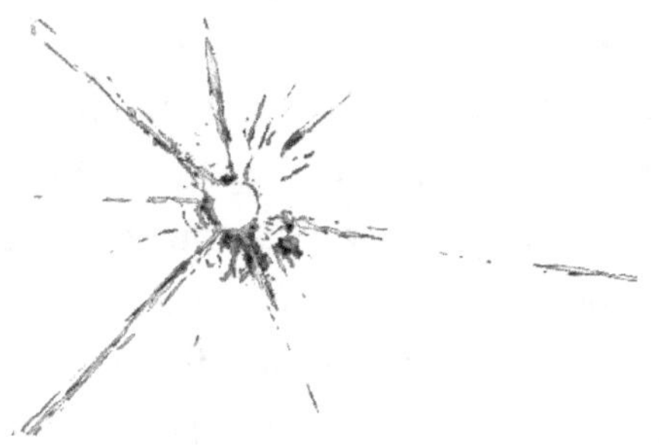

Chapter Thirty

"I'm going to find the *cobardes* who came after my daughter! There's nowhere on this planet that they can hide from me!"

Dorian couldn't remember the last time he'd seen his grandfather so irate. Actually, he could remember, he simply didn't want to remember. He also understood where he got his temper from, and observing it from the outside had him making a note to do some self-evaluation in the coming months.

Luciano was screaming over his Bluetooth earpiece, demanding that his people in California get to the bottom of things. "I don't care if you have to bribe the fucking fire captain, find out who did this or so help me … you don't want me coming there to find out!"

"Abuelo, calm down. You're going to raise your

blood pressure to dangerous levels, and you don't need that right now." Dorian stepped into the living room where Luciano was holed up. He was acutely aware that they were the only ones in the room; not many wanted to be in his line of sight, for fear that *El Jefe Supremo* would find something to chastise them over. "You just yelled it yourself: you got people on the ground seeing about this. We can focus on some other stuff, like finding out where my father is."

Luciano turned and gave Dorian a look that would have turned a normal man into a quivering idiot, begging for forgiveness for speaking out of turn. "I love you, DK, but your father … he handles things on such a fucked-up level that I won't put it past him that he is behind all the shit that's going on. Ground zero, he is."

Dorian wasn't naïve about there being no love lost between his father and his maternal grandfather. Fathers of daughters were never truly trusting of the men that were connected to their most precious gifts. Still, he needed help in figuring things out. "Abuelo, I know you still hold Dad accountable for the craziness from when I was a teenager and I asked for your help all those years ago, but he's been a legit square for the past decade while I handled the weapons dealing."

"I don't believe for a moment that he just decided to drop into the suburbs and act like he doesn't want this life anymore." Luciano took a sip of his brandy as he continued to marinate over his thoughts. "Just like you; your mother told me that you were starting to make moves to leave that world. It isn't going to be easy to leave, kiddo. It will manifest itself into something else just to remember what that high feels like."

Dorian wanted to rebut, but the truth stared him down worse than the barrel of a gun ever could. He hated when his grandfather dropped in on him and made him face the man in the mirror, but he didn't have a choice in the matter. "I already have other passions that popped up before I took over for Dad. Who's to say I can't get back to that once I handle the transition?"

Luciano let out a full-throated laugh that brought other people into the room, including Isabella, who wanted to know how the conversation had turned so jovial in such a short amount of time. "I tried, before you were born, and I tried again when you were in high school, and look at where I am now? It's either in you, or it isn't in you. We're not normal men, DK. The problem I had with your father was that he tried to be someone he wasn't. That's how he got snatched all those years ago, and he probably got snatched before someone tried to take my daughter out."

Isabella interjected into the conversation. "Papi, I know you never really liked Donovan, but this is bigger than your hatred of him now. He's missing, again. We need to figure out who is doing this and why they're doing this after all these years."

"Mami, we'll figure this out the best way we can, same as last time. I got more eyes than I did when I was younger, so this shouldn't take too long," Dorian replied. "There's a lot more going on than you're aware of right now, but I promise we will figure this out. Now, do you remember if Dad was talking to anyone out of the ordinary over the last month or so?"

Isabella shook her head. "You know your father; he was a creature of habit. Same friends. Same connections. He rarely left the house, and when he did, it was only when old military buddies were in town to visit."

Luciano scoffed. "Even after all this time, I never knew what you saw in him. His original play was bogus, and somehow you chose to believe him anyway. What exactly do you think is supposed to happen now?"

Dorian slipped in Luciano's space, meeting him eye to eye. "What is going to happen is that we will find Dad and then figure out why all this is happening so we can dead it once and for all."

Dorian's cell phone rang, startling everyone in the room. He took a look at the number on the phone and immediately picked up. "Kale, talk to me. Did Harry get through? When and where is the meet?"

"You're not going to believe this, DK. He wants to speak to you directly." Kale's voice sounded solemn, like he didn't want to give him the rest of the information. "He says he has your father."

Dorian didn't flinch. "Give him the number."

"Already ahead of you, sir. He should be calling any minute now."

Isabella noticed the change in Dorian's body language and grew worried. "What happened, baby? What's going on?"

Seconds later, his phone rang again. He held his index finger up to quiet the room as he answered the call. "Wraith."

"There's no need to stand on ceremony anymore, Dorian Bentley." Rainier's voice was distorted, a move that Dorian expected. "You know why this phone call is happening, so, let's get to business."

"The fact that you insist on calling me out but you hide behind distortion devices lets me know I'm dealing with a coward. How about you deal straight up?"

"That's interesting talk from a man who takes great pains to conceal his own identity, don't you think?"

"Obviously I didn't do that great of a job if you're aware of who I am. I need to do better at returning the favor."

A text message caught his attention almost as soon as the conversation began to heat up. Yaya was on her game, letting Dorian know she'd picked up the signal. *He's trying to use ghost servers to mask his location. Keep him talking, I'll only need three minutes to lock in.*

"There will be no need to do so at this point. This

will be simple: I will give you the location of where to meet, and you and I will negotiate the dissolution of your organization in exchange for your father's life."

Dorian gritted his teeth as he tried to keep his anger at bay. He had to buy Yaya as much time as he could to get what he needed. "You know that's not going to happen. You need to come better than that. What you're asking for is beyond the realm of reasonable."

"That's disappointing. I guess I need to kill him now."

Dorian wasn't impressed. "All this to get my attention, to get me to shut down because you can't beat me, and you give away your only bargaining chip? Fine, do it, and I'll come with everything I have to wipe you from the face of this earth."

"You could have done that when I had Harry kill Juan Carlos," Rainier pointed out. "Or were you too busy trying to keep your girlfriend safe to worry about payback?"

"I can't do anything about the past, and as of this moment, you have my word that every resource I have available is focused on you. Please know that nothing else matters to me except erasing you from every equation I have in play right now."

"You can try, but I don't think you can protect everyone around you. I have my people with eyes on … Samara, is it? She is quite the exquisite creature. She would make an excellent piece in the Saudi King's collection."

Dorian was ready to cut loose on Rainier when he received another text message in the midst of the call from Yaya. The moment he read it, he grinned at what it meant. He took a few more minutes to read the entire contents of the message, all but ignoring his adversary.

He's in Brazil with you, sir. Barely five miles from your location. We can get assets to sweep and extract on your word.

"What's the matter, Bentley? Cat got your tongue?" Rainier continued to taunt. "If you're trying to trace my location, it won't work. I've been bouncing my signal this entire time. I bet it's telling you that I'm in Joburg with you, huh?"

Dorian smirked, realizing that Rainier had made his first mistake. "Just tell me where you are so we can settle this nonsense. This is starting to bore me, and I don't have time for games. I have an empire to run."

"I don't think you're realizing the gravity of the situation. Have you forgotten what it will take for you to retrieve your father? If you think this is a game, you're sorely mistaken."

The final message was from Yaya. He almost laughed out loud when he read it, but he kept his composure. *Sir, the extraction team in place now. Say the word, and we will deploy.*

Dorian decided that it was time to play mind games, now that he knew the team was ready to go. "Oh, but I do. In fact, I have my team in place to see about you in about five minutes for extraction. That's how much I realize the gravity of the situation. Your mistake is thinking I'm still in Joburg. Just like you, I can be anywhere at any time, without you knowing about it."

"You're bluffing. I'm not where you think I am."

"You're currently about five miles from my current position, in Rio. If you look outside of your window, you will see three motorcycles that have been posted up at the base of the driveway while we've been playing this game of who's dick is bigger."

There was a pause on the other end for a few moments. Dorian politely waited, checking his timepiece to give Rainier time to figure out how things could end up. "Do I have your attention now, or do I need to really get your attention?"

"I see I've underestimated you. Fair enough. Meet me at Fort Copacabana in an hour. Come alone, no back up from your grandfather's men or it will be the shortest reunion in history."

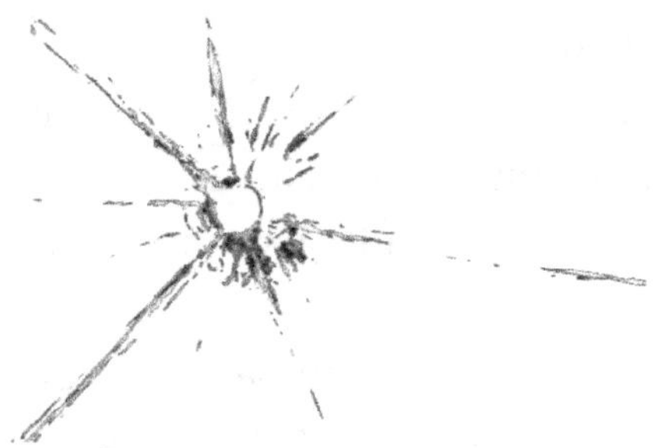

CHAPTER THIRTY-ONE

Dorian found himself standing at the turret of Fort Copacabana, split between the guns historically called Barroso and Osório, which were a part of the infamous the 18 of the Copacabana Fort revolts. It was the first revolt of the *tenentista* movement, in the context of the Brazilian Old Republic. The rebellious officers turned the fort's guns on Rio. To suppress the revolt, the Brazilian government brought the battleships São Paulo and Minas Geraes. On 6 July São Paulo bombarded the fort, firing five salvos and obtaining at least two hits; the fort surrendered half an hour later. The fort was now a museum, but he didn't see any other location that would suffice for the meet.

He wasn't sure whether there was much of a significance of meeting at this particular location, but he made sure that if they were going to meet, it needed to be on a neutral location, and in a wide-open area. He was almost certain that Rainier would not honor the terms of the meet, but he didn't have a choice in the matter. If things went south, they wouldn't have to worry about local police interference until it was too late to do anything more than identify the bodies. This would be where everything would be revealed, once and for all.

He saw two figures approaching from the beach, entering from the rear of the fort, which mildly surprised him. What didn't surprise him was the man who accompanied his father. In fact, he was about as noncommittal about his emotions as he could be, and his facial expressions did not give him away, either.

"I didn't want to believe it when my people told me. When I had some time to think about it before you arrived, it all made sense," Dorian commented as General Locke and Donovan stood in front of him. "I guess neither of you could let go of your former glory, could you?"

General Locke never flinched. "Sorry, kid, you were drawing too much attention. We had to step in to reset the balance."

"So, there's no point in negotiating anything at this point. This whole ruse was concocted because you can't handle the fact that you were both put out to pasture." Dorian's irritation rose to the surface, and he didn't bother to mask it at this point. "Sooner or later, I was going to find out my father was Rainier and that you were helping him the whole time. How did you think this was going to play out?"

Donovan's stone-faced demeanor was something that Dorian didn't account for. He stood there, analyzing Dorian like he was looking at him for the first time. "How this should have played out was for Harry to take you all out so we could continue from where we left off. Since he didn't have the guts to end you, I'm going to do it."

Dorian's incredulous look almost elicited a chuckle from Locke. "Are you high or something? I'm your son, what would possess you to think about killing me? What about Mom?"

"Your mother is the fucking reason we're even here at this moment in time. If she hadn't—" Donovan's voice trailed off as he growled in anger.

"If she hadn't what, Dad?"

"We can shut all that down right here and right now. I am not your father."

Dorian scoffed as he heard that comment. "Now I know you're high. That's bullshit and you know it."

"Oh, but I wish it was. Otherwise, it would be hard as hell to pull the trigger."

Locke couldn't take the smirk off his face. "I'll admit, it had me a bit thrown off myself. All these years and nobody had a clue. I wonder who was the better covert operative, your mother or your father."

"I'm gonna need you to keep your comments under wraps, general. You just might make it out alive if you do." Dorian was not in the mood for sardonic humor, especially from someone who had no business opining. "Stay in your lane."

"For a man who is currently outnumbered, you've got a lot of nerve making any demands."

Dorian ignored Locke, focusing on Donovan to figure out what exactly was going on with him. "So, tell me, how am I not your son? I get the whole reason you wanted to create this Rainier persona now. Hell, Harry had to tell me as a last-ditch effort to keep me from killing him for betraying me."

Donovan shook his head. "He never could keep a fucking secret. I'm surprised he didn't divulge the other bombshell that I was hit over the head with almost forty years after the fact."

"Okay, let's play this BS game of yours." Dorian was at his wit's end over this new line of questioning. "If you're not my father, then who is?"

"The one man on the planet who has been more of a father to you than anyone. Apparently, even more than I was to you."

Dorian balled his fists, moving toward Donovan with the intent to punch him. "That would be my grandfather, you sick son of a bitch. Try again."

"No, *you* should try again," Donovan seethed. "You're focusing on the wrong man. Who was there for you while I was in the field? Who's tried harder than anyone to keep you out of harm's way all this time?"

The hairs on the back of Dorian's neck stood on edge as his mind raced through the possibilities until they reached the final conclusion. His eyes widened as the answer cut through him like a hot knife through butter. "Juan Carlos? Uncle JC? That's not true. He's had nothing but the utmost respect for you both. He's never so much as looked at Mami the wrong way."

"Harry would disagree with that statement," Donovan replied. "He was there in Joburg when your whore of a mother was kissing a man I thought was a friend. He told me of the way she looked at him, how it motivated him to shoot him when he thought he couldn't. He isn't the man you think he is, but I do know one thing: he is your father."

Dorian felt like his heart had been ripped in half. His mind ran through all of the things that happened when he was younger. He remembered distinctly when Donovan couldn't make it to an important high school debate championship that he eventually won, but Juan Carlos was in the audience with Isabella. By the time he came back to reality, he looked at Donovan, whose scowl was evident on his face.

He had to push his emotions out of the way for now, there was a pressing matter that needed to be addressed. "I'll deal with the other stuff later, I guess the current conversation at hand boils down to why you're pissed with me and my team. Don't you realize that we're the ones on top now?"

"You were never going to be on top, Dorian. Sure,

you found some ways to innovate how the weapons trade needed to be done, but this was never your world to rule. Despite all the schools I sent you to, you were always playing checkers."

Dorian chuckled for a moment, looking at the two men in front of him like they were the ones a step behind. "First Harry, and now you two. For all of the talk about this not being my world, I've been able to make moves and develop connections that you never could."

Locke nodded. "You're right, and now that those connections have been made, we can slip right through and continue with those connections. After all, no one knows who the Wraith is, remember?"

Dorian was speechless for the first time in the conversation. Once he found his voice, there was no doubt in his mind what needed to be said. "So, now that this smoke and mirrors routine is over, what do you think I'm going to do right now? You both know that I'm not giving up my operation, so, I guess you've got your own decisions to make."

Donovan pulled the gun from behind his back, pointing it at Dorian, the scowl never leaving his face the entire time. "Fine, then it's time for you to die."

"You first, Donovan."

A shot rang out in the dark, striking Donovan in his chest, left center of his chest, dropping him in seconds. General Locke immediately looked to take cover, but Dorian took out his gun, pointing it directly at him. "I don't think you're gonna want to move right about now, general. Remember what I said about staying in your lane so you don't get killed? This might be one of those times where you might want to stay right where you are."

The general literally stopped in his tracks, his eyes locked in on Dorian's near point-blank distance from him. He still had his weapon in hand, but realized that Dorian had the advantage.

Dorian heard Yaya's voice over his earpiece. "We've got eyes on the secondary target, sir. Primary target is down for the moment, but not eliminated. I also have the guest you requested on com. They have been engaged since arrival."

"You're not going to get away with this, you know that, right? Do you know that the fuck you think you're doing?" General Locke kept his hands up as his eyes continued to search in the darkness to find where the shot came from. "You're threatening a fucking four-star general and a member of the Joint Chiefs of Staff. The minute I'm Stateside, I'll make sure you're disavowed and prosecuted."

Dorian grinned, placing his index finger toward his ear. "I'm sure that you trying to make such a maneuver would be unwise to execute, am I correct on that, Ms. McAvoy?"

Locke was confused over the reference, glaring at Dorian with contempt. "Who the fuck are you talking to?"

Dorian turned on the speakerphone on his satellite phone, pointing it in Locke's direction. "Would you like to introduce yourself to the general?"

"I'm sure the general knows who I am, just from the sound of my voice, but for the sake of refreshing his memory, this is White House Press Secretary Lea McAvoy. I believe that considering the revelations that have been made, I believe Vice President Warren and President Yeager would be very interested in your extracurricular activities and your explanation of those activities."

General Locke's face lost all of its color as he began to realize what the sound and tone of her voice meant, especially considering her proximity to his bosses. "Now, now, Ms. McAvoy, there is no need in informing them about this. They have enough going on right now as it is."

"I believe the general has gotten the point, Lea, thank you for your assistance in this particular matter. I'll see you at my mother's next showing?" Dorian asked.

"Mrs. Warren and I can't wait. The last piece you pointed out for purchase went very well in the house," Lea replied before disconnecting the call.

Dorian heard faint groaning coming from his left. He looked down and saw Donovan struggling to breathe, clutching his chest. He stood over him, with gun in hand, and waited for Donovan to look up. "Any last words?"

"I'll … I'll be waiting … for you in … in hell."

"You'll be waiting a long time, Donovan. Make sure you give me the full tour if I come through for a visit, okay?" Dorian mentioned before he squeezed the trigger twice, watching Donovan's body expire. He turned toward Locke, his stare seeming to bore holes through the general's body. "Now, you have an answer to a question, and how you answer that question will determine whether or not you meet the same fate as your former partner."

"Just because you think you have support doesn't mean I can't burn you on the way out the door."

The general remained steadfast in his positioning, until the barrel of the gun in Dorian's hand was pressed against his temple. "What's the lie you usually tell soldiers' families when their loved ones are killed under suspicious circumstances again? From Ms. McAvoy's tone, you're skating on thin ice with the Administration. The spin on this would be absolutely brilliant, I would imagine."

General Locke closed his eyes, contemplating the next words to come from his mouth. "Okay, okay, you win. Once I'm Stateside, it's business as usual."

"Double the order at the same price, just for the inconvenience of all this drama down here tonight."

"Are you out of your—?"

The sound of a bullet whizzing past them and burying itself in the concrete a few feet from them jolted Locke from his original thought. Dorian shook his head in disapproval. "Care to try your words again? The mic is still hot."

"You son of a … fine, double the order, no uptick on the payment."

"Good man, because the impatient person on the other side of this conversation doesn't like you very much, and she's rather overprotective of her employer." Dorian chuckled. He lowered the gun and placed it behind his back. "Now, this meeting never happened, this conversation never happened, and that man on the ground never existed. Agreed?"

"Agreed. I'll take my leave now, and I'll expect to hear from you in the next 48 hours?"

Dorian nodded as he mocked a salute. "Until the re-up, general, sir."

Chapter Thirty-Two

"Daddy, DK is here! DK is here!"

Harry wanted to sound as enthusiastic as his daughters were over the unexpected arrival of their "big brother," but he couldn't avoid the sense of dread over the inevitability that his appearance meant. It had only been a few days, but spending them reconnecting with his daughters and reconciling with his ex-wife had been more than he could have dreamed. Sooner or later, he thought, the dream would end, but he'd hoped it would end later rather than sooner.

He watched as Dorian acted like he didn't have a care in the world as he kissed his ex-wife on the cheek and bear-hugged each of the girls, materializing his apologies for the long absence in their lives in the form of very expensive gifts that ensured that all was forgiven. He wasn't sure if Dorian was being sadistic on purpose or if he was genuinely happy to see his family. He almost wanted the façade to end as soon as they were no longer within earshot or line of sight.

Dorian disengaged with the girls as he looked in their father's direction. "I need to have a word with your father for a few. Can you make sure you can keep your mom occupied until we're done?"

Both girls nodded as they took their mother's hands and dragged her from the living area, leaving Dorian and Harry to their devices. Harry sighed heavily as he offered one of the chairs to sit so they could have the conversation he'd been dreading for nearly a week. "Before you say anything, I want to say thank you for allowing me to see my family again. I didn't think I would have a lot of time to spend, so I tried to make every day count."

Dorian nodded, his face showing no emotion whatsoever. "I have had a few days to mull over what I wanted to say to you, Harry, and I'm not exaggerating when I say that that was a difficult internal conversation to have. We've been through a lot, you and me, experiences that go back to when I was a teenager."

Harry nodded, intent on listening to what Dorian had to say instead of focusing on the final conclusion.

"I tried to separate the emotion from the argument I continued to have with myself, and the one thing that stuck with me at the end of the day was those two girls upstairs," Dorian continued. "I never did tell you how we figured out where they were, did I?"

Harry shook his head, leaning forward in the chair, silently urging him to continue.

"Interestingly enough, there was another party who needed me to step away from an intimate situation regarding her employer." Dorian leaned back in his chair to continue to recall the way the conversation with Trinity progressed. "She outright told me who had your daughters, and did so in exchange for disappearing from her lover's life and purview. I had to exact a heavy price to extract them from the situation they were in, but that's what you do for family."

Harry exhaled, realizing that things could have truly gone awry if he had succeeded in removing Dorian and the rest of the inner circle. "So, what happens now? I realize I owe you my life, and if you're here to collect on that, then we need to make this as painless for my family as possible."

Dorian raised an eyebrow, wondering where that line of thought came from. "Harry, if I wanted you dead, you wouldn't be here. Those theatrics in Joburg were not for show; Ishmael had every intention of erasing you from existence, and I had every intention of letting him. Jessilyn saved your life with a single phone call."

Harry nodded, acknowledging the angel that manifested in his firstborn. "I know I sound like a broken record, but I need to make this right. I don't know how to do that, but I need to, for my own sake and sanity. Whatever you say, I'll do it."

"What you can do is do right by your family," Dorian advised. "If I've learned anything after what has happened in the past couple of weeks, it's that family is everything. I almost took that for granted, and it almost cost you your life. Be the man your daughters need you to be, and be the husband your wife deserved the entire time."

"I hear you, loud and clear, youngster." Harry closed his eyes, the weight lifting from his shoulders with each deep breath he took. "You said that Juan Carlos didn't die. How was that possible? I was certain from the bullet wounds I saw that he was done."

"Funny thing about JC; he has this stubborn streak in him." Dorian considered his own words carefully, considering the circumstances. "He's still in a coma, but the doctors are saying that he should be able to pull through. It's just going to take some time."

"I wish I'd said something sooner, DK. I guess my pride got in the way," Harry admitted. "I couldn't take the chance of losing them to—"

"Donovan Bentley," Dorian finished.

Harry did a double-take. "I've never heard you refer to him by name, as long as I've known you. Does that mean that he told you what happened?"

Dorian sat quietly for a few moments, regarding the question that was posed. "I'm still trying to wrap my mind around what he told me, and what he told me that you witnessed before you tried to kill JC. I have to ask the question: how in the world did you two come to such a conclusion?"

Harry looked skyward before resting his forehead against his clasped fingers. He looked toward Dorian, doing his best to be as delicate as he felt he could be. "Donovan had his suspicions, I would imagine. What you might not have been aware of, DK, is that they weren't the picture of a healthy marriage in a lot of respects. He was gone … a lot. Left her to her own devices, he did. And when a woman like your mother has the ability to avail—"

"Step carefully, Harry."

"I'm not trying to besmirch your mother's honor, kid." Harry held his hands up in mock surrender. "But they started off on the wrong footing. He pulled some shite that he shouldn't have to gain your grandfather's favor, and it sort of went downhill from there. They put on a good front for everyone, but it wasn't hard to see, for folks who wanted to see. I know what two people look like when they're in love, and it just didn't look that way."

"So, you're saying that someone else was supposed to be with my mom?"

"Yeah … she was already pregnant with you when they got married. She was involved with JC for a time, too, from what I remember. In fact, I think they were supposed to be together, before your father convinced your grandfather that he could take better care of her."

Dorian rubbed his temples. "I don't know if I can

deal with much more of this. If what you're telling me is the truth, then the possibility does exist that Donovan was not my father."

Harry stood and walked over to where Dorian sat, picking up a folder from the desk drawer before sitting down. He pulled up the chair he sat in to lend a comforting hand on Dorian's shoulder, presenting the contents of the folder. "DK, there's more … before he sent me on that suicide mission to try to take you and the boys out, he told me that he'd taken a DNA sample to find out for himself. He already knew; that's where the whole plan got hatched in the first place. He didn't tell me until after I tried to kill JC when I told him I saw Isabella with JC at the airport."

Dorian made a mental note to have a conversation with his mother as soon as he was done with Harry. He rose to his feet, stretching to get the stiffness out of his system. The past few weeks had been extremely rough, and whether he wanted to admit it or not, he was emotionally exhausted from it all. He needed something positive to focus on, and he knew where to get that in the immediate moment. "Go and get Jessilyn and Angelica. I need to catch up to speed with what's going on with them. I need some normalcy for a little while."

"Sure, DK, I think I understand what you mean," Harry replied before heading upstairs to grab the girls. "I think we could all use a bit of that for a little while."

CHAPTER THIRTY-THREE

Dorian touched down in Rio with a head of steam, determined to clear as much of the haze that now hung over his entire existence. His head swirled after his visit with Harry, and no matter how much good it did him to spend time with Jessilyn and Angelica, it didn't assuage the emotional damage to his heart. In one moment, he knew exactly who he was. In the next moment, everything he'd known had been thrown into chaos.

Two people knew the truth, but he'd eliminated one of those two people. It left him to have to get the tough answers from the other person, but he wasn't sure if he was up to the task. So much had happened, but he needed to know, for his own sake and sanity.

From the moment he stepped onto the compound, his only concern was finding his mother. He'd all but bypassed everyone else to figure out where she was inside of the massive estate. His grandfather could barely get a word in; all he could do was follow Dorian until he reached his final destination.

While he was happy to see his mother, he was distracted, more interested in getting to the crux of the conversation he'd had in his head for the past twelve hours. "Hi, Mami."

Isabella's eyes lit up at the sight of her son. She rushed over to hug him tightly. "Hi, baby, I'm so glad you're home. Where's your father, is he okay?"

"Mami, there's some things we need to talk about." Dorian motioned toward the couch for them to sit. "There's a lot to unpack, and I need help with some answers that only you can give at this point. There are some things that were said, and they're very disturbing."

"Baby, you're scaring me. What happened to your father?"

Dorian closed his eyes for a moment, bracing himself for a different set of emotions to flow from both his mother and his grandfather. He took a breath and exhaled. "If you mean Donovan, he is no longer with us. Things didn't go as planned."

Isabella's shock and Luciano's indifference were on par with what he'd expected, but having them in the room would prove daunting as he navigated his own feelings on the matter. He suddenly wasn't so sure that he wanted to have the conversation he'd planned on having, but he also didn't feel that there would ever be a good time to have it, so, he decided that ripping the bandage would be the best strategy, no matter how much it would hurt in the immediate moment.

Isabella hugged him tightly, wiping the tears from her eyes, but it wasn't lost on her as to how her son referenced his father. "Why did you refer to your father by his first name? You've never done that outside of family. What's going on?"

Dorian bypassed the questions. "We'll get to that in a minute, right now, I need answers to some questions."

Isabella raised an eyebrow. "Questions about what, exactly? You're still not explaining to me what happened to your father, baby."

Dorian did his best to keep from exploding, but there was only so much he could take. "Donovan left me with some disturbing news before I took his life."

Isabella gasped. "Why would you kill your father? Are you insane? What would possess you to do such a thing?"

Luciano, who'd been silent up to this point in the conversation, scoffed at the notion. "This doesn't make any sense. Why would you kill him, DK? You damn near worshipped the ground he walked on your whole life. What could possibly have happened to make such a decision?"

"Donovan was not my father," Dorian stated, letting the words linger in the air for effect.

"As it turned out, he was the man known as Rainier, the man who wanted me dead so he could take over my operation."

Luciano leaned against the fireplace mantle, letting that tidbit of information sink in. He made his way to the door, resigned to leaving his daughter and grandson to work through the rest of the conversation. "I'll be in my study if you need to talk, DK. You and your mother, it seems, have a lot to discuss."

Once he left, Dorian focused on the confused look on his mother's face. He sat down next to her, trying to get a gauge of where her thoughts led her. "Your husband wanted me dead because he found out I was not his son. Any idea where he would get that notion from?"

Isabella hesitated, taking her son's hands in hers. She faced him, doing her best to keep as much of a brave face as she could. "I don't know what would make him think you're not his son, baby. There's no way that he couldn't be."

Dorian took the folded papers from his suit pocket, doing his best to avoid slamming them in Isabella's lap. "I'm exhausted with all of this, so, I'll get right down to it. Donovan, somehow in the recent past, had my DNA tested against his without either of our knowledge. You can read the results for yourself. Harry gave them to me after Donovan gave them to him, in case I didn't want to believe a word out of his mouth after he revealed who he truly was in this whole mess."

Isabella perused the contents of the paperwork, her lips trembling with each word she read. "He wouldn't have had a reason to do this. There's no way he could have known, unless—"

"Unless, what, Mami? What happened?"

Isabella was too consumed with her own thoughts to hear her son. "Oh, God, he couldn't have found out. There's no way, we were careful."

"He did, Mami, and he tried to kill you because of what he found out."

"Wait … what happened in San Diego? He set that up? He tried to kill me?"

Dorian nodded. "Yes, and he tried to kill the only other person who he could tie to his wife's betrayal."

Isabella's anger rose to the surface. "Betrayal? Donovan was the one who's to blame for all of this!"

Dorian wasn't prepared for the outburst as he gripped Isabella's hands tighter. "Mami, calm down. There's obviously something that I'm missing here for you to react like that. Now that I think about it, why did Abuelo leave? What's the real story, what are you not saying?"

Isabella put her head in her hands, trying her best to settle herself. She could barely make eye contact with her son as she took a series of deep breaths. "The man you knew as your father popped into my life when I was deeply in love with someone else. Papi, however, decided that Donovan was the better suitor for me, regardless of what I thought or felt."

Dorian shook his head. "He wouldn't do that. That doesn't make any sense."

"Times were different back then, baby. Arranged marriages and unions were the norm when I was younger, especially among the elite." Isabella kept her eyes closed as she continued to recount the past. "All Donovan had to do was have the right connections and the type of money to keep me used to the lifestyle Papi always provided and that was about it. Your abuela spent years trying to convince me that I would eventually fall in love with Donovan the way she'd eventually fallen in love with your abuelo."

Dorian stayed silent for a few moments, leaving the pause to linger between them. "Let me guess … Uncle JC was the man you were in love with."

Isabella nodded. "I almost defied Papi by running away with him, but I couldn't do it. I spent two days with him … and I wanted badly to tell Papi that I didn't want to marry Donovan. I just couldn't do it."

"So, how … how in the world did you and JC deal with being away from each other? How did he become my godfather? I have so many questions right now." Dorian lifted her chin so she could meet his sympathetic gaze. More puzzle pieces continued to fall that presented a larger picture than he'd anticipated. "It must have been torture to be away from someone you loved so much."

"Carlito was placed on Donovan's radar by Papi,

years later. I guess it was his way of trying to make up for the impossible position he'd placed me under." Isabella managed a small smile. "Your abuela gave him a lot of grief after we moved from Rio. It was hard to say if he was forced into the mix with Donovan, but somehow, they made it work so well and became such good friends that he eventually became your godfather."

"But, wouldn't that be a worse fate, having him so close and not being able to act on any feelings you have?" Dorian wasn't sure whether he could handle much more of the conversation. There was so much that he'd not been aware of that he felt like he'd misjudged the situation and misplaced his anger after the fact. "That had to be torture for the two of you."

"It probably would have been, but Donovan was more interested in keeping up appearances. I was the trophy wife, but we rarely, if ever, were intimate. He was too busy with the real whores he thought I didn't know about while he was out in the field." Isabella frowned as she remembered that aspect of their marriage. "Carlito and I took advantage of the time Donovan spent away, which is why Auntie Shay spent so much time babysitting you growing up. It was the only way to keep things out of your line of sight, to keep from confusing you."

Dorian sighed. The reference to the escorts and prostitutes struck a nerve, causing a visceral reaction that he tried to suppress before Isabella caught on. He didn't realize how much influence Donovan had over his life until that moment. Listening to how Isabella spoke so lovingly of Juan Carlos made him miss Samara terribly; he hadn't checked on her since before he flew back to Rio.

The questions wouldn't stop coming, no matter how much he wanted them to cease.

"Wait, if it was that bad, why didn't you just divorce him? He was never interested or involved in the things you wanted to do anyway. It would have at least taken the stress and the burden from your shoulders."

Isabella laughed for the first time in their exchange. "A Catholic girl divorcing her husband because he wasn't satisfying her? I would have never heard the end of it from the family. It was better to just be discreet; Auntie Shay had a girlfriend for years before your Uncle Marcos died. Most importantly, I didn't want you to think less of me for leaving him. You idolized him so much when you were younger."

Dorian raised Isabella's hands to his lips to kiss them. "Once I was on my own, there would not have been much that I could say if you decided then to divorce him. I am not that little boy anymore. I saw more once I was older than you might have realized. We have always been honest with each other; I would have understood if you decided to leave. I just want you to be happy."

"Yes, we have always been honest, you and me," Isabella replied. "I should have done something about this a long time ago. Maybe we might have avoided everything that has happened and my Carlito wouldn't be in the hospital fighting for his life."

Donovan took a deep breath. The next question in his mind felt like lead rolling off his tongue. "So, do I have to ask the burning question that's in my mind right now?"

Isabella gave up a nervous giggle as she turned to face Dorian. "No, you don't have to ask, baby. Juan Carlos de Silva is your father … your true bloodline, your real father. He is the only man I was ever with before Donovan."

A flood of emotions threatened to overwhelm him. He thought back to all those times during his childhood and teenage years where he remembered Juan Carlos being at some of the more defining events in his life, instead of Donovan. His mother always made up some plausible excuse over why his father couldn't make it, when his father was actually there the entire time. All he could do was manage a grin as the idea of Juan Carlos being his father coursed through him, warming him to his core. "I guess, now that I think back on it, I shouldn't be surprised. Deep down, I guess I always knew. I feel like I should be relieved, but I don't know how to feel just yet."

"You shouldn't be surprised, baby. He always looked at you like the son he never had."

"Does he know about me, that I'm his son?"

Isabella shook her head. "I don't know how he may

react to the news. He may hate me for not telling him until now."

"Mami, he's obviously in love with you, even after all these years, and he has never let on to any of us that he was," Dorian remarked. "We all have a chance to catch up on lost time, and you can have the love you have always deserved, without having to hide anymore."

Isabella blinked a few times at the suggestion. "Are you sure, DK? This has to be a lot to take in right now."

Dorian's phone rang, interrupting the conversation. He took a look at the caller ID and immediately recognized it as the hospital providing care for Juan Carlos. "Yes, this is Dorian … he is? Wonderful news, we'll be there in the morning."

He turned to Isabella with the widest grin possible and hugged her tight. "We'll get a chance to find out tomorrow. He's awake."

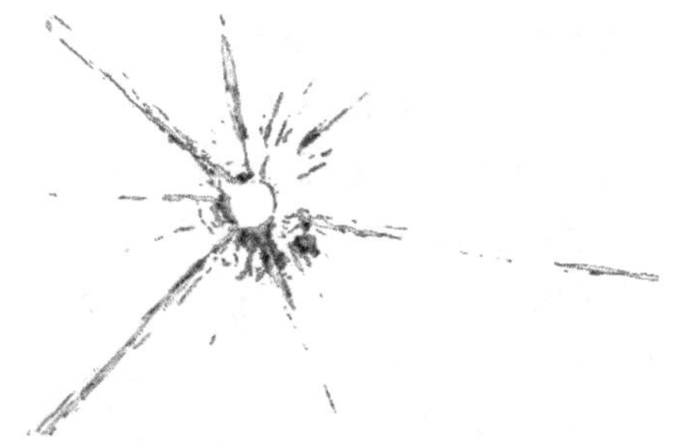

Chapter Thirty-Four

"What's the last thing you remember, Mr. de Silva? You've been through quite the ordeal."

Dorian sat in the corner as he observed the doctor going through the preliminary checkup with Juan Carlos' vital signs and reaction to stimuli. Watching Isabella sitting by his side, looking both concerned and enamored with him brought an uneasy smile to his face. Once the doctor left, it would be the beginning of a very enlightening conversation for his father and mother.

"I was at the airport saying goodbye to Bella, and then … fuck, Harry shot me. Got me good, too." Juan Carlos rubbed the nearest bullet wound in his chest, wincing over the memory that was now embedded in his mind. "He was about to finish me when I heard sirens wailing in the distance. I saw EMTs when I finally passed out."

"Well, I have good news. We were able to extract the bullets from your wounds, so, there is nothing that would suggest that you won't make a full recovery. You're a lucky man, Mr. de Silva. I'll leave you to your family." The doctor shook Isabella's hand before turning to Dorian, who escorted her to the door. She smiled as she nodded to his silent question. "We've made sure he's been well taken care of, per your explicit instructions. He will be able to walk out of here with no ill effects."

"Thank you, Doc. I am in your debt. He means more to me than you know," Dorian replied. He placed two thick envelopes in her hand, patting the top of her palm. "Please ensure that Nurse Iminathi gets the other envelope. This one is for you, for taking care of him. Let me know if you need anything at all. I'll make sure it happens."

The doctor smiled and patted his hand. "Thank you, Mr. Nagi. I'll keep in touch."

Isabella rubbed the back of his hand against her cheek, closing her eyes at the sensation of it against her skin. "I still can't believe Donovan tried to have you killed. I didn't think it would come to something so drastic."

Dorian shook his head, content to filling in the blanks over the motive. "He tried to have mom killed, too. There's been a lot of things going on that have just come to light in recent days, and for him to reach this particular point, something had to snap inside of him."

"Well, I'll be the one doing the snapping now," Juan Carlos roared. "I'm gonna bury them both right next to each other. I won't even pull the sneak attack nonsense that they tried to pull on me. I'll make sure they see me coming."

"Carlito, please, there's been enough bloodshed." Isabella squeezed his hand to get his attention. She waited until he focused on the concerned look on her face before she continued. "There's a lot that we need to talk about, and I don't need you going off half-cocked trying to get your pound of flesh."

"What would you have me do, Bella? I can't allow this to go without reprisal!"

Dorian pulled the other chair up to the opposite side of the hospital bed. Juan Carlos began to speak, but he held his hand up to stop him. "Whether you realize it or not, we were all being played by two men. One of them, unfortunately, you will not be able to get your reprisal from. However, his partner in this whole scenario, I saved for you—General Locke."

"Wait. Donovan's dead?" Juan Carlos asked. His eyes narrowed as he lifted himself to a more comfortable position on the bed. "Who killed him?"

"I did."

"Why? Why would you take that from me?" Juan Carlos glared at Dorian, searching his eyes for anything that would make sense to him. "Why would you kill your father? That's the last thing that I would have expected from you."

"I'm going to need you to be patient with me while I explain things. Can you do that?" Dorian's emotions were palpable, and he had a difficult time trying to find the words to unravel the last near forty years of all of their lives. "It is important that I try to get this out as best as I can."

Juan Carlos' eyes softened, recognizing the turmoil Dorian was going through. He hadn't seen this side of him since he was a teenager. "Okay, DK, for you, I'll listen."

Dorian nodded, taking a deep breath to gather himself. "The reason that Donovan contracted the hit on you was two-fold: the first reason was to convince me to shut down the operation so he could take over again."

"And the other reason?"

"Donovan found out about you and mom. He somehow connected the dots to your involvement with each other."

Juan Carlos' eyes widened, shifting to Isabella's eyes before he switched back to face Dorian. "That's not possible. Harry didn't even know. He saw us at the airport after Bella left, and the look on his face was sheer shock. I know Donovan didn't know, but I figured Harry would have told him after he shot me. And why would he want you to shut things down? None of this is making sense."

Dorian continued to rattle off the details,

suppressing the shift in his emotional spectrum. He wanted to get to the punchline, but the full picture needed to be shown. "Donovan had been plotting with Locke this entire time. They came up with the Rainier persona, finding every opportunity since before Cameroon to cause as much havoc as possible before moving in for the potential hostile takeover."

"Wait a fucking minute. Donovan was Rainier?" Juan Carlos' wheels started spinning, going into detective mode. "So, Locke was the one feeding him the intel on our movements. That explains a few things. But, how does Harry fit into the puzzle? He wouldn't have had a reason to try to kill me. We've been doing this for too long for him to turn like that."

"Yeah, about that. Donovan managed to have Harry's daughters kidnapped while in Ireland. He used them as bait to get him to erase all of us, me included, with the supposed promise of putting him at the top of the new organization."

"I'm still not understanding why he would want to kill you, DK? You're his flesh and blood. He'd have to be out of his fucking mind to want to kill his own son."

Dorian paused. The next words that came out felt like glass cutting his tongue. "I'm … I'm not his son, JC."

"Okay, I know that these drugs are strong, but I know I'm not hallucinating. You are Donovan Bentley's son."

Isabella interjected into the conversation to take

some of the burden from her son. "Carlito … as much as this is going to come as a shock to your system, it is time for the truth to come out. The truth … the real truth … is that the man that is sitting at your bedside is your son."

Juan Carlos snapped his gaze, looking at Dorian like he'd never seen him before. He continued to study his face, looking at his features again, blinking rapidly when he recognized himself in Dorian. He brought his hands to his mouth to stifle the audible gasps and series of profanity-laced comments that threatened to come from his lips. He couldn't stop looking at him.

"My … my son? Bella, he's my son? How … how could you not tell me? How long have you known?" Juan Carlos' shock and mild disappointment was mixed with the joy in knowing that his godson was now more to him than he'd ever dreamed. "I have so many questions."

Isabella shed tears as she tried to explain. "Carlito, I had my suspicions, but I was never sure. I didn't want to cause any more confusion than what may have come without any real proof. Once DK told me how Donovan found out, there was no doubt in my mind that it was you."

Dorian had finally been able to get his emotions under a measure of control, grabbing the railing to steady himself. "So, now that we know the truth, I guess I get to call you … Dad?"

Juan Carlos paused for a moment, letting the

significance of that reference sink in. "DK, I've always seen you as a son. I've watched you grow up; hell, I had a hand in raising you in a lot of aspects. We have so much time to make up for, so much I want to tell you about your true bloodline. Nothing in life has made me happier than in this moment."

Juan Carlos then turned to Isabella, taking her hand in his and kissing the back of her palm. "I should say almost nothing. Bella, this might not be the best time to ask this question, but I need to ask. Will you spend the rest of your life with me? Will you be my wife?"

"Yes, Carlito. My heart has always belonged to you." Isabella leaned to kiss Juan Carlos, much to the delight of their son. "It is beyond time to make this family whole. First, we need to get you out of this hospital, so we can make this a reality."

Dorian gave his father a hug, feeling a weight being lifted from his own shoulders. "To complete this circle, I'll be heading back to the States to take care of a matter of changing my name."

Isabella nodded in agreement. "I think this is the best decision to make, considering what we know now. It will be a fresh start, and I'm sure a certain *belleza* who will need to be brought up to speed, too, huh?"

That caught Juan Carlos' attention. A smile spread across his face as he realized the significance of the moment. "Oh, you've been holding out, son? I can't wait to meet this young lady. I mean, if I'm going to be a potential father-in-law, I might as well act the part, huh?"

Dorian shook his head and laughed at the symmetry and irony. It didn't matter who it was, that generation always had a penchant to couple their kids and sit back for the grandchildren to arrive. "I'll introduce you to Samara once I've had a chance to acclimate her to all the changes that have happened. I haven't had a chance to see her or talk to her since all of this went down. As soon as she's up to speed, I promise we'll sit down as a family and you can interrogate her all you want."

He kissed Isabella across her forehead and shook Juan Carlos' hand, leaving them to their privacy while he made a quick call. He headed to one of the private rooms so he could hear the conversation he needed to hear after such a long and emotional ride. He needed her to be the first to hear everything that was going on.

He'd barely had a chance to sit down when the call connected. Hearing Samara's voice was exactly what the doctor ordered. "God, have I missed you. Ishmael has been keeping me up to speed on things. Is it finally over?"

"Yes, *querida*, it's finally over. There's so much I need to tell you, so much has happened. I don't know where to start." Dorian closed his eyes as the emotions began to flood all over again. "I'll have Ishmael bring you to me here in Joburg so I can explain it all in person. I can't wait to see you."

"I'm dying to see you, too … among other things."

"We'll have plenty of time to make up for all of that

as soon as you get here."

"You promise, Daddy?"

"I promise. I'll see you in the morning."

Chapter Thirty-Five

Samara couldn't believe everything that Dorian spent the past couple of hours explaining to her. It felt like its own unfolding drama that one of her favorite authors would have written. Truth was stranger than fiction, and all she could do was help her beloved figure out all of the emotions that he felt as they came.

"What I can't figure out is, why would Donovan want you dead? You had nothing to do with what happened before you were even born?" Samara cuddled against his chest, doing her best to soothe him. "Something must have really snapped inside him to carry this all out so elaborately."

"I don't pretend to understand it, but at this point, I'm still trying to wrap my head around the fact that JC is my father, my *actual* father." Dorian exhaled as he let those last words linger in the air. "I mean, everything that I've known since I was young, it all gets turned upside down in the course of a week. What am I supposed to do now?"

"There's no real rulebook on this, *querido*," Samara replied. "You said it yourself, he has been like a second father to you; he was your godfather before this new information came to light. Things have changed a little bit, and there's still some things that need to be worked out and adjusted to, but the most important thing is that he loves you like his own, and now he truly gets to prove that and build a relationship with you as father and son."

Dorian grinned as he stroked her hair. "When did you have such a sage bedside manner? I feel like another weight has been lifted off my shoulders just talking this out with you."

"There's a lot about me that you get to find out about. We have a lot of time to make up for ourselves, you know." Samara turned to lay on her stomach to face him. "Just like there's a lot about this new you that I get to see, now that you've made your decision to turn everything over to Ishmael and Kale."

"Am I doing the right thing? I feel like I haven't left things in the best condition for them. They're able to handle themselves, they probably have been since I've had to deal with this madness with Harry and Donovan."

"Yes, you're doing the right thing. The unknown is going to scare anyone, and you're not immune,"

Samara remarked. "It was probably scary when you first took over for your father all those years ago. It worked out then, so, why shouldn't it work out now?"

Dorian shook his head. "I should have told you about my operation a long time ago. It wasn't that I didn't trust you, but I was so accustomed to keeping things so close to the vest and playing the double life card that I couldn't get out of my own head. Can you forgive me for keeping you in the dark?"

Samara pressed her fingers to his lips before he could utter another word. "I already had a clue of what you did for a living, but it wasn't my business at the time because we were only what we were at the time. Once you told me you loved me, all of that changed, which means that what I know now is all I needed to know. There's nothing to forgive."

Dorian's satellite phone rang, interrupting their conversation. He picked it up, recognizing Ishmael's number, and sat up to take the call. "What's going on, kid? Everything good?"

"All good, DK, just letting you know we'll be at the estate in fifteen minutes." Dorian could hear the rumble of the engines in the background, lending credence to Ishmael's response. "Kale and Yaya are with me, and I have the other party you requested for the transition meeting."

"Good man, I'll see you in fifteen minutes." Dorian disconnected the call, giving Samara a curious look. "I want you with me during the transition meeting, do you think you're up for it?"

Samara grinned. "I think I am definitely up for it. I will admit, Ishmael sort of gave me a rundown of how things worked. We had a lot of time to chat while he was keeping me safe."

"I guess I shouldn't be too surprised about it. Ishmael trusts you because he knows I trust you, even when I've not exactly shown it myself," Dorian explained. "He has a knack for reading me that very few people possess. I think that's why I'm entrusting him with running things for me."

A series of knocks on the front door synced with them getting dressed to greet their guests. Dorian didn't worry about receiving the guests, as the staff was still in house for the day, so he knew they would be moved into the space that was set aside. By the time they'd gotten to the great room, Dorian did a double-take over the persons who were in the room.

Yaya was there, as expected, Kale was there, as Ishmael explained during the phone call. What had him questioning his vision was the fact that Ishmael was there, but the young man who was sitting next to him was, quite literally, a carbon copy of him. Dorian continued to study the two men, trying to figure out something other than the obvious, while trying not to look like he'd been shocked with a cattle prod.

Ishmael read Dorian's body language and adjusted his introduction accordingly. "I can tell that you're trying to trust your eyes, so let me go ahead and cut the confusion in your head. Dorian Bentley, I would like for you to meet my twin brother, Ibrahim. Ibrahim, this is the head of the operation, Dorian Bentley."

Samara looked at Dorian, Dorian looked at Samara, and exclaimed in unison, "Twins?!"

Ishmael cracked up laughing, with Kale joining in the laughter along with Yaya. "Yeah, it was an adjustment for them, too, and they said you would probably react in the same way. You all knew I had brothers, but I never really said I had a twin brother, so to speak. But, like I told you when you were considering the shift, I only had one person I could trust."

Dorian shook through the initial disbelief and adjusted to what Ishmael was explaining, taking a seat as quickly as he could to sort through his thought process. Once he wrapped his head around things, he nodded in agreement over Ishmael's assessment. He turned to Kale and Yaya and addressed them. "Kale, Yaya, considering that, I assume, you both had a few days to adjust to this revelation, what do you think about this? Can you flow with this?"

Kale nodded. "I'm good. He's every bit like his brother."

Yaya nodded, looking over at Ishmael before focusing her attention to Dorian. "I'm okay with it. From my perspective, it helps with the mystique of the moniker even more than when we were rocking with you at the helm. It might actually have us be in literally two places at one time."

Samara patted her hand on top of his, nodding at the premise that Yaya presented. "She has a point, baby. It might widen operations and have things really take off."

Dorian agreed. "I will need to let you know of the things I had to do, specifically with the French government, in order to extract Harry's daughters from the situation that Donovan and General Locke put them in to try to get him to take us out. You need to be aware of the hoops that you might need to jump through until things settle down with them."

"Trust, DK, there won't be any problems. We should be able to have things clicking in no time." Ishmael fist-bumped Ibrahim as they nodded to each other. "We have a whole plan in place to take things to a whole other level."

"He's right. My brother has been bringing me up to speed on how things were being run, and we've already figured out a nuance to get things rocking," Ibrahim remarked. "We can split the planet, while keeping each other abreast of what is going on when and where necessary. In fact, I've already asked Kale to find a sniper to cover me during transactions while he keeps Ishmael intact."

Dorian nodded. "Do you have anyone in mind, Kale? I mean, considering there's gonna be a huge shakeup at the top with both Harry and JC retired, I think finding someone you can trust is more important than ever."

Kale grinned. "I already have someone in mind, and it's simply a matter of getting them up to speed. It should be a seamless transition, once you get a chance to get a feel for everyone before you retire."

"Good, I will leave you to that aspect." Dorian turned to his tech expert to focus on her for the moment. "Yaya, I'm going to need you to keep up with these two, it sounds like they're gonna keep you busy for the foreseeable future."

Yaya gave a playful dismissive wave as she considered her response. "Sir, they will have to keep up with me, I'm used to the pace that you worked on, and even if it is the two of them, they don't hold a candle to you."

A collective "damn" coursed through the room as Samara giggled at the loyalty Yaya showed to her soon-to-be former boss. She looked up at Dorian with a smile on her face, realizing that things were being drawn to a close. "Well, now that that's handled, I guess that means I get to have you to myself for a little while, huh?"

"Yeah, I guess I'll have a bit of free time on my hands," Dorian replied as he softly kissed her forehead. "Any ideas of what we can do with that free time?"

"I think we can come up with a few things to do, Mr. de Silva."

Ishmael cocked his head to the side in a "record scratch" moment. "Wait a minute ... Mr. *de Silva*?

What in the identity crisis, plot twist hell is going on here?"

Dorian shook his head, a nervous laugh escaping his lips. "I'm still trying to get used to the whole thing myself, but I'm going to have to sit down with you all in the next few days to explain what happened in Rio. It's a lot to take in, trust me."

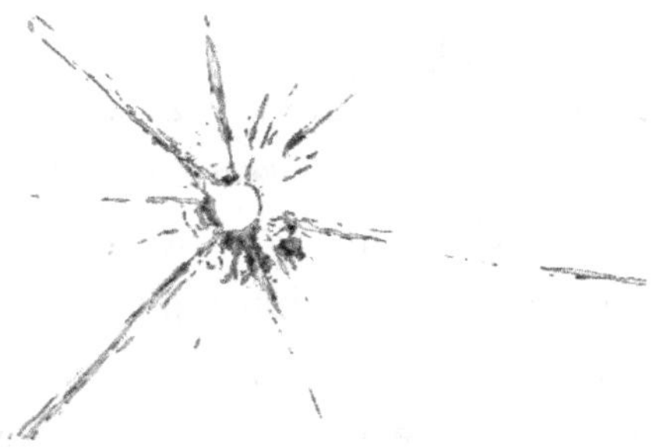

Epilogue – One Year Later

Dorian sat on the deck of their home in Rio, the home they'd been slowly, but surely, building over the course of the year. Juan Carlos and Luciano sat with him, enjoying a few cigars and liquor, marveling at the spacious landscape of the back yard overlooking the Atlantic Ocean. Dorian paid a premium for the view, and the privacy; he realized living in the city would not be prudent, especially considering the exciting news that brought half of the city to his home.

"Twins??? Damn, son, I didn't know you had that in you!" Juan Carlos exclaimed as he took a sip of the cognac in his glass. "I guess that type of potency runs in the family after all."

"Papi, chill, I was just as shocked as you are now. It's gonna be a rough couple of years for me as it is," Dorian replied as he took another pull of his cigar. "I don't know what I was thinking. I'm not ready to be a father yet, and now I got twins to worry about?"

Luciano's laughter echoed against the large trees that framed the property line. He smiled as he reminisced over his younger days. "Don't worry, grandson, I'll be able to tell you all you need to know about dealing with twins. Your mother and aunt are twins, you will be fine if you listen to me."

Dorian's head was still spinning as he thought about his new normal. A boy and a girl, at the same time, as a first-time parent. The simple thought of it was more terrifying to him than any hot zone that he'd ever entered into. All he could think about was making sure he didn't screw up too much, but it was comforting to have parents and grandparents to help with the concept.

He turned to Luciano and clapped his hand on his shoulder. "Oh, don't worry, I'll be leaning on both of you. Hell, this is one of those times where I can't fake it until I make it."

"Kid, none of us, and I mean, not a one, has ever known. All you can do is take it one day at a time, and do the best you can to keep them out of harm's way until they're about, oh, thirty or so." Juan Carlos winked at Luciano as he explained himself further. "I still kept you safe, like you were my own flesh and blood, because you reminded me so much of what I wanted my son to be. To now know that you were mine the entire time is equal parts satisfying and irritating.

There's so much more I need to teach you."

Dorian nodded. "This last year has been enlightening on so many levels, Papi. To have met my other abuela, all the other family that I never knew I had. Even the ones who kept an eye on me when I was dealing with the madness in the favelas. It's all so wild right now."

Luciano reached out and shook Juan Carlos' hand, giving a nod in his direction. "We really hadn't had a chance to really sit down and clear the air between us, either, JC. With our kid standing here right now, I want to apologize to you for allowing my short-sightedness ruin what obviously was a deep and wonderful connection between you and my darling Isabella."

Juan Carlos shook his head. "What was done, was done, sir. We will still have a full life, thanks to the money we've made and being able to get out before either of us got our tickets punched. I've always loved your daughter, and that won't change now."

"I'm happy to hear that, son," Luciano replied, catching both Juan Carlos and Dorian off guard. Luciano grinned for a moment, realizing the significance of the gesture. "I never had any sons, so, to truly be able to have one of my daughters' suitors be able to have that attached to him, it is a blessing for this old man. I look forward to formally welcoming you to the family in the coming weeks."

"Thank you, sir."

"No, you no longer get to call me that. It's Papi, son.

Period."

Dorian broke into laughter. "Checkmate, Papi. Abuelo is pretty rigid about what he expects. Get used to it."

"I'm beginning to realize that, kid." Juan Carlos squeezed Luciano's hand, sealing the silent acknowledgment between them. "Say no more, Papi. I'm happy to see what the future holds, especially when I'm finding out how much of a celebrity my soon-to-be wife is already. I better find a way to keep making money."

"Speaking of making money, how does it feel being out of the mix for the past year?" Luciano asked both men. "I know I have my times when I want to get my hands dirty, but I'm an old man now, I can get my lieutenants to handle things until my successor is named. What are you two doing to cope?"

Juan Carlos didn't hesitate in his answer. "My life has been consumed with a lot of catching up for lost time. I've made the money, now it's time to enjoy it before my grandkids start to take over and money gets rerouted."

Dorian wasn't as jovial about the question. "Honestly, I don't think I miss it, at least, not entirely. There are some days where the itch hits hard and I miss the bullets and adrenaline rush. I just stay away from all the international news outlets where I can, but the boys still keep me abreast of what's going on."

"Good move, kid. Besides, I figured the crew was

still keeping you in the loop." Juan Carlos took another sip from his glass. "What's going on now?"

"Last I heard, Ishmael was in South Korea, and Ibrahim was in North Africa, moving into the Afghan region. It seems things are circling back into full swing, and they have been busy with a lot of different sides wanting weaponry," Dorian replied. "They've put damn near everyone else out of business. No one can understand how the Wraith can be damn near in two places at once."

"Yeah, I'm sure Locke has been keeping them loaded down with all the business they've been drumming up."

"Oh, I didn't tell you?" Dorian snapped his fingers as the mere mention of his name jogged his memory. "Vice President Warren got word about what Locke had been doing and had him resign his post on the Joint Chiefs of Staff and all but forced him into retirement. He's an ordinary citizen now."

Juan Carlos' eyes narrowed. "I think I need to take a trip to take care of something in the next couple of weeks."

Dorian recognized that look as he took a folded piece of paper and placed it in his father's hand. "Consider it an early wedding gift, Papi. And I have people who will swear that you were with me when the time comes. I got you."

Luciano nodded. "Take care of business. He needs to pay for what he's done."

"Speaking of taking care of business, gentlemen, your son needs to be put down for the night. I already have his sister sleeping, but he seems to have a reason to want to stay up." Samara padded in with the giggling bundle of joy in her arms. She placed him in Dorian's arms and kissed his forehead. "Good night, *mi niño bonito*, Mami needs to sleep while she can."

She tiptoed to kiss her husband, leaning into his ear so the other men in the area couldn't hear her. "Hopefully if Papi can get the other little one to sleep, he can put his adoring wife to sleep properly. I love you, *mi querido esposo*. Don't be too long."

The minute Samara left, Luciano and Juan Carlos read their body language. They looked at each other and started laughing as they headed out the door. Dorian was confused as he watched them leave him with his son. "What happened to helping me when it came to dealing with the twins?"

Luciano turned for a minute, took one look at his great-grandson's eyes, and shook his head. "Sorry, kid, but I know that look. A boy needs his father, and only his father, in moments like this. You will be fine, and he will be asleep in no time. Just talk to him; he may not understand you now, but he will, in time, because by the time he can understand you, your words will flow like butter."

Dorian shook his head as he laid his son against his shoulder, listening to his breathing as it slowed and deepened. Before long, he was lightly snoring, leaving

Dorian to his thoughts over how his life had changed over the course of the past year. As much as he tried to convince his father and grandfather that he was finding ways to cope, the truth was a different circumstance. He could only hope to find something to replace the adrenaline rush, but he had three good reasons to earnestly get used to his new normal.

His phone buzzed, which startled him for a moment. The area code and number caused a smile to spread across his lips. He gently placed his son down and covered him to protect him from the gentle breeze flowing through the deck to pick up the phone before it stopped ringing. "This is an unexpected pleasure. I was expecting you to be dealing with the current mess going on in North Korea."

"That is true, but I would be remiss if I didn't call to say congratulations on the new bundles of joy, pretty boy." Lea's voice still dripped with the same essence of sensuality that he'd always enjoyed. "Besides, my Sir has been handling things behind the scenes to help the POTUS shine in the spotlight. It won't be long before things are settled down in that region."

"I'm sure my people have been assisting in that measure, too."

"Yes, they have. In fact, we've been restructuring things a bit to give them a more clandestine, yet prominent, profile within the DoD," Lea replied. "Your man Ishmael is quite the charmer, and quite business savvy, and his proposal in light of General

Locke's removal and retirement is one that my Sir is looking forward to implementing. It would be to our added advantage to have you join in on the new endeavor."

Dorian chuckled, realizing the veiled attempt to stroke his ego. "As much as I would love to, I have other endeavors that no longer involve the US Government. I made it clear to Ishmael and Ibrahim that it is their show now, and from what I've been hearing from them over the past year, business has never been more profitable."

"Suit yourself, love, but I would have loved working with you in a more direct capacity."

"I'm sure you would have, but I have a family to look after now. Priorities have shifted quite a bit. In fact, I have been putting my energies into more, shall we say, enlightening endeavors."

"Hmm, you have my attention, but I think that might be a conversation for another time." Lea's voice took on a more practical tone as Dorian heard more people entering into the room over the earpiece. "Mr. de Silva, I look forward to finding out more about this new endeavor. Perhaps Vice President Warren might be able to offer some assistance, perhaps a collaboration, in the future?"

"Yes, Ms. McAvoy, my wife and I would be very interested in sitting down with you and the vice president to hammer out details," Dorian followed suit, presuming that he was on speaker phone for others to hear. "I'll make sure that we go through the proper channels to ensure we get on his calendar. It has to be a bit maddening at the moment."

"I will ensure that you're placed at the front of the docket, once things have settled down," Lea acknowledged. "I look forward to seeing you and your beautiful wife soon. I've got some down time scheduled in a few weeks, and I would love to meet the woman who has, for lack of a better phrase, retired my most prized asset."

"I look forward to it, too. We'll see you soon." Dorian disconnected the call, picking his son up and heading into the living room. He turned on the television to generate a bit of white noise while he settled back in to ensure the young one was sound asleep. He couldn't stop staring at him, relishing this first of many father-son chats that he looked forward to having over the course of his lifetime.

"Marco, I have so much to tell you when you're older, so many things that I have to teach you and your sister. There are things that you will learn in this life that won't make sense to you, but I think that between your grandfather and your great-grandfather and I, we will be able to give you the best of us all. You and your sister, Nova, will be loved and protected, so help me, God."

Dorian kissed Marco across his forehead, carrying him up to the kids' bedroom to settle him in, before heading to his bedroom to finally rest for the night.

ABOUT THE AUTHOR

Shakir Rashaan is the author of the national bestselling novel In Service to the Senator, Unthinkable, The Devil's All-American, the national bestselling series the Nubian Underworld, the Kink, P.I. series, and the upcoming novel, The Paramour Code (Nubian Underworld #5) in March 2021. He is also developing projects under the pen name PK Rashaan. You can find out more about Rashaan at www.ShakirRashaan.com.